PRAISE FOR
LILITH SAINTCROW

"Simply put, Saintcrow doesn't f*** around."

— CHUCK WENDIG, AUTHOR
OF *WANDERERS*, ON *AFTERWAR*

"Incredibly timely, well written and important.... A testament to Saintcrow's skill."

— *LOS ANGELES TIMES* ON *AFTERWAR*

"A true faery story, creepy and heroic by turns. Love and hope and a touch of *Midsummer Night's Dream*. I could not put it down."

— PATRICIA BRIGGS, AUTHOR OF THE MERCY
THOMPSON SERIES ON *TRAILER PARK FAE*

"Painfully honest, beautifully strange, and absolutely worth your time. Lilith Saintcrow is at the top of her game. Don't miss this."

— SEANAN MCGUIRE, AUTHOR OF THE
WAYWARD CHILDREN SERIES ON *TRAILER
PARK FAE*

"Lilith Saintcrow spins an incredibly imaginative and delicious tale with vivid language and a story you will not be able to put down. I loved every minute!"—

— *DARYNDA JONES ON TRAILER PARK FAE*

"Honestly, I wish I'd written it."

— *CHUCK WENDIG ON TRAILER PARK FAE*

"Unique, twisted, lovely, and raw. Just fabulous."

— *FAITH HUNTER ON TRAILER PARK FAE*

FLEDGLING & ARCHON

FLEDGLING & ARCHON
TALES OF THE SANGUINANT
BOOK III

LILITH SAINTCROW

Fledgling & Archon

Copyright © 2025 by Lilith Saintcrow

Ebook ISBN: 9781641973700

Trade paperback ISBN: 9781641973762

For M. S., who made it through.

CHAPTER 1

Becoming a bloodsucker had fixed her knee problems—which was, so far as Simone could see, the only good point.

Well, there was also not needing bifocals, plus her tinnitus had outright vanished. The resultant sensory sharpness was a curse in its own way since there were so many things she would rather not see or hear. Especially when she got through the door of yet another boot-scootin' shithole and found that, as dismally expected, the entire bar stank to high heaven *and* there was another vampire present.

Five bucks to you, Barry. Her finder would be thrilled that his sucker-map algorithm was still tiptop. If it was indeed computer wizardry and not some kind of low-level psychic whatsis, which Simone did not quite rule out.

There was a whole lot she refused to disbelieve these days.

She gave every pair of peepers under cowboy hat or faded baseball cap plenty of time to take in her arrival, then stalked across a slightly sticky floor with a little extra strut in her Levi's. Each light bulb hanging in a dust-crusted fixture seemed to have at least two flies perambulating lazily below and the corner jukebox was a knockoff Wurlitzer currently thumpwailing some generic Hank Williams clone. All the boots in the place were just as run-down as her own deeply vintage Tony Lamas, *except* for the brand-new glossy black numbers with shiny toecaps worn by the vampire at the end of the bar.

No doubt the locals thought he was just a weekend-rodeo stranger; his camouflage was as good as her own. The vamp stared over his brown glass bottle of domestic pisswater like he couldn't believe *another* bloodsucker would have the temerity to walk into this dive.

Sandy-gold hair flopping over his forehead, check. Those narrow, close-spaced hazel eyes, checkity-check. Her sense from the blurry security camera footage was correct, too—he *felt* like a young one, and looked like he'd been bitten in his late twenties.

Honestly once she'd hit her late forties everyone looked like a baby. Of far more interest were the dark, microscopic flecks on his denim jacket and the quickly snuffed crimson pinprick in each pupil.

Well, I've certainly got his attention. Which was never a problem; vampires seemed a gregarious bunch, despite what the forum posts said. Of course, she probably had a leg up by being a fellow bloodsucking evildoer.

The dry spot at the back of her throat scratched, lightly. "Whiskey, please." She tried a polite smile on the grizzled, plaid-jacketed bartender, whose bushy greying eyebrows twitched in what could have been surprise.

Me too, buddy. Here she was, plain old Simone Deschants of Trenton City, looking well over thirty years younger than her actual age and fitting into her college jeans as well. It was a miracle, Lord have mercy—but the price was steep.

"Uh." The bartender's pupils were blessedly human, dilating as faded blue irises shrank. He seemed nice enough—sad, yes, but that was to be expected in a place like this. "What kind, ma'am?"

Asking for the most expensive firewater would be showy,

and too much for her slender budget as well. She had to remember who she was, despite the…

The fangs. And the thirst, and what it made her do. "Good old JD's, please. Thank you."

She turned as the bartender busied himself, letting her gaze rove, marking the position of every critter in the room. Mostly male, only two waitresses—both with the type of high, crunchy hairsprayed bangs she hadn't seen since high school, Christ this place was a time capsule—and a couple ladies in what was their going-out best, including large bright plastic earrings. She even caught a breath of drugstore perfume from a blonde in an embroidered chambray shirt, who was staring owlishly at this new babe on the block.

For a moment Simone actually felt pretty.

Except she wasn't in search of booze, a line dance, or a cowboy to take home for riding. Her business was with the man-shaped thing at the end of the bar, the monster staring fixedly in her direction—and those spatters on his jacket, all but invisible to human eyes.

Not to her, though. And she could smell it, red and iron-rich, stroking that terrible, insistent patch at the very back of her throat.

Blood.

Four packs left in the fridge, she chanted inwardly. It wasn't going to be enough, but maybe she could get more once she was out of this pissant burg.

God knew she'd done far more difficult things in the past few years.

So she gave the barkeep a crumpled bit of legal tender, told him to keep the change, and held the other vampire's gaze as she downed her whiskey, exhaling softly afterward as the brief alcohol sting faded. Christ, she couldn't even get drunk nowadays, though lots of the others acted like blood itself was pure-d Everclear.

Once again she was grimly unsurprised that booze didn't ease that fucking dry spot. Nothing did but the red stuff, and even the bagged variety only imperfectly.

The vampire at the end of the bar was trembling. Oh, *that* wasn't visible to the normal folks, either; the liquid in his bottle barely moved, a few bubbles shaken free of smooth glass sides. But he stared at her like he'd just found new meaning in the universe, and Simone wondered why they all acted so oddly. Was it just because she was perpetually new in town? Did they get bored looking at normal people's faces?

Doesn't matter. Naturally vampires were more visibly different to her now; she could see the matte-poreless skin, the wild shine to their eyes, the gloss of their hair. Regular, happy ol' people had imperfections, pimples, scars, bedhead, wrinkles.

It wasn't fair, it wasn't just, it wasn't *right*. But there was nothing she could do except her self-chosen job, so Simone simply gave the bartender another half-apologetic smile and headed for the door.

She knew the other vampire would follow.

It wasn't quite a one-horse town—eight stoplights, the nearest hospital reachable by half-hour highway drive, three churches and four honky-tonks on the main drag. Outside the imaginary village limits, grassy plains stretched westward until purple mountain majesties decided enough was enough and put a stop to that nonsense, thank you very much. The wind sweeping across miles and miles of almost-nothing tasted like grass, cows, wildlife, an occasional tang of balsam or river, and forever. Hard diamond stars glittered endlessly, but she had no time for beauty or philosophy because the bloodsucking fucker was mean as well as fast, and her claws might have a hard time getting through his skin.

Sure, he was 'young'—but now that they were both on the

move it was clear he was a bit older than *her*, which seemed to make the bastards far more difficult to deal with. Her only hope lay in the fact that he was also weirdly uncoordinated, almost too excited to fight properly.

Every bloodsucker she'd interacted with went shaky-psycho when they got close to murder, and Simone didn't have time to think about why *she* seemed to have missed that boat.

It could be a function of accumulated age? Or maybe she just didn't notice her own altered perceptions. Both horrifying prospects, to be sure.

Getting her prey to the town limits was simply a matter of running fast enough; a carefully chosen gully yawed to her right, precisely on schedule. She plunged into its arms, twisted in midair, bounced from side to near-vertical rocky side, dodged half-seen or merely sensed obstacles, and when he attempted to hit her from behind she was almost, *almost* surprised.

But not entirely, and she had a bit of experience nowadays when it came to ripping up vampires. Plus, visiting this very ravine right after dusk had given her a good idea of its layout— not to mention the tangle of abandoned barbwire rusting comfortably in its crooked elbow, perhaps deposited by a long-ago flash flood.

She dropped flat just in time; the blond bastard sailed right over her into the mess. A yip like a surprised coyote, followed by a thrashing and a sweetly metallic scent.

More blood. *Vampire* blood.

Okay, he's not so old as I thought. Great. But she couldn't wait around for a motherfucker to die of tetanus.

He stagger-streaked from the iron cobweb-tangle, arms outstretched and claws out. Her own fingernails were extended —tough, razor-sharp, and more than ready.

The hardest part was shoving away a lifetime's worth of training—*you can't do that, girls don't hit people. Use your words. Be nice!*

Fortunately, her body's hateful new instincts knew what to do. She just had to get out of the way.

Plus, before catching a bad case of vamp-itis she'd been on the downhill side of fifty and the rocks of a bad divorce besides. There wasn't a lot of *nice* left in Simone Deschants, taking her maiden name back in a big way and dodge-weaving close, left hand flickering to open up a big ol' steaming rip in the monster's guts.

During each and every fight she remembered the thing that had infected her, how it had screamed when morning sunshine filtered through the church basement window. She heard those cries once more as she tore at the drunk-staggering bloodsucker, ducking and bobbing, claws ripping over and over until finally, eventually the wet rot racing through its tissues turned to glittering dust.

Another monster went *poof*, caving in as she caused more damage than preternatural flesh could heal until nothing was left but irritating iridescent particles, grit working itself finer and finer into every crevice. Simone backed toward the gully's wall, rubbing her hands together frantically, shaking out her hair, and finally brushing at her clothes with maybe a little more force than necessary.

The grainy stuff itched, but only briefly. Worst of all was the way her conscience dug its spurs in. Maybe this guy had been attacked one night, turned just like her, and was only trying to survive. Maybe one day Simone herself would go nuts from the thirst's constant scratching and have to be put down like a rabid dog.

She leaned against the ravine's wall, ribs heaving though the fight was indisputably over. "Sorry," she heard herself whisper, over and over. "Sorry, I'm so sorry, I hope it's better now. I hope you're at peace."

A crowd of dry, twinkle-giggling stars watched avidly from overhead, along with the low-hanging, evil-grinning gibbous moon. Neither cared about her silly little emotional pangs. Good ol' Ma Nature was beautiful, sure, but she was also a stone-cold bitch. Maybe vampires were simply an evolutionary niche, biology getting day-drunk and deciding to have a little fun.

Simone let the soft, frantic catechism of regret drain away as she braced herself against the ravine's wall, calculating the hours left until dawn.

Just enough time to get home and check in.

CHAPTER 2

Taverns, hostelries, inns as a whole smelled far better than they used to, or perhaps his nose was simply dulled with age. Yet the wanderer hesitated before crossing the street, forcing himself to *focus* through the shifting, distracting kaleidoscope of night's wonders.

Neon signs buzz-blinking, shower-shadows of multicolored light competing with the lamps and blinking traffic-control devices. Arteries and veins of paving turning to dirt as they unraveled from the township-clot, starred at the margins with houses staring blankly at wonderful vistas of grass and weather. A cool breeze redolent of plain and mountain, thick with the ever-present tinge of car exhaust. Mortal heartbeats thundering through the mechanical cascade of pipes, buzzing galvanism, tinny music, chatter, and clatter; the song of wind through tall grass and quiet murmur of high-summer watercourses diving for shelter providing orchestral backdrop.

The wilderness called; for a creature so old and frayed, solitude was an imperfect refuge at best. Yet that was better than the alternative. He almost turned to stride away before remembering his purpose once more—a stranger, an *intruder* tainting his current territory.

The fractures and slippage weren't so bad here. In mortal cities the crowding of prey was a constant quasi-irritation; in these lightly settled environs, however, he could visit a few isolated homesteads upon an eve, feeding carefully to avoid glut. Or he could simply linger unseen outside one of four taverns, harvesting the drunken, leaving them weakened yet still breathing. The effort of restraint helped fight the accretion of mental and physical dust upon his joints and brain-folds, hardening slowly to stone, but the wanderer suspected he might be too old to die in the usual manner of his kind.

After all, neither the great fire of the Sun nor open flame itself could kill him. Hazily he remembered how he had discovered the latter fact and shuddered, his fingers driving into the crumbling concrete flank of what had possibly once been a greengrocer's as he tarried in comfortable shadow, again attempting to remember why he was here, now, in this particular place.

Intruder. He clung to the single word, the concept threatening to slip from a mental grasp grown increasingly clumsy—and worse, timorous.

The process was accelerating. He would soon be too slow and absent to survive even a fledgling's attack, unless mere reflex was enough to ward off such an ignoble end. An elderly, arthritic dragon, shambling through the dust-heap of centuries—no, a *dinosaur*, that was a good concept, meaty, endlessly interesting. Was he ancient enough to remember such beasts?

It seemed likely. He remembered thinking the mortals' steam-carriages were like unto wyrms, snorting and heaving, and fleeing at least one of the things not so very long ago. But no, there was another word for it—*train*, like a noblewoman's dress or retinue, like teaching tricks to a dumb beast. In other languages the connections were different; he had to focus hard upon the current tongue.

Once again the wanderer almost turned away. Later he might brood upon how close he had been to failure, true-death, the treasure whispering past his aching, clumsy fingertips. But at the last moment, recognition of the insult arrived once more —a trespasser, an interloper in the small realm of one who had survived open flame, by the thunderbolt, by the wounds of God!

So he forded the street's cracked pavement river and pushed at the caupona's door...

No. *Tavern* door, this was a watering-hole, not a sleeping-place. The close, almost-pleasant fug of mortal breath and yeasty inebriation puffed outward in a silken cloud. A golden thread buried in the breeze's depth halted him upon the threshold, a long glassy moment between screaming chaos and a precious, crystalline moment of lucidity.

What is that?

Spice and night wind from exotic harbors, a hint of green sap and the faintest stinging touch of mortal alcohol. Sense-impressions flooded the fractured mess his brain had become, layering quick and deft as a master painter's brush—a glance from wide dark velvety eyes, brown curls fragrant as cedar bark, a soft musical murmur he could almost, *almost* hear.

The bartender drew breath to shout at a ragged scarecrow standing spellbound in the doorway; the wanderer's attention fastened upon that stocky mortal, who wisely swallowed whatever he had been about to say.

Marvelous, wonderful clarity. The smell was intriguing, enchanting, wonderful. Yet more than that, it peeled away a thick layer of accreted dust, sharpening every visual edge and burnishing the entire room from its slumped, wheezing music-maker—*jukebox, that's what it's called*—to the glistening blue-black flies under hanging lanterns abuzz with galvanism, the spotted mirror behind shelves of liquor to the worn, dust-creased boots of tired mortal males. Quite a few curious glances settled upon the wanderer; he wondered if his cloth were too anachronistic for even simple country folk used to keeping their opinions to themselves.

Layered against that beautiful, phantasmal perfume was the

more-familiar intruder's scent. Perhaps *that* was why the trespasser lingered? But if so…

Well, you will simply have to kill him. Not a difficult task. His gaze roved the tavern's interior, marking every living thing, and the mortals would never know how close they brushed against death that night—a feast before battle was always tempting. The golden thread was a frail fence and enticement all at once, drawing him away from such dangerous pleasures.

She—the scent was unmistakably female—had lingered here for a short while, dyeing the air with beauty. A shudder passed through his frame; he turned, allowing the constant whistling wilderness-breath to sweep the door closed. Let this clutch of mortals live another night; there was time and enough to drink the entire continent dry if necessary.

Later. Once he had run the most important prey of millennia to ground, and disposed of whoever now held her.

Following a single auriferous thread, the wanderer stepped into the road, loping easily along painted yellow stripes. Buildings blurred to either side, and he plunged past the frail glow modern mortals used to hold back the night.

Remember, remember, he chanted as he ran—almost unnecessary, since the evaporating waft of delicious scent waxed and waned, yet thankfully never quite disappeared. No attempt to mask at all, though the trespasser's spoor was intermittent, showing some recognition of elementary safety measures.

He could not tell if the strangeness was in his own looming unreason or the trail itself. Stars overhead sang to themselves in high tinkling voices, a yellow moon leering, gazing upon the earth's teeming face with interest but no mercy. The trail veered, plunged into the mouth of a gorge, and only the angry reek of recent death stopped the wanderer from leaping straight into a rusty tangle of mortal iron.

Not that it could have harmed him; his hide was ancient, more durable than daylight. But had he been so foolhardy his clothes would have been reduced to shreds.

Now the wanderer could not remember what he wore, or whence the garments had been stolen from. A question literally immaterial; when he met the bearer of that wonderful perfume, he would no doubt seem a bit odd. What mattered was getting close enough to fill his lungs, let the fact of her presence sink in so he could think clearly for a few moments. The constantly fracturing mess inside his skull would coalesce, and he might even be able to remember his own name.

The intruder to this territory had been less than cautious; this, the wanderer could understand. With that lovely, enticing, magical fragrance filling nose, brain, branching vein-channels, it was a wonder either of them had been able to run without stumble-staggering like new foals. No trace of whoever had killed the trespasser, which meant the valuable prey's protector was old and canny—and yet, they had let her slip away?

A sanguinant did not use their greatest treasure as bait. Never, never. It was simply not done; he knew that, as he knew little else about this confusing present time. So, a bauble slipping from a powerful grasp, temporarily adrift until reclaimed? Perhaps, yet her trail led from the gorge as well, *still* with no masking.

How was it possible? The wanderer was missing something crucial, and would most likely die as he challenged another archaic, powerful sanguinant for the prize.

If, that was, a creature like himself were capable of true-death. Was it accuracy, hubris, or further insanity to have doubts upon the matter? He had, after all, survived the fire.

For once, remembering that terrible event did not distract him from current surroundings. Slipping between the whispering speed and nearly invisible mistform at places which seemed ideal for ambush, he was more alert than he had been in… oh, two centuries, at least?

How long had it been, precisely, since the quaking riven earth, the walls of flame breathing like living creatures, the agony as their caress swept over him, robbing him of any claim to logic or sense? He knew not what day it was, what year according to which calendar, or even what this mortal country now named itself. The language of its inhabitants eluded him at the moment as well, yet the scent was working upon him in tremendous fashion, for he dimly sensed what he was missing. Great gaps torn in his knowledge, his reason, his very *self*, and he could not entirely blame a city soaked in flames.

Those who lived long became as stone, physically and in all other ways. Unless…

Unless you are strong enough to kill the protector of that scent. Why do they not mask her? Such a simple precaution.

A cold, rational, *sane* thought, one he clung to as he ran.

He veered down a gravel side-road, which widened to a small, irregular trampled space abutting the green skein of an aestival-vanished creek. The metallic scent of water was barely a drouth-choked trickle, and a large rectangular shadow loomed. The shape was possessed of wheels as well as two large night-blind eyes watching him, curiously insectile, glossed with starlight.

Ah. Glass, front-facing. Along the thing's flanks were irregular hints of golden glimmer.

Candlelight? Here?

It was a camping vehicle, he realized slowly, halting at the very edge of what had to be a place for locals to park when the creek was high enough to hold fish, or dabble toes in a cool flow. The scent was very strong; she had been resident some while. That realization peeled another layer of insanity from his encrusted mental processes, and the resultant jolt was almost as pleasant as the great gripping lungfuls of golden-brown spice he took in greedy gulps, waiting for her protector to show.

Nothing. The night wore on. His senses, muffled by age and madness, whetted themselves with each new draught of scent.

The distant murmur of her voice was just as he had imagined, a soft sweet song capable of enticing any sanguinant into the whirlpool, onto razor rocks. A desert wanderer would follow that whisper over the sands until the carnivorous flame-spirits feasted upon his bones; a fur-clad steppedweller would ride every horse he possessed to foundering in pursuit.

Inside the vehicle, her muffled laughter, edged with something… anger? Disdain? He could not tell. The wanderer, now invisible even to those of his own kind, was patient. Each soft, controlled breath, freighted with her magnificence, was whetstone to a rusty edge. Perhaps he could gather enough sanity, enough flexibility to fight effectively when her guardian appeared.

Yet why, *why* would any sanguinant announce her presence like this? Did they not grasp the risks? Impossible. Even a fledgling knew to conceal, protect, jealously shield such a nonpareil.

Unless… was she alone? Which made no sense either, for who had meted out death to the trespasser? One of *her* kind did not engage in combat; it was simply unthinkable. No sanguinant would ever allow such madness.

The vehicle moved slightly, rocking on rubber wheel-feet. A flimsy fortress indeed, and no hint of invisible seals. Either the wanderer was missing a critical element of the scene and her protector was even now stealthily preparing for the kill, or…

Was it possible? It would be a miracle, an insanity in and of itself.

Clicking, sliding metal. A rectangle on the vehicle's side flung itself open, dim golden glow limning a slim shape. A bounce, a hop, and she folded down to sit on a low, handmade wooden stepstool, clearly accustomed to the maneuver.

A cat poised to watch unwary prey would have seemed frenetic next to his utter motionlessness, breath and pulse both in abeyance, his own scent thoroughly masked. In fact, another of his age and experience might have sensed something wrong in a single frozen patch amid the flow of night, camouflaged in long grass and scrub bush greedily seeking the creek's hidden damp.

Between starshine and candleflicker she perched, lithe and graceful, long fingers rubbing at her nape under rippling dark hair just the color he had scented—cedar bark, matching the spice of her scent. Sandalwood, clove, cardamom, cassia, all rich and wonderful savours mixing to fill his mouth with the tingling honey-numbness of change and analgesic agents, his true teeth sliding free without a single betraying crackle of shifting bones. His eyes burned, dry and avid; suppressing the pinpricks of kill-glow required an effort of will he was unused to making.

The wind, capering across miles of empty rolling grassland, wrapped him in her warm, enticing fragrance. Another layer of dust peeled from his perceptions; he marveled at how dull his senses had become.

And oh, was she not superb? Wide dark eyes under winged brows, her cheekbones starkly shadowed, a sweet bow of a mouth drawn with some emotion he could not name, her slim-ness very obviously tense even as she sighed and gazed at the distant horizon.

He realized the vehicle was deliberately parked to afford her quite the artistic vista, which bespoke some planning. And her thinness was not that of fashion; her scent held a faint edge of burning sugar, caramel turned too dark upon high heat. She was not properly fed, and no smoky screen of another sanguinant's possessiveness hung upon that gorgeous, compelling aroma.

Can't be. His mind trembled upon the edge of fracture once more; the sensation retreated as he allowed another trickle of air past his nostrils. Even the most momentary relief was worth unending devotion; a sanguinant would pay any price, perform any feat to have unfettered access, to be near the source of that surcease.

It simply cannot be.

Yet it was. Sitting before him, in jeans and a soft, clinging long-sleeve shirt, an actual, unmistakable leman pointed her booted toes and sighed. "Fuck," she said, conversationally—an old word, perhaps older than himself. He almost twitched, looking for her interlocutor. Or did she speak to herself, as the lonely were supposed to?

He had, as the madness waxed over seasons and mortal years, babbled in the depths of night or cave. He had sung, hardly realizing the voice was his own, and howled during storms when the thunder-gods hurled bolts earthward. But *she*, she was too beautiful to ever know such things.

"Might be a good idea," she continued, softly, ruminative. A lovely voice to match the rest of her, a low restful alto, the sweetest song imaginable. "No harm in trying, I suppose." A long pause, as she leaned against the vehicle and tipped her chin up, examining the sky. The lovely line of her throat—so tender, so exposed, a pleasant torment.

Young. Barely fledgling. The sure instinctive sense of another sanguinant's age spoke, clarion-loud inside his own veins. And it added, *Unclaimed.* That was the important part.

Had she killed the trespasser? Impossible, and yet... so was she. An unclaimed leman, *deva, aima-glyza, imprima,* sitting within his reach, staring at the starstrewn sky. Dawn grew close; she should be behind invisible seals, in a secure, silken nest. His blood surged at the thought, an iron bar with its claws sunk deep in his belly, reaching to the base of his spine. Diamond nail-flickers raced up his back, nerves and strong ancient muscles tensing by imperceptible fractions.

Unblinking, he watched. If her protector existed, they *must* strike now. Yet no trace of another sanguinant lingered upon her, unless it were the fading tang of violent death—the trespasser's. She *must* have been responsible; there was no other explanation. Perhaps their mutual opponent, drunk upon the very glory of her, had been singularly easy to dispatch.

The wanderer was very nearly thus himself, though another invisible layer of madness dropped from him with a stunning silent crash. He longed to flicker across the space, his teeth sinking into that naked, tempting pulse, carry her through the door into the vehicle, and…

She sniffed, heavily, rubbing below her pretty nose with the back of one hand. A strange, almost childlike motion, before she rose and re-entered her egg-thin castle walls. The door slammed, and he was left to wonder if she had indeed been weeping.

Where was the one who had granted her the Dark Gift? Had her protector been challenged and killed? If so, why had the victor not claimed her? A leman was not left to wander.

They were, simply and starkly, too precious. Already the wanderer was more awake and aware than he had been at any time since the fire. And—even more of a gift—the thought of the burning city, the heat, the sounds, the smell of roasting did not drive him to restless motion, seeking escape from an internal enemy.

Dawn comes. A fledgling's unconsciousness was deep and utterly vulnerable, beginning at sunrise. Did she know how to set seals about her place of rest, or was she intending to sleep in this… this tin can? It defied belief and insanity both.

Scraps of that maddening, glorious perfume twist-trailed about him. He longed to fill himself at the font; he *craved* a much closer acquaintance. The fear that somehow she would vanish, that this was a hallucination preceding true-death, did nothing to aid him in discerning the most efficient course of action.

Balanced between caution and the mounting urge to claim this fragile, fabulous, utterly maddening miracle, he waited for dawn.

CHAPTER 3

HER EX-HUSBAND, WHILE ONE OF THE GREATER ASSHOLES GOD HAD inflicted on both earth and humankind, was also indubitably correct in one small way: there was, as Curt always said, nothing fucking like getting home from work and cracking a cold one.

Of course *his* choice of poison had been fancy IPAs in sweating brown bottles, not pouches of human blood stamped with lot numbers and antigen information, but that was beside the point. Simone didn't even feel self-conscious about the fangs, the sucking sound, or draining the goddamn thing like a Capri Sun with a missing straw; she lived alone now, and that was one of the great gifts of both divorce and attaining the grand age of a half-century plus. She could belch, scratch, sing, scream, walk around naked as a jaybird if she pleased, and nobody would or could say a goddamn word.

Getting back to the RV and cautiously circling to make sure nobody else was around was habitual by now. So was climbing inside, opening the fridge, and letting out a giant sigh that would've driven Curt up the wall. He'd want to know just what the hell she had to be unhappy about, or he'd make some kind of passive-aggressive remark about her sagging ass. Not that his was worth any prizes, but like most men he considered himself aging like fine wine instead of turning into pissy, melted Play-Doh.

Thinking about her ex-husband was a bad sign. Besides, the general fix-up vampirism seemed to have done on her entire body could not have left her hindquarters out of the equation; she hadn't fit into jeans this size since gaining her freshman ten. Her tits seemed to have perked up bit by bit too, as the vampirism settled into her body, though her stretch marks were still faintly visible.

Her childhood scars had vanished; the old mole on her left instep remained. Which was interesting, but not the type of information online forums reveled in.

Simone touched a match to a few tealight candles—saving battery charge in an old RV was plain old prudence, not aesthetics—and fired up the sleek black laptop as she finished draining the blood bag. Cold going down her throat, the liquid hit a point behind her breastbone and exploded with welcome heat, her body recognizing at least part of what it wanted.

Biting actual people was relatively easy yet filled her with deep shaky loathing, and the nausea was even worse since she apparently couldn't vomit anymore. Maybe she was like a bird and would swell up and die with a bit of Alka-Seltzer in her gullet; of course, she didn't pee either, and the liquid diet was probably responsible for the fact that she didn't crap.

She kept quiet about *those* biological changes, even with her finder. None of his damn business, and besides, keeping track of every bathroom in range was a good habit for more than one reason. Just like paying attention to nearby cell phone towers; this spot, while secluded enough for her purposes, was just on the edge of a spire serving the nearby town, and the rechargeable booster on her RV's roof had done signal service since the day she'd stolen and hooked it up.

Of course Barry Jessup was awake waiting on a live hunt's

result, despite any and all time difference; he picked up the video call almost before it finished bouncing through the VPN. The laptop screen glowed; her bespectacled, ginger-haired, potato-nosed sometimes-business partner blinked into the camera on his end, a massive whiteboard behind him bearing a tangle of arcane notations, scribbled reminders, and fluttering Post-its or printed photos.

"You're late for check-in," he said, accusingly. Hell of a greeting.

"This line of work isn't about punching a timeclock." Simone restrained the urge to pinch the bridge of her nose, simultaneously glad she'd finished the blood pouch and wishing she could allow herself more. Her throat was better, sure, but that awful dry spot still ached. "You can cross one mosquito-ass cowboy chucklefuck off the list and file for the bounty, though."

To his credit, he didn't ask precisely *when* the event had happened, since that could have been a clue to her current location, VPN or not. "Did you get any footage?"

For Chrissake. Everyone wanted to record everything these days, it was a goddamn disease. "It's not always possible, Barry."

"Easier to get paid with proof, you know." He blinked several times, a night creature disturbed in its burrow. "You could set up a—"

"I killed it, what more do you want? Just pull up the Wyoming files and get to work tagging the sumbitch who stole that poor Clanton guy's boots." Simone didn't have to work at sounding both tired and disgusted; forcing herself to look through autopsy reports of vamp victims was part reminder of why she was doing this in the first place and part corrective against becoming a murderous psychopath herself. Or at least, so she hoped. "Christ. What crawled up your ass and died?"

"Nothing yet, thanks." Barry was gifted in seeing the downside to any situation, which was probably why he was still alive.

He had too much pessimism to go running after vampires himself, working as a job-finder and collections agent for others not similarly gifted with good sense. Plus, he collected a reasonable commission off every bounty. "It's just that everyone nowadays wants to wait thirty days before paying, or longer."

Yes, ol' Barry was an entrepreneur *par excellence,* and didn't seem to care she had one foot in the enemy's camp, so to speak. Why not overlook such small matters, since it earned him a good fifteen percent? And by now Simone was reasonably sure he wouldn't send a fanatic fellow vamp-slayer after her.

Not unless I royally screw him on a bounty, that is. "Why don't you make them pay up front?"

She knew the answer, but like most men, Barry enjoyed repeating himself. The call-and-response could even be relatively comforting.

"I'm not rated for escrow." He rubbed at one patchy-stubbled cheek and attempted what might pass for a winsome smile. "Plus, casualty rates are too high. A relief to see you, by the way."

Yeah, well, nice of you to say so. "Uh-oh. Who went down?"

"Professionalism forbids." Any hint of levity vanished. Barry's mouth pulled even more bitterly tight at either corner as he pushed his glasses up, fingertips stained with dry-erase ink. His other hand was busy tapping at an offset keyboard; he turned to glance at yet another screen. "Aha, here we are. So, you got that Rocky Mountain fuck, huh?"

"If you're referring to the messy bastard working north-northwest from Cheyenne over the past two years, yes. Told you it was mine." It had been disturbingly easy to track the monster, as a matter of fact.

And even easier to lure him to the gully.

Her finder's unkempt coppery eyebrows turned into Teton-peaks. He tapped some more, now with both hands, clickety-clack. "No problems?"

"There's nothing *but* problems in this sort of thing, my man.

Anyway, you can cross him off; he matched the security footage and was wearing the boots from the September victim." Those nice, bright Tony Lamas, glinting in the bar.

Shit. Her throat was full of hot sourness.

"Did the boots poof too?" Barry sounded only mildly curious.

"They did." One of the many mysteries of the night life. "Wish I knew why the clothes go with the vampire, but oh well."

"Okay." Barry made a face; he had an almost superstitious aversion to calling the monsters what they fucking well were. Of course, he refrained from calling her a leech as well, or any other derogatory term. Other than the usual banter between coworkers, that was. "It might take a day or two, and if you're in Wyoming…"

"Am I?" Simone forced a smile. "You know I like to play it safe, Barry."

"Yeah, yeah, I know." His face eased all at once, holding a puckish grin instead of pained grimace. "But I've got something that just might interest you."

Uh-oh. "Like what?" Her finder was an inveterate matchmaker. He claimed to think certain groups of heavily armed assholes crazy enough to go hunting murderous folklore wouldn't mind having one of the things they usually attempted slaughtering around to help out. Some of the offers were reasonably attractive—but Simone was done with men, and double-done with groups of them.

Especially groups possessed of a plethora of guns, bad coping mechanisms, and trauma nightmares. Her first and last attempt to join a team had ended almost as badly as her… as the initial infection.

Simone suppressed a shudder. Which was getting to be a habit lately.

Barry paused; it was clear he saw her expression change. "Nothing like that," he said, finally. "Not a crew possibly needing your, uh, unique and particular skills. But our angel investor's still interested in your whole deal."

"Wasn't aware I had a deal." Her chin set, and she was aware of scowling at the laptop. Her face on the screen was pale, pore-less skin gleaming; go figure, now she looked okay on camera and all it took was bags of human blood bought on the black market.

Or stolen from a hospital, though her conscience pinched hard either way. Figuring out how to acquire what she craved was unsettlingly easy, pulling off the acts even more so. Her own propensity for monstrous behavior was deeply troubling. If she wanted to survive, though, there was very little choice.

For all the liberation in becoming a possibly immortal blood-sucker, her options were still distressingly narrow.

"Just listen, will you?" Barry sped up, looking to get the entire spiel out before she lost interest—or took offense. "He circled around to the offer again; he'll pay just to meet you. Your record means that even if you're not exactly what he's after, he'd still like to talk—"

"Barry." Simone heard the bitchy little warning note to her own voice, and for once didn't feel bad about it. "You really shouldn't be bragging to this rich nutjob about your friend Jane and her vampirism infection."

"We both know Jane's not your real name." Barry dead-eyed the camera, probably fancying his expression a variety of fear-some glare. He looked about as dangerous as a narcoleptic prairie dog. "And your, again, *unique* set of skills means you've cleared more bounties alone than most pro teams do without fifty percent casualties at best. But since you're asking, I've kept several of your personal details out of it because I'm not a sleaze, for fucksake."

"No, you're a real prince." Simone mulled over whether prairie dogs could indeed be considered dangerous—they were rodents, so the biting had to be taken into consideration. It was the kind of question the internet had been created to answer.

How the world had changed since her childhood. She might look younger, but inside she was creaky and dusty as an abandoned farmhouse.

"The guy'll put down serious cash just for a meet," Barry persisted. "That's all, an hour of your time, anywhere in the continental US. He's legit, and he's looking for a cure."

For a moment Simone couldn't believe her new super-sharp, tinnitus-free ears had just relayed something so nonsensical. "What, he got bit too?"

"No, no, not like that. He's a literal *billionaire*, man." His bloodshot eyes lit up—he'd probably been waiting for her call-in, poor guy, knowing she was on the trail of at least one active infestation somewhere west of the Mississippi. "Got a whole lab up in the Rockies near Aspen, hush-hush, and could be government involved."

That sounds like a conspiracy theory. Or a really bad B movie, take your pick. Simone shook her head, hair sliding over her shoulders; getting out of her work ponytail was a wonderful event each evening. "If he's got all this juice and government help, why isn't there a cure yet?"

"Well, most va—ah, most bloodsuckers seem to be really *into* it, you know? But for those, you know, like you…"

The Simone on her screen now had narrowed eyes, and she was glad her resting bitchface was holding up. In fact, it seemed to have gotten a lot better since infection, which was a blessing since she looked so much younger now. "What gave you the idea I wasn't into being a bloodsucking monster, Barry?"

Not that she was, but so much of surviving in this line of work was putting up a fuck-you front. Showing any weakness was a no-no, even to so inoffensive a male specimen as this.

"Come on, Jane." Barry was flat-out wheedling now. Plenty of his job was dealing with touchy male hunter egos, and it showed. "Just meet the guy, show him you're the real deal. That's all he's asking."

More than I'm willing to give for free. "And I suppose he's paying after thirty days?"

"Nope." A shit-eating grin stretched his lips now. And it was official, Barry Jessup looked like a cat with a tummy stuffed full of canary. "Up front, once you commit to time and place."

"How much?" Another thing good girls weren't supposed to do—drive a hard bargain. But being middle-aged on the inside was a goddamn blessing, Simone thought; it gave a woman that most valuable twofer, experience *and* perspective. Almost a shame the magic only happened once men started finding you invisible or unfuckable.

He gave a number, and Simone laughed.

In fact, she damn near howled. A cascade of chuckles almost shook her out of the bench, the entire RV rocking a bit, candle-flames shivering on their wicks. "Nice one," she finally managed, wiping theatrically at her smooth, bone-dry cheeks. "Oh, Jesus. You really had me going for a second, Barry. Whew."

"I'm not joking." Now it was his turn to scowl—the canary had attempted an escape from digestion, maybe. "That's after my commission, by the way."

Oh, Lord. Simone's smile stayed fixed, though she wasn't feeling very humorous at the moment. "Yeah, and if you believe that—"

"A *vampire* is gonna lecture me about believability?" The scowl was back; Barry's forehead puckered like a piece of cloth run the wrong way through a cheap sewing machine. "I fucking checked this motherfucker out from tits to balls, Janie. He's *for real*, and he just wants to meet you. Maybe he gets off on talking to monsters, I dunno."

A low blow, but she probably deserved it. And Barry hardly ever called her *Janie;* neither of them liked to be anything but businesslike.

It was just better that way.

"Maybe he does," she agreed, before the silence could get awkward. "I'll think about it, once the bounty for this most recent escapade hits my account. Clock's ticking, my man." And she hung up without further niceties or polite little fictions.

A dick move? Maybe. But also incredibly liberating. Closing the laptop afterward was anticlimactic. So was heading to the step for what she still thought of as a smoke break, despite shedding any and all nicotine habit when she left college—along with drive-in movie dates and reading a book per week.

She ought to get back into that last one. If vampires lived as long as folklore said, she'd have plenty of time to absorb all the literature Curt always sneered at, plus any romance novel or spy thriller which caught her fancy as well.

All she had to do was decide. Maybe even audiobooks, since plenty of her time was spent driving.

It was a beautiful night. The stars no longer looked quite so menacing and the wind was full of subtle beauty, its fingers playfully combing long grass in seawave ripples before touching her loose, messy hair. This was her very favorite part of the working day, never mind that she'd probably never see the sun again.

Not unless she started to go murder-crazy, that was. Would she have the strength of will to off herself before she was a danger to others?

"Fuck," she said, drawing out the word long and soft. The night listened, as if it cared what she thought about anything; the feeling was immediate, not quite unwelcome, and downright unnerving.

What if there *was* a cure? Examining the idea from several different angles returned the depressing verdict that the government would probably suppress news of that miracle even if they didn't start trying to make vampire soldiers, just like they suppressed news reports about the monsters preying on humanity.

One argument in the online forums was that regular people didn't *want* to know, and the interests of public peace required not peeling up the carpet to see the bloodstain squirming with maggots underneath. Others thought the governing bodies themselves were either full of monsters or beholden to them, which was either paranoia *par excellance* or par for the course. Either way, Simone had decided, it amounted to the same thing. A difference which made no difference, so to speak.

Game it out a little more. Subtracting government from the equation left a rich man—always one of the worst monsters in history, needing no help from any myth or folklore. This shady billionaire was probably looking for a way to weaponize the whole bloodsucking deal, not to mention seeing if the vamp-blood cure for shot knees, tinnitus, astigmatism, or several other run-of-the-mill medical annoyances could be made to turn a profit.

Wouldn't one of the bloodsuckers have figured out a way to reverse vampirism by now, if it were possible? But they all seemed to go psycho instead.

Why didn't *she*? Or was she just living on borrowed time? Still, if she attended the meet carefully, after receiving even *half* the number Barry had given…

"Might be a good idea," she told herself. "No harm in trying, I suppose."

The dirty yellow taste of a lie lingered in her mouth. Any pleasure in watching the sky and listening to the wind's low wandering song was soured by her own conscience as well as that persistent, unsettling sense of being watched. Her sharp vampire senses caught nothing wrong, not a hair out of place in the vast panorama of sky, grass sea, and distant dark mountains; the sensation was atavistic, not to mention creepifying.

Maybe she really was beginning to go down Psycho Lane. There was no way to confirm just yet.

She barely needed the clock in her bones to announce dawn wasn't far off. The metallic note of deepest darkness had leached from the wind's back, and now moving air held the subtle promise of another late-summer day creeping for the horizon. At least she was relatively safe during sunlight hours, with very little danger of a nosy sheriff wandering by. Finding good parking was an art she was well-practiced in by now.

Fuck it. She bounced to her feet, climbed back into her approximation of a home—better than the cushy ranch-style she'd shared with Curt, since it was completely hers, no matter how tacky—and embarked on the familiar ritual of getting ready for bed.

It wasn't as soothing as usual, but that was to be expected.

CHAPTER 4

A VOLCANIC DAWN SWELL-SHIMMERED UPON THE EASTRON HORIZON, throwing up gouts of red, gold, pink, orange. Safe in the shadow of long grass and dry anemic shrubs, the wanderer waited. During the deepest darkness, further layers of killing dust had sloughed free of his vision, his hearing, even his sense of touch as he caught lingering traces of her scent in the clearing. It was an agony to wait as night faded, and even worse to anticipate a heretofore-unseen protector returning.

Yet he had paid in painful coin for a marvelous, entirely worthwhile certainty. She was indeed unclaimed, and furthermore intended to sleep inside the vehicle. No sign of invisible seals, and even less of watchful, wrathful attention from another sanguinant. Now he was curious as to how such a mythical, beautiful creature came to be wandering about in this manner, and longed to hear her tale.

Was she simply waiting for a worthy guardian? He was savage enough to survive both fire and madness; he wondered if that was enough to hold such a nonpareil.

Mistform was denied to him between sunrise and dusk, but he could nevertheless slip soundlessly across gravel, a shadow in strengthening sunlight. The glare of Shamash's eye scratched almost pleasantly along any bit of exposed skin. He vaguely remembered that at first his own eyes had watered and stung even on a cloudy day, but now the discomfort was minimal.

He had been daywalker before the disaster, he knew that much. For once, thinking upon the event did not drive him further into mental fracture. He could even separate threads of earlier languages from the spare, drawling tongue now current in this part of the country, heard as he watched mortals go about their brief, fascinating lives.

Occasionally his hide twitched, though, remembering old hurts. The great fire's scars had been agonizing as they healed. He did not care to think upon the ocean of blood necessary to fuel that repair; he had drunk deep and often, risking the killing frenzy of glut. Lifted free by her scent, the peeling away of successive carapace-layers brought memories swirling where splintering chaos had once reigned; his ratiocination was shaky and the rest of him deeply distracted, the risk of overlooking simple dangers magnified for some short while, but he was certain of a few things now.

Yakum, he no longer remembered his mortal life or clan, nor his becoming sanguinant. *Dì èr*, he was somewhere upon the westron side of a rich, varied continent, and had held this territory for a century plus-some-while. *Tertius*, he must learn quickly of the world's current state.

Most importantly, nothing could be allowed to harm this sweet, toothsome brown-haired leman, or jeopardize his claim. A prodigy had appeared in his steadily degrading existence, a salvation which now must be taken, cared for, sheltered.

Kept.

Lack of mistform thankfully did not mean he was denied other abilities. The vehicle's side door was locked, though the mechanism was simple and yielded to the invisible pressure any sanguinant capable of reaching Elder status could deploy in varying proportions. A better deterrent was something which felt to his mental grasp like an iron bar, resting in brackets—so she did take some few precautions with her bolt-hole.

Good.

Not nearly enough, however. It was indeed an iron bar, and he settled it carefully back in its serviceable, slightly uneven handmaids. Had she bolted them on herself? The fragrance of his new prize enfolded him, strong and sure, stripping away choking dust and killing calcification, sending pleasant shivers through ageless flesh.

Cramped yet ruthlessly tidy, a complete house upon wheels in the style of home-ships or some nomadic caravans. A tiny galley innocent of dirty dishes—she did not require mortal food, though such fare could be pleasant, even luxurious to sanguinant—and cabinets of thin pseudo-wood, blinds fitted into and drapes drawn over every aperture. Even the glass-eyed front, where a driver and passenger would sit at relative ease as the carriage raced over paved roads, was shielded by ingenious lids made of cardboard, thin metal rods, and reflective fabric. Windows along the sides also bore extra curtains, turning the vehicle into a dim, breathless cave.

A tiny watercloset to the rear, bearing the dry faint tang of bleach. She was a cleanly creature; he took another long inhale and her scent worked into the bottom of his lungs, teased at his fangs, reknit the aching shards inside his skull more firmly. Unfamiliar peace swamped him, banishing the rage, the grievous terror and numb apathy, the unrelenting torment of an incomprehensible world.

On a shelf above the driving-seats, a cavern arranged very much like a trundle bed emitted drenches of that soothing, magnificent fragrance. The subliminal hum of her presence, a divine creature slumbering—a fledgling, caught in the grip of daylight rest, saw and felt nothing until dusk.

No trace of another sanguinant, nor hint of any presence save hers. A sleek black item upon the small table which could be used for meals or converted into another bed was... he groped for the term.

It was not the *tele-vision*, a wonder he had grasped even while mad, as it was like the kinematograph—a technological marvel spoken of in tones of wonder just before his catastrophe. But another deep, drenching inhale and he had the proper term. Yes, a wholly modern thing, *com-pu-ter*; he had noticed the glowing screens as he watched mortals through windows or at a distance, attempting to absorb what he could of prey-habits as he struggled against the madness. They had smaller varieties now as well, wondrous devices fitting in pockets, their bright glass faces apparently hypnotic even if the attraction escaped him.

He hungered to learn more, to listen to her explain this strange scientific sorcery, to become conversant, then proficient, then skilled. Leman did not suffer calcification, did not become rigid and hidebound with time. Ever curious, ever sensitive, they moved through eternity's wasteland, transforming sterility to lush garden—and their bonded protectors shared in that priceless gift. To have a leman was to be immune from the trap of kill-craze during glut, banishing the languor of multicolored visions which starved a sanguinant by fractions, to shake away the stultifying curse of numb, accreted age.

Such miracles were of necessity rare, and invaluable. No sanguinant would ever willingly let one fall from their grasp. Discovered when mortal, they were to be bitten and claimed immediately; to find one protected by another sanguinant was to challenge for possession and be either victorious or dead.

Yet here she was, an inarguable fact. The sense that he was hallucinating before true-death shook him at intervals, dispelled each time he filled mouth and nose with that wonderful fragrance.

As in so many cautionary tales, he must see again to believe. Perhaps he would be struck down for his daring; all the same, he was helpless to turn aside.

He did not precisely need the ingeniously constructed ladder leading to her couch. Yet he used it anyway, moving with patient stealth so complete he barely stirred trapped, motionless air. His pulse thundered, disobeying the command to silence, but there was no one to hear.

Only a fledgling fast asleep, her lovely skein of cedarbark hair spread across a flower-patterned pillowcase. One tender arm thrust under pillow and head, dark eyelashes a fan against her cheekbones; she had not even taken her shoes off. The flush of rest colored those thin cheeks, her mouth in repose far less somberly drawn, her free hand limp and carelessly close to the bed's edge. A trace of gleaming upon her pretty fingertips caught his attention, and the wanderer froze.

Death-dust. So she had indeed been present at the trespasser's demise. A leman, so young and yet capable of such violence? His sense of her age in the Blood was now nearly exact, and if she were more than a half-century in darkness he would... what?

Eat my hat, he had heard mortals say. What an amusing phrase; now he could appreciate it. Especially since he was wearing one—or was he? Yes, he possessed a battered greyish piece in the style of this territory, camouflage acquired from he knew not where like the rest of his raiment, removed with punctilious manners so soon as he entered her domicile. He had set it upon the table next to the *com-pu-ter*.

No doubt he was a ragged, sorry sight. His existence had for some while precluded such luxuries as a proper nest, though he had small tomb-lairs aplenty and even the earth itself would hold one of his age at need. Nor had he bothered to amass certain things necessary for a leman's comfort. To do so was a new challenge, one he must and would rise to.

For a moment, the enormity of what was occurring shook him to the very floor of consciousness and body both.

He had survived. The storm of flame and agony was past, a long night of insanity broken; the fever was done and a cool hand pressed to his brow. He studied his rescuer's face once more, lost in wonder. Impossible to say which he adored more, the peace of her repose or the wonder of her awake, displaying a kaleidoscope of thought and emotion like swift-changing weather upon plain or mountainside. Drinking her in, each breath nailing him more firmly to a coherent, understandable world once more, he also realized he knew neither his name nor her own.

All in good time. His true teeth were free now, each faint breath sliding painfully past, and though a fledgling's sleep was often mistaken for mortal death he sensed the infinitely slow tide-change of her sweet, beckoning blood. She did not stir as he crept, inch by fraction of inch, onto the bed. Slow as sinking quicksand, he slithered to embrace his deliverance, and the first touch was hesitantly reverent.

Arranging sleep-heavy limbs was no difficulty. Nor was tipping her chin aside—she was tall for a woman, fitting perfectly against his own neglect-wasted frame—and finding the near-imperceptible pulse. His fang-tips hovered uncertainly as a new thought intruded upon careful, one-pointed concentration.

Such a blessing, the ability to focus again. To have considerations instead of mere murderous distraction.

First the bite, then the claiming, a sanguinant proverb. Yet she was unconscious, clearly ill-fed, and had endured the trespasser's violence to boot. To wake and find herself suddenly…

A faint thrum was the growl beginning deep in his ribcage, provoked by the thought of a now-gone intruder laying hands upon her. The need struck, dark and terrible, every inch of cloth against his skin a fierce irritant, and even the mating-thrall was a vivid, razor-edged pleasure after so much terrified numbness. How long had it been since he had felt the urge, a full erection uncomfortably bound and gagged?

Must protect. Yes, that was the overarching goal, yet when a thoroughly modern fledgling awoke, what would she think of attentions paid during her somnolence? It did not matter; a leman *must* be claimed.

And yet.

His control slipped, instinct striking snake-quick. Had she a bonded protector still living, his teeth would have been unable to pierce, but his fangs sank into glorious yielding.

Molten syrup, clear and fine as the strongest unwatered wine. So hot, so sweet, so *good*; the essence of heat and beauty hit the back of his throat and slid down, spreading through every vein and artery bright-quick as lightning, lingering in a deep haze.

The second gift of a leman—an immediate addiction, a single mouthful rendering all other blood into tasteless sludge. Necessary and nutritious, certainly, but the temptation of glut was wholly erased in a moment, since what could compare to *her*? He would never feel the craze again, the Sanguinant's Thirst narrowed to one very specific flavor.

If he had not already cherished the scent which repaired his sanity, the taste of her would have provided worshipful reverence. Oh, yes, now he understood the whispers through the demimonde, the proverbs translated into any language those of the Blood knew. Most held leman to be a fiction, yet he held one in his very arms and his fangs sank deeper as he pulled a second mouthful, the growl rattling every surface of this tiny habitation.

A welcome obsession, a rock catching a falling man's hand, a rope clutching a drowning swimmer. She burned through him, the blood carrying sadness, an eternity of lonely nights, a complex pattern of emotion and instinct making up a leman.

His leman. And by every god or spirit ever honored he longed for the next step, to rid them both of clothing and take her in time-honored fashion.

One last pull against her veins, the burnt-caramel edge far more pronounced now. She was on the very edge of starvation, tissues ready to self-cannibalize. To take more would be a criminal misuse, unworthy of a man granted a miracle.

It required a great deal of will to withdraw, to clean the slight wounds with his tongue, healing agents spread with lingering care. To lie still, eyes closed and unfamiliar serenity filling him to the brim, as his arms tingled with the feel of her and the rest of him burned with pleasurable almost-pain.

The sun had mounted quite high, pressing against thin metal walls. A single finger of its light would cause irreparable harm, but she had shielded this small cave well. He had some few hours to prepare for her waking; he must re-accustom his tongue to her native language, acquire better clothing, begin arrangements for her comfort and protection.

Licking his lips, absorbing every last trace of her taste, his nose buried in her tumbled hair and her scent wrapping about his very bones, he reveled in the sheer luxury of finally thinking clearly.

If he left her vicinity, how long before the killing dust grimed his senses afresh? He sensed unreason crouching outside the small bright circle of her presence, and the prospect of suffering a splintering, howling madness again was unpleasant at best.

Be precise. It is terrifying, and to be avoided at all cost.

So. He would leave her to rest under his own invisible seals, test how far the effect of her grace extended, make what arrangements he could, and return at speed.

Another luxury—to have a direction, a series of tasks, a *purpose*. The largest difficulty would be in tearing himself away from this most beautiful of enigmas.

He set his jaw and began the process of doing so, inch by laborious, resisting inch.

CHAPTER 5

SINCE HER INFECTION THERE WAS NO LEISURELY AWAKENING, lolling in bed half-conscious. Instead, a switch flipped and Simone was *up*, alert and aware to a degree she'd never before considered possible. No coffee or tea necessary, and that fact was both useful—no need to waste time—and sort of maddening, because a mug of something hot and caffeinated was one of the better ways to start a day.

Of course, her days were nights, but that was beside the point.

Rolling off the bed and landing feather-light in the RV's central aisle was surprisingly easy; she hadn't needed to practice more than once, and that initial attempt had gone perfectly. Running her fingers through her hair, she took a deep breath. Yawning hadn't gone the way of bathroom visits, so she gave herself a good one every evening.

The dry spot at the back of her throat was worse. Simone stretched, turning this way and that, shook her hands out. No need to check the bathroom mirror, really. The vampire movies got one thing right—being infected gave you clear skin and a great 'do right out of the gate.

Maybe that was what Barry's billionaire friend was after. Leech-based beauty treatments.

The RV's claustrophobic familiarity felt a tad different tonight. She sniffed, experimentally—no, nothing off. Her hearing, exquisitely sensitive as well as blessedly tinnitus-free, filled with absence. Not even the usual low moan of wind brushed her eardrums. Of course, that was probably just edited out by her brain, since she'd been hearing it all throughout this particular bounty.

Still, she couldn't shake the feeling that something important had changed, an invisible shift just barely under the threshold of sharpened perceptions. But everything was as it should be— jumbo crowbar over the locked door, her laptop right on the table, the three bags of O-positive on the mini-fridge's shelf looking smug and self-satisfied, knowing they weren't enough. Simone straightened, closing the fridge, and stood for a moment, her brain racing furiously.

Nothing. You're paranoid, you know how it is every time you finish a real job. Killing drunk-acting vampires was hardly a confidence booster, to be honest. Each death was horrifying, seeing the things they did to their victims a stark reminder of her own infection as well as what could potentially be awaiting her in a few more years, and even if she considered herself more a vigilante or an exterminator there were definite ethical drawbacks to either.

Her existence abounded with slippery slopes.

Plus, the thirstier she got, the more her nerves frayed. Maybe at some point that would overpower her instinctive revulsion at the act of drinking from a human, even a pushy guy at a bar or nightclub. How often had she actually gotten her fangs in someone, now?

Twice, and both times she'd been so goddamn afraid of possibly not being able to stop. That she'd rip a perfectly normal human being open like a bag of potato chips and leave them dead, just another statistic for the cops to file under *weird story, but unsolvable, let's go have some doughnuts.*

The fact that she *had* stopped, that it actually hadn't been that difficult, wasn't a comfort. A lot of things weren't hard until *boom, sorry, you're getting old, your knees and your marriage don't work anymore, and forget getting up from the couch without making an old-lady sound, bitch.*

She moved automatically, taking down her canvas messenger bag, stuffing the laptop in its big pocket, checking the pathetically thin roll of emergency cash and two fake IDs, the switchblade she hadn't needed yet, the ashwood stake she'd tried before discovering her claws worked better than anything else. She glanced at the bathroom door—there was her jacket, hanging right where it should be, but…

That was closed when I went to bed. Wasn't it?

Now she couldn't remember. She would sense if someone else had entered her space. Wouldn't she? She was out hard during daylight, sure, but once conscious her nose was like a bloodhound's.

Still, Simone's instincts were screaming. The creepy sense of being observed by an invisible gaze was muted yet persistent, and sent a cool trickle of dread down her spine. Something was definitely wrong, growing worse by the second.

You're paranoid. It's the first step in going crazy like all the other—

A faint rustling under the shell of silence, like chiffon brushed by a fingertip. The very softest hint of warm breeze inside the RV's sheltered stillness, where nothing but her should be moving, and the consciousness of another living, breathing being nearby was sudden, undeniable, and utterly terrifying. Her back prickled, and she had to concentrate in order to turn her chin, the rest of her following with dreamlike, wooden slowness.

Watching horror movies, she'd always mocked the agonizing snail-speed rotation of the camera to reveal a monster. She'd since found out it actually felt that way, body and perceptions trapped in a torrent of clear, heavy goop weighing on every limb, straining against fear and simply hoping the bad thing would go away before visual data arrived at the brain to make it un-ignorable.

A tall, lean shadow, with a shock of dusty dark hair. Bright blue eyes under heavy near-horizontal brows, a long aristocratic nose, and of all things, he was holding a stiff, new black Stetson in both hands. He stared at her, head cocked slightly, and he was *unquestionably* a fellow vampire.

In her RV. Standing, in fact, between her and the cockpit, as if he hadn't needed to go through the side door *or* the driver's and passenger's. As if he'd been there the entire time, just invisible.

Now she could smell him. *Male, brunet, been outside for a while*, her nose cataloging impressions swiftly, along with *new clothes right off the rack, didn't wash them* and the information that his boots were brand-new as well. Not that she would have thought otherwise, since they were shiny and uncreased, though thankfully not expensive black Tony Lamas with bright silver toecaps.

More than that, he *felt* ancient, in that funny instinctive way she could guess at the age of bounty targets—a riptide of pure force, deceptively placid on the surface, far older than any other bloodsucker she'd come into contact with. A horrifying hush filled the RV's interior, slopping against the ceiling, and Simone's lungs refused to work normally. Her exhale was chopped into little bits as she straightened, caught in panic-soaked slow motion.

Her lips trembled, her throat dry as Death Valley.

Door. All she had to do was throw herself backward and buttonhook to the left around the edge of the under-sink cabinets; the crowbar was basically to dissuade humans bent on daytime theft, but if she could reach and use it as a weapon…

The other vampire just *stood* there, examining her. Those black jeans were so new they still had shelf-creases, the braided leather belt similarly just-off-the-shelf. His shirt was like hers, thermal cotton waffle-weave, but black as sin and stretched over shoulders a little too broad for the rest of him. He looked half-starved and stringy, but that was no indication; the instinctive sense of old, deep, controlled power was over-whelming.

This is going to end very badly. Simone stared, waiting. Time ticked by, caught in silent stasis, and the thought that maybe this creature was simply playing with her was utterly horrifying in its own way.

"Fine," she heard herself say, dully. "Kill me. Get it over with."

In a way, it was almost a relief.

Whatever Simone expected, it wasn't the continuing slow appraisal, his gaze moving down to her toes and back up, fastening on her face.

He cleared his throat, an oddly human sound. His voice was hoarse, as if disused or broken from screaming—or as if he was dry-thirsty as her own desiccated self. "There ain't no need t' fear, pretty girl."

Oh, there is. There absolutely is. Simone thought about the door again, and nearly gasped when the vampire leaned forward. A subtle movement, but marked to her sharp, inhuman senses.

Wait. He's talking instead of just growling and snapping his fangs.

"Where is your protector, hm?" His long, capable-looking fingers tightened on the hat's brim, pressing felt with exquisitely gauged pressure. "Your Maker, the one who gave you the Gift?"

Is that really what you want to know? And what did he mean, *protector*? There had been no protection involved, just the attack, the... the assaults, the biting, and the fear.

Remembering the agony, the terror, her own screams, the rattle of handcuffs... no. She *refused* to think about that. "Dead." The word shook, and the rest of her trembled as well. The spot at the back of her throat dilated, prickling terribly; if she got out of this, even all three bags in the fridge at once wouldn't be enough to erase the dryness.

Who are you kidding? This guy's gonna tear you apart, just like you ripped up that motherfucker last night.

"I am sorry," he said, gravely. He certainly wasn't acting like the other vampires, weird and violent-drunk. Was it just a phase the young ones grew out of? "It must have been very frightening."

Could this be the one who had infected her attacker? Some of the folklore had funny ideas about lineage; it was the only thing that seemed to make sense. If he was, though, had he been tracking her down for five fucking years? Her brain attempted to process that question, plus the fact of another vampire actually *talking*, hit a sheer wall made of blank panic, and gave up. Simone threw herself toward the door.

Or tried to, at least. The vampire blinked across intervening space, iron-hard hands closed on her, and even though she was doomed, there was nothing to do but fight.

CHAPTER 6

For example, now he knew straying from her side provoked an almost immediate return of painful mental splintering plus the deadening of every sense, growing progressively worse with each passing moment; he knew that simply taking anything he wished from a mortal merchant or home was still so easy as to be an afterthought; and he knew that mortals still actively avoided and ignored anything they felt instinctively to be truly strange, even in broad sunlight.

However, he was still no closer to understanding where his leman had appeared from, or precisely what had happened to her Maker. And he certainly had not expected such an immediate, violent response, though now he could well guess how a scent-drunk fledgling eager to claim a treasure could conceivably be dispatched by such a beautiful, desperately feral creature.

Unless the recent trespasser had been her Maker? Unlikely, and he could not ask at the moment. She twisted in his grasp, striking out with lovely quicksilver grace; perhaps her former protector had encouraged violence? It was possible; the wanderer could even allow it likely. Sanguinant were powerful predators, many well used to indulging sadistic fantasies upon helpless prey.

They all began as humans, and the Dark Gift allowed no few of the species' worst impulses to run wild.

Easy to lay hold of her, his own force thoroughly controlled to avoid any pain or damage. To cage her in his arms, enjoying the wild struggle pouring through her slim frame, rubbing against him with soft, frantic abandon. She was silent, perhaps in desperation—though a leman had to know what would happen next.

Wonderful to hold something so tender, so fragrant, his grasp a bulwark against the outer world. A strand of her hair ran across his lips, dyed and flavored with that glorious, mouthwatering scent; clasped hard against him and lifted free of the floor, she sought to kick, clipping the booth holding the table. Veneer splintered, dust puffing up. He lifted her a little more—this variety of mortal construction was too flimsy to harm her, but he would not, *could* not take even the smallest chance.

"Shhh," he murmured, seeking to soothe, to find the sweet flawless shell of her ear and hopefully calm all this furious motion. He searched for words, his grasp of this time and place's language better since he had spent the afternoon half-listening to the mortals in the nearby town, but not nearly so complete as he would like. "Easy there, little lady. We'll be knowin' each other better soon, but—"

She gave a short, inarticulate scream, struggling with fresh strength, and her claws were out. Fabric tore, a prickle dragging along the outside of his hip since she could reach nothing else with her arms pinned. Did she wish to pierce his skin? It would not happen unless consciously allowed; an Archon's hide was exceeding tough.

Had her former protector trained her to accompany feeding with violence? Such games were not to his taste, but if she required he would certainly provide. The caramel edge to her scent intensified, the note of burning growing unacceptable. She would damage herself soon, and that could not be allowed.

Enough. His strength and speed far outstripped hers; nevertheless, he sought to be gentle. He bore her down, the narrow strip of worn scratchy carpet between cabinets and the booth-and-table rushing up to meet them, then he had her pinned to the floor. Capturing both her wrists was another simple maneuver, as was his knee between hers, pressing with just a fraction more strength than she could summon.

She froze, dark eyes staring at him through a deliciously mussed tangle of silken hair. This close he could see the green and paler chestnut threads in her irises, taste the flood of her breath as her ribs—beautifully curved as cathedral arches—heaved. A high flush in her cheeks, though not nearly so much as there should be.

Simply not enough blood to fuel a blush, he realized. The urge to feed her was nearly overpowering yet paled beside the thrall rising in his bones, snarling and clawing unmercifully.

"Just kill me," she whispered, her lips shaping the words with fascinating little movements. The feel of her slenderness under him was so entirely enticing he almost missed the meaning of the phrase. Why would she— "Just do it, please, for God's sake, I don't want to live like this anymore."

He thought she had somehow managed to stab him, despite both her arms being trapped and a fledgling's strength literally incapable of damaging one so much older. A thin, pointed spear pierced his chest; after a moment he identified the feeling as *heartbreak*, painfully glorious after centuries of numb, grinding insanity. "Nah." His voice, rough from screaming and lack of use, was a harsh bark after the music of hers. "It'll done be better, I swear. I'll make it so."

But first... All thought foundered, the thrall rising to swallow him whole. Cloth tore, and the first real brush of her skin against his sent a jolt all through, crown to soles. His new garb tore free in ribbons, hers just as easily dealt with, and the curve of her belly was a downy delight. Such velvet, once all the irritating obstacle-veils were ripped away, and her thighs parted almost easily. He let go of her wrists, and she attempted to strike and claw him again—he accepted the blows, each a brushing enticement.

Coffin-narrow, the space precluded much movement, be he was still able to hook his fingers in the soft hot hollow under one of her knees, pressing it aside into the foot-space under the table. Sliding forward, the hungry yearning tip of his phallus finding a scorching velvet at the very core of her body—

She burst into fresh frenzied motion, or tried to. Whatever she meant to say was lost as his mouth found hers, his true teeth suppressed though her fangs were well in evidence, and she sought to bite him even as he sealed his lips to hers, drinking any cry, scream, plea. He was a well, every surface eager to echo her, and he tried to slow down, to take some measure of her arousal.

Fear was twined with the survival instincts, both braided through the mating urge. Hot slickness eased his way, her scent darker now, even more intoxicating. She moved, he responded, and the first thrust was sheer paradise. The second was even better, if that were possible, and he was lost in a welter of sensation. Her hips rose, an involuntary, betraying twitch, and his body eagerly answered, driving deep.

Time stopped, meaningless in scorching, velvet eternity. Trapped, she writhed beneath him; the secondary prong of a male sanguinant's mating form questing for the most sensitive bundle of nerves either mortal or his own kind possessed; he found her rhythm and pressed advantage unmercifully.

No quarter, no mercy, nothing but the blind urge to *take*. Nothing mattered but the throaty, mellifluous cries of her release, the rhythmic, strangling pulse as she finally reached the summit, wracked by the little-death of pure pleasure.

The imprinting roared through him, a crimson roar like the long-ago fire robbing him of both sanity and coherence. It was not the honeyed spasm of his own physical release, yet the sensation was strangely akin. How had he lived for so long without this sheer, stunning, divine relief?

His leman shuddered into quiescence, though her true teeth were still out and the terrible burning note of malnutrition in her scent could not be borne. He freed his mouth, lifting his chin to expose his throat, and as he pressed still deeper into her hot, throbbing core she took the invitation and struck, sanguinant instinct fighting for blind survival.

And he let her sweet, sharp fangs pierce his skin.

His leman gulped greedily, clutching his shoulders, drawing starving-hard against his veins. Each burst of suction tore through him, tightening every muscle and nerve in an ancient, preternaturally strong body; he only regretted that he had not fed more deeply before returning, in order to grant her a greater measure. As it was, he gave enough to skirt the edge of actual weakening before denying her fangs, though it pained him to force his skin closed and hear the tiny, mewling, dissatisfied noise made deep in her throat.

"Enough, darlin'," he crooned, rubbing his chin against her cheek, an absent caress. "More later, an' t' spare." Each word was a dry rasp, but he cared not a whit.

It was done. His leman was claimed. He was conscious of her arms loosening, her hands falling from his shoulders, and her lapse into stillness. Ragged breathing, her eyes half-closed, perhaps languid with desire's aftermath.

He hoped it had been adequately pleasant. And that it had elided every trace of her former protector—*dead*, she said, and that was good.

Very good. The thought of any other sanguinant touching this miracle was enough to rouse a killing rage deep enough to eclipse anything he had ever felt before, since the fire or before—though he could remember only scattered scenes of that dim, vast, rustling archive.

For now, he was content. And, as soon as she was ready to speak, perhaps he would learn her name.

CHAPTER 7

SIMONE HAD EXPECTED BRUTAL DISMEMBERMENT, MAYBE HER THROAT torn out, a brief burst of agony before she went dry-poof just like the bounties, a whirl of glittering dust and so long, that's all she wrote.

Not… not *this*, whatever it was. She hadn't come so hard since well before her marriage, and never with anyone else. Maybe her post-infection dry spell had been saving up for a big blowout, or maybe the clitoral stimulation had done the trick? And all on the floor of an RV she'd bought for cash in a lemon lot just outside Lorraine, Kansas, for God's sake.

At least she'd cleaned every inch of the interior more than once, usually while thinking about how to go about another bounty. It was a relief, a luxury, having nobody's dirt but her own to deal with.

Horribly vulnerable, to be sprawled under someone like this. Terrible to think that he'd gotten what he wanted and next he'd kill her, she'd have to go to hell knowing that her last hour on earth had been spent… like this.

She might even be laying on his stupid hat, which was deeply, mortifyingly funny in the way only life-threatening bullshit could be. And oh, hadn't she learned the value of screaming dark hilarity, of laughing when it became too much to take?

Any woman surviving long enough in this hateful world knew that particular exchange rate.

Silence, except for her own breathing and a deep, slow thudding. A leisurely two-tone thump, long pause, another thump, all falling into dead air. She still couldn't hear the wind, and that should have clued her in—but how on *earth* could she have guessed at a vampire just blinking into existence with no warning? Her senses were acute, and she'd clocked every other bloodsucker she'd come across with no trouble at all.

Or had she? *That* was a fucking terrifying question. If one could fly under her radar, others could too.

And she'd been doing so well.

Come on. Think. Simone stayed very still, hoping against hope the old vampire would somehow forget about her. Or maybe fall asleep, like her attacker had after the initial assault? That floppy-haired bloodsucker had done terrible things to her, but not like this. For one thing, during the first attack she'd been bleeding from several shallow cuts, which had seemed to drive the bastard even deeper into violent, drunken psychosis.

Her breathing evened out. That strange thumping was like a heartbeat—his? Why hadn't she heard it before he resolved out of thin air? Did he have what he wanted? Was this some kind of vampire handshake, the etiquette when meeting a really old bloodsucker?

The last five years had been weird as shit, but this had to win some kind of prize.

Sure. Just gotta live long enough to cash the ticket in. Now she was painfully conscious of reclining on cheap nylon carpet, and maybe he wasn't done because he was still…well, still apparently, entirely erect, and stuck so deep every small after-orgasm vaginal twitch reminded her of the fact.

She was trying very hard not to think about the taste in her mouth, either. Or the warmth spreading through her, the horrible dry spot at the back of her throat vanished for the first time since she'd changed into full vampire—because that metamorphosis hadn't happened all at once, oh no.

That would have been too easy.

Still, once this particular vampire's blood touched her lips, it was like yet another switch had flipped. She'd very nearly forgotten what was happening with the rest of her body while she gulped greedily at a burning, delicious flow, and the taste wasn't flat iron like the blood packs or even the complex mix of emotion and strange flashes of insight from the two humans she'd tried drinking from.

No, this vamp's blood was different things in quick succession. Blueberry pie, still warm from the oven. The first few bites of a *really* good bacon cheeseburger. An almond latte, Christ how she missed coffee. An orange-and-vanilla popsicle on a hot summer's day, the puttanesca sauce from that Italian eatery that had closed in Midtown ages ago. All good things, most favorites she hadn't tasted in years—or decades as the case may be.

Wait. Did I kill him, guzzling like that? Or maybe he was passed out since she'd taken down his blood pressure? But she could hear his pulse and he wasn't unconscious-limp. Instead, he was considerately keeping most of his weight braced and balanced atop her.

As if sensing the question, he shifted slightly. The movement caused a ripple through her entire body, something poking at her post-coitally sensitive clitoris, and Simone gasped.

"Easy," the old vampire murmured, his breath touching her hair. He still sounded like he'd gargled gravel for breakfast. "I'll feed you agin' soon, darlin'."

This was the first time any other vampire had actually *spoken* instead of just staring as if hypnotized or making quasi-drunken noises, their fangs out and their eyes laser-locked on her. And save for the hoarseness his accent was no different than the bartender's last night, right down to the marked, flat drawl.

Jesus, I just got fucked by Gunsmoke Dracula. It could have been funny, if she'd felt like laughing. Simone didn't like the thought of a vampire sounding *human*. But at the same time, she herself sounded reasonable enough to pass—or so she hoped.

Barry certainly seemed to think so. And oh God, how she wished she'd hung up on the video call and started driving, making miles before dawn.

"Are you going to kill me now?" The words quivered in her no-longer-dry throat. So much for sounding brave, but she needed to know.

At least she had her wind back now. He was terrifyingly strong, worse than any bounty she'd ever come across—there was a *reason* she stuck to the young ones—and the appearing-out-of-thin-air thing was a definite advantage on his part.

All of which meant she had to be sneaky, play for time, and hope to hell he felt like monologuing his evil plans. Generally it wasn't hard to get a man talking about himself; she hoped she still had the knack.

"'Course not." The old vampire moved again, withdrawing slightly as if shocked. "Thought I'd ask yer name, an'… an' talk."

Little late for that, mister. "My name?" Simone sounded blank, dazed, and hoped he was buying it. Even if she wasn't quite playacting she certainly *felt* a bit dizzy, along with a deep warm sense of physical well-being she hadn't experienced since…

Good God, she couldn't think of when. Even right after becoming full vamp, discovering she could run at near freeway speed and jump at least a ranch-style house with a single bound. Experimenting to find the limits of her new status had been kind of a blast, to be honest.

Then she'd found out about the thirst. Each and every burst of superhuman ability had to be paid for, naturally. It fucking figured. Simone twitched, knowing any attempt at escape was most likely useless, but he moved again.

"Whate'er you like." The old vampire pulled free with slow care, each movement precisely controlled. It wasn't so much the strength as the restraint, Simone decided, and though staying motionless was probably a better option she couldn't help herself.

The moment it was possible she scrambled away toward the rear of the RV, nylon rasping her palms and bootheels—not to mention scraping her bare ass, because he'd ripped her jeans right off. He's shredded his own pants as well. Plus, she had indeed landed on his hat, which was sadly crushed.

Mr. Old Vampire rose with that same eerie, controlled grace, eyeing her mildly as she fetched up against the narrow closet next to the bathroom. She'd gone right past the side door, and cast a quick, longing glance in its direction.

You could just go straight out the wall of the RV. With fresh strength from several gulps of super-old-vampire blood, it was more than possible. Her nether portions gave a twinge, unused to all this activity; for breaking her post-divorce dry spell, this was certainly a landmark. *Don't be hamstrung by convention, Simone.*

"I wouldn't do that, now, darlin'." The old vampire should have looked ridiculous, pantsless with a considerable hard-on she might have admired under other circumstances, wearing only a torn thermal waffleweave and those brand-new boots. But there was nothing funny in the way his head cocked slightly, like a cat watching a struggling mouse—or the sheer sense of age and force spreading from him in an invisible, undeniable haze. "Y'all oughta know I won't hurt you."

I don't know that at all, thanks. Simone pulled her bare knees up and hugged them hard, grateful she still at least had her own shirt on. "You're old." Her voice wouldn't work quite right; the words shook like an old woman's limbs in the aftermath of a bad stomach flu. "Is… is that why you're not crazy?"

Although you could just be hiding it really well. And if you're sane, what the hell did you just… just fuck me for?

"Oh, I been crazy for a long time. Couple centuries,

mayhap?" He looked very comfortable, all things considered, as if this was his RV and Simone a new, slightly tiresome guest. "But you fix that right up, pretty little leman."

Oh, shit. It occurred to her that maybe sucking on blood pouches had kept her from going cuckoo like other vamps, and now she'd just taken in a few pints from a monster who cheerfully admitted to being around the bend. Even more terrible was the realization that he hadn't used any form of protection.

What if the staggering, fangs-out craziness of other blood-suckers was a strain of rabies, or an STD? How long did she have before she went foaming, biting, barking psycho?

He'd gone motionless again, watching her with those bright, interested blue eyes. Her bag was still on the table; the few spare outfits she had were in the closet behind her. How far could she get? He was so *goddamn* fast.

Be smart, Simone. Be very smart, for however long you've got left. The fear was wine-red, familiar, a hateful constant companion. "How the hell did you get in here?" The words shook; it was so goddamn *quiet*. The longer this went on, the more wrong that one tiny detail seemed; her RV could have been flown into orbit and plonked on the moon, for all she knew.

"Through the door—leastways, the first time." A smile bloomed, spread slowly across his lean, almost-handsome face. "You don't set no seals. Dontchew worry, I'll take care o' that."

Christ, he sounds like he's auditioning for Bonanza. Or a Clint Eastwood movie; she briefly wondered what ol' Clint would think of all this, and maybe that was the first sign of losing her goddamn mind. "What the fuck do you *want*?"

He shrugged, his erection leering at her from under the shirt's hem. "Well, now, your name would be a good start. And y'all can maybe find—"

Simone's nerves snapped. She *felt* them give way, a twang like overstressed guitar strings finally parting. Or maybe it was the impact, because she used every last inch, ounce, and gram of speed and strength she owned, throwing herself sideways at the wall next to the crowbarred door...

...and was flung back with corresponding force, slamming into the cabinets across the RV that held just-in-case camping gear and a few unnecessary weapons. She slid down, and didn't have time to land because the old vampire had flickered across intervening space to catch her, iron-hard hands closing about her arms.

"Never, *ever* do that again," that rough, gravelly voice said.

The hit rang her chimes pretty good, but other than that it accomplished precisely nothing. The old vampire seemed pretty concerned, which was a laugh and a half, and after a thorough examination, turning her this way and that while she tried to shake the dazement out of her skull, he guided her to sit at the table.

Simone, perched in one half of the booth, stared bleakly at the barred door. Now she could almost-see a sort of shimmer like rippling hot air over distant summer pavement, still reverberating with the force of impact. *Invisible seals*, he called them, and she'd seen that kind of thing once before.

In the concrete-walled church basement, as a matter of fact, while the floppy-haired vampire who had infected her snoozed away the day, Simone handcuffed to an exposed piece of rebar in the corner.

This old vampire clearly had no trouble getting through the shimmer—vanishing briefly and popping back into sight bearing a brown paper bag full of spare clothes, all brand-new as what he'd ripped off before nearly fucking the life out of her. She couldn't quite figure out what that level of preparation said about his sanity level, or her own.

She wanted very badly to open up the closet and get herself another pair of jeans, but if she so much as glanced in that direction he stopped, giving her a long, considering look. So she hunched, miserable and bare-legged, wondering if postcoital cooch-juice was going to stain the seat cushion's worn red-and-cream velour.

At least she wasn't leaking vampire sperm? That was something to be grateful for, Simone decided, and watched him pick up the crushed hat, working at the felt to push everything back into shape. Even his hands looked strong, broad palms and long fingers, muscled forearms visible since he'd pushed his sleeves up.

Sinewy, deceptively lean. She preferred stockier types, bonus if they ran a little shorter than usual—not that she'd ever had a chance to pick and choose after college, really, because she'd married Curt almost immediately. And any interest coming her way after going full vamp didn't count.

Hitting fifty had been a type of relief, once the worst of the divorce pain died down and she could think again. It was even freeing, after a fashion, to relegate any male attention to *kid waiter wants a bigger tip* or *thanks but I'll fantasize instead, fantasy is safe.* Plus, an older woman who had won the alimony battle could invest in a toy or two, delivered in discreet packaging, and simply take care of her own needs without any fuss or bother.

Her one attempt at painting the town red after the final hearing had ended ingloriously, with a crazy, nonverbal psycho of a vampire snatching her right as she began to unlock her old white Toyota, sitting sedately in a corner of the Barrel Roll parking lot. For all she knew the car was still there, and dear God but she never wanted to think about that particular evening ever again.

Tonight was shaping up to be a serious contender in that department, too. And she'd only just woken up.

"Oh, now." A big black smear appeared in front of her, folding down on itself—the blue-eyed vampire, fully dressed, sinking to crouch in the tiny space between her knees and the sink cabinets on the other side of the aisle. "What's wrong, darlin'?"

What the fuck do you think, you fucking bloodsucker? Simone shook her head. Her hair was a mess, even if vampires were blessed with sleek, tangle-free locks, and it slid over her shaking shoulders.

He said something else, low and melodious—either a foreign language, or he was babbling in tongues. The contrast with the aw-shucks cowboy drawl was shocking, and wrung a strained giggle from her throat; she hastily swallowed the small noise, her hand flying up to clap over her mouth.

He caught her wrist halfway through the motion, caging it securely. Once again, his strength wasn't nearly as frightening as the control. It didn't hurt, but she couldn't break free short of chewing her own arm off.

"Y'all been awful scared, I reckon." The cornpoke-and-cowboy accent intensified—he sounded local, right down to the syrup-slow delivery. His warm, hard fingers were gentle enough, sure, but she also remembered the leashed, casual power as he held her down. "But nothin's gonna hurt yew now. That's a promise, darlin', an'—"

If she were younger, she'd play along like you were always supposed to with a man who could hit you. Her entire life plus five years of living as an undead bloodsucker rose up inside Simone, ignited somewhere behind her breastbone, and filled her head with an unsteady ringing noise. Or maybe she had a bloodsucker concussion from hitting an invisible wall.

"Will you *stop* with the bullshit accent?" she hissed. "It's not funny."

"This is how they talk," he said, quietly. "The mortals I been listenin' to, at least; I ain't had time f'r others. Don't know yer language real well yet."

Each word sounded like it hurt, scraping his throat raw on the way out, and now she felt like an asshole. But she wasn't the one who had burst into *his* halfass approximation of a house, no sir, and now she had to wonder if he'd been watching her beforehand.

For how long? Had he seen her kill the other bloodsucker in the gully?

"But I'll learn," he added, grimly. All expression had left his face, and those blue eyes burned. "Soon's I can, to please you."

It was utterly fucking ridiculous. Her go-bag was right on the table, practically at her elbow, and if she could just get past him and through the shimmer-wall, she could... what? Run bareass through the night, hoping he wasn't fast enough to catch her?

That did not sound very intelligent at all. Neither did provoking him, especially when she wasn't sure what his plans were. If he was going to snap and poof her...

But he was talking again, each word carefully spaced. "I'm set on learnin' e'erything about this-here modern world. You'll help me with that, sweet leman. Right now, though, I need t'hunt. Y'all can stay here, locked under seals, or take me to where the mortals are. Whiche'er you like."

Oh, hell. Simone couldn't even wonder why the hell he was calling her a terribly accented *'lemon'*; it was no weirder than anything else tonight. The *'need to hunt'* bit was concerning—had this guy been responsible for the victims they'd attributed to her earlier bounty? But no, there was security footage about the younger one, who had seemed almost to delight in carnage; her visitor seemed a little too self-possessed to make that kind of mistake.

A chilling thought. So was playing chauffeur to a vamp while her nethers tingled and her mouth was full of a strange, spice-candy aftertaste, like dessert after a buffet of every delicious meal she'd ever eaten.

However, if he let her get behind the wheel, she had a chance or two of escape. It was selfish to prioritize her own hide over the humans this vamp could probably drain in moments, but at the moment Simone didn't care.

"I'll drive," she informed him, pulling against his hand. He let go—but only after a moment of keeping her wrist trapped, no doubt just to prove he could. "Can I at least get dressed?" *You ripped up my favorite jeans.*

She didn't add that bit, but he nodded as if he heard anyway. Was he telepathic? Christ, she hoped not.

"Yes ma'am," he said, and rose slowly, balanced and controlled as a cat all the way through the movement. "Anythin' you please."

CHAPTER 8

HE WOULD CERTAINLY HAVE PREFERRED HER HALF-CLAD IF AT ALL, but his new treasure seemed rather... high-strung. She had thrown herself against the seals without hesitation or restraint, and he had been too momentarily shocked to do more than catch her after impact.

The wanderer now had a number of dark suspicions about her former protector's tastes and proclivities, and he was almost sorry the other *sanguinant* was dead. Whoever—or whatever—had tormented this lovely creature until her responses were so full of flinching fear deserved the most lingering of punishments before finally breathing its last.

Even the fact that she was fully claimed, her new protector of ancient strength in the Blood, did not seem to comfort her.

Or perhaps he was laboring under some cardinal misapprehension, as he seemed to be in the matter of her language? A leman was so very precious, deserving of the most careful treatment. Had her former guardian instead been gentle, had she felt affection for them, and did not wish to sully the memory by accepting a new suitor? Difficult to tell. Her fascinating hazel eyes were wide with caution; her gaze roved, clearly weighing every avenue for escape, and the wanderer had not felt so interested, so *exercised*, in a very long time. The very presence of an *imprima*, a *deva*—he could now remember more names for what she was, in at least four languages and another tongue long dead—tore successive layer after layer of dead age from mind and body both, honing him to a keen edge. The pleasure of anticipation, of moving to forestall almost before she could think of possible flight, was completely, intensely luxurious.

Her scent now lacked any hint of malnutrition, though she was still painfully thin, visibly anxious. And the new smoky haze-tint to her fragrance was his own blood in her veins, a mark of warning—and possession.

A continual wonder, watching her move gracefully through the small house-on-wheels, every motion denoting the ease of long familiarity. She yanked on underthings and a pair of denim trousers taken from a narrow closet, kicked the ruins of their torn clothing under the table almost violently, tied her hair back with casual roughness… but moved with slow, tentative caution to take a keyring from the large waxed-canvas pouch. The *compu-ter* was inside that bag as well, its black plastic edge peering out, and that was thought-provoking. So was her stripping away the shield over the vehicle's front glass eyes, folding it with quick motions, stowing the result in a handy cubby.

And glancing at him all the while, as if she expected punishment. That was troubling, but he would focus upon encouraging some small measure of trust in her new sanguinant, bit by bit.

It was an intriguing prospect, and one he welcomed.

The vehicle's design was wholly ingenious, and her casual movements gave each piece of modern innovation fresh luster. He often witnessed the mortals steering similar vehicles, large and small, but had never been inside one during movement.

He missed horse-drawn conveyances—far easier to enter, to feast within their jolting once they shifted past chariot to coach, and easy as well to exit unremarked. The innovation of greater speed meant more damage to mortals when such repasts provoked startlement in the driver, leading to collision or other accident. Messy, and unsatisfying in the extreme.

She dropped into the main seat, glancing repeatedly at him as he took the other, and he waited for direction.

"Seatbelt?" she said, finally, indicating the strap buckled across her own chest and lap. The word trembled, though her expression was entirely beautiful, mutinous, brittle bravado. "It's safer."

Safer? Did she think him a fledgling like herself? Outside the glass, the night was barely underway. It had not taken long to claim her, yet the entire universe was now entirely different, possessing a new central axis. The wanderer studied the view while reaching for the buckle, fastening the tough, smooth ribbon as he had seen her do, with a satisfying click.

"And the… that invisible stuff. Seals, right?" She swallowed, hard, her pulse fluttering. Indeed she was keeping to adorable, trembling calm only by a thin margin. "Is it going to move with us, or…?"

She was extremely intelligent; he looked forward to following her through the centuries, ambling in her wake as she discovered each new era's secrets and hidden delights. He was almost lost in contemplating that starry prospect, but she required an answer.

More to the point, attempting to move this contraption while the seals held fast would indeed be a mistake.

"No." A moment's worth of attention, an internal shifting, and the familiar stillness of a sealed space vanished, a low brushing of wind now audible. The material of the conveyance's outer shell was sensitized now, and would take less effort to ward later.

Sheerly wonderful that he could *think* of later, no longer trapped in a maelstrom of chaos. Every moment in her company was peace, every breath freighted with divine grace. He seemed to remember long-ago mortals believing the mad were touched by gods; all he remembered of his own insanity was the pain, then the numbness, the constant striving to endure one more terrible dusk, one more empty dawning, one breath further, a single heartbeat—

"Hello?" She was even more anxious now, the word spiraling up uncertainly. Her pulse, a sweet thunder, now almost humming-quick. "Uh, Mr. Vampire, sir?"

"They don't travel," he said, trying to pronounce the words as she did, following her vocal patterns. "Surprised your Maker didn't teach you how. You must be… young, in the Blood."

"You mean, being a vamp? Five whole years." She inserted the small metal key, twisted it as he had seen mortals do. A shiver, a shudder, a rumble of combustion; the engine roused at her touch—what item, animate or the opposite, would not? "You're the first one I've met who actually *talks*."

A pair of remarkable assertions; for a few moments, he thought the madness had returned or his ability to understand her tongue faltered. He had thought her less than a half-century from receiving the Gift, certainly, but five small years was not even an eyeblink.

More important was the other detail. "How many others you met then, darlin'?"

"A few. They all growl and try to bite me." She busied herself with dials and switches, glancing frequently at him as if expecting each movement to bring swift retribution—and the wanderer did *not* like that. Yet she still clung to thin, nervous calm, and every conversational exchange was at once a revelation, a gift, and a victory. "Uh, can I ask you something?"

"Anythin' you like." What would he deny his new prize? Nothing, save self-harm or escape. Now her behavior made more sense—so young in the Blood, mortal instincts and the urge to flee what was essentially a predator would occasionally strike. He must be careful, coax her into recognizing his intent to guard.

To cherish.

"How old are you? If that's, you know, something I can ask."

Even more tentative, as she pulled a small lever. A mechanical thump, a shuddering, and the contraption was freed from stasis, lurching into wallowing motion. Gravel crunched under the rubber rounds, and he watched carefully as she used the wheel to steer, her right leg twitching as she switched between floor-pedals.

What a marvelous dance.

"I…" How to explain? "I don't know, 'zactly. There 'us a fire."

Electric floodlights cut a swath before them, glittering on raised dust and dazed, swooping night-insects. She had parked not only to take advantage of the view but also positioned the vehicle for easy egress along the gravel road, most intriguing. Care and forethought in one so young—why was she so surprised he could speak?

Of course, incoherent raving had been his lot before her arrival. Fledglings catching her scent would be reduced to utter drunkenness, an Elder deeply distracted by the lovely miracle; a daywalker, even though of might surpassing both as sanguinant o'erpassed mortals, would become entirely fastened upon the need to bite and claim.

Miraculous that the city's burning had not killed him, doubly so that the wandering afterward had failed to do so, and now a leman. Truly he was fortunate, even among the children of the Blood.

She stared out the front, as if wholly absorbed in her task. Or, more likely, not daring to inquire further, since her scent now held a more definite edge of fear—tormenting, teasing, poking at the mating-thrall. A surge of hot protectiveness ran through his marrow; the animal in him wished to remove whatever was frightening her before offering comfort in unmistakable, highly specific fashion.

He would take her again after hunting and before sunrise, he decided. Slowly, with great care, attending to her smallest pleasure.

"Whole city burned down," he added. Perhaps he could entice her to further questions, more clues. "Flames hurt me bad, but I 'us already daywalker so…"

That earned him a sweet, startled glance. "Daywalker?"

"It takes a bit o' doing, to stand in th' sun. But some manage it." Age was a prerequisite, though not entirely the measure of such a feat, he thought. Even with his memory and reason fractured, he had retained an instinctive grasp upon sanguinants' ways and methods, if only to hold both territory and his own survival. "Your Maker din't tell you?"

"There wasn't a lot of conversation." Her knuckles had turned white. The wheel groaned softly before she swallowed, convulsively, and loosened her hold. The vehicle swayed, rumbling into a turn, and bumped up onto a paved road. In the distance a lone streetlight leaned, beaming an orange message-glow toward cracked concrete.

She was growing more fearful by the moment. The vehicle hummed, gathering speed, and whooshed past the streetlight onto a long dark stretch of ruler-straight country road. His suspicions about her Maker became even bleaker, and the concomitant fury crept a little deeper into his bones.

"Well, now." He tried for the quietest, most soothing tone he had ever heard a mortal male use, hoping it was enough. If he could remember anything before the fire, perhaps it would be better… but he was forced to use what little he had. "How 'bout you tell me what did happen, darlin'?"

His leman was silent for a long moment, pressing a lever on the column holding the wheel, then leaning slightly forward to touch a button on the instrument panel. The long, thin-walled carriage accelerated once more, settling into a high happy hum. No wonder the mortals liked these conveyances so much—the sense of smooth speed gained by simply pressing a pedal was satisfying, though relatively slow compared to an Elder's ability of skimming along topographical features or riding the night wind in mistform. The deep hum of the wheels was pleasant as well.

How long had she traveled in this fashion? Five years was nothing, yet she had no measure of time save the mortal.

What had *happened*? How could a leman, a fledgling, be wandering unclaimed? The more he learned, the more puzzled he became.

"No," she said, quietly. "I don't want to talk about that."

There was a metallic click, and she wrenched at the wheel. A scream of metal, a sudden coughing sound, and the world turned over rapidly.

A bright orange blossom of flame filled his vision, a rush of heat, the acrid smell of petrol.

CHAPTER 9

It did cause her a pang or two to start the self-destruct sequence; she'd had that little gift installed by a mechanic Barry knew in Illinois, a woman in clean, pressed blue overalls who took cash and asked no goddamn questions.

Don't go blowin' yourself up now, you hear? Laughing while she said it, but Miz Kendra's big brown eyes had been cold and considering, and she had never turned her back on Simone.

Which had been kind of... not irritating, but a little sad? Attempting to learn a bit about engines would have been pleasant, but some sure instinct—feminine, not vamp—had said that Kendra knew goddamn good and well what Simone was now, and didn't like it.

Still, bloodsucker money spent like anyone else's. And Simone had paid with a smile.

No, hitting the seatbelt's catch and throwing herself sideways through the door with a screech of metal, a tinkle of glass, and a hard high snapping sound wasn't difficult. Nor was hanging in midair for what felt like a very long time, her body arranging itself to take the landing hit. Her reflexes were on point, and the old vampire's blood had given her a shot of pure power, so she overcompensated and cleared the eternal barbed-wire fence at the side of the road, easy as pie.

The hard part was hitting and veering in a curve, boots nearly smoking as grass whipped to either side, her body achieving balance instinctively. The space between her legs was still a little tender, giving a harsh throb as she found her stride, running not quite flat-out but at a pace she could sustain for some while and almost tripping because of the newfound strength and speed filling her muscles.

Wow. He must be really *old.* All his talk about daywalking and a burning city—useless to think about it right now, she had to hope the RV's tanks, recently topped-up, would provide enough boom-and-burn to kill the other vamp, or at worst slow him down.

Simone ran, focusing on breath and form. She'd hated PE class with a passion, attempted aerobics and other sweaty indignities to try keeping her weight down all through her marriage, and would never have believed that *running* could ever feel good. Then she'd gotten infected.

Now the low song of cloven air rushing by her ears, night's invisible fingers combing her hair, lungs working hard, full of sharp, intense bursts of scent… oh, it was *glorious*, even the fear beating in time to her laboring heart sweet and wonderful, because it meant she was alive.

That she had, for however short a time, escaped yet another trap.

She'd felt the same fierce, terrified exultation that morning so long ago, staggering away from the abandoned, ramshackle church, nearly naked and blinking heavily in thin cloudy sunshine as the floppy-haired vampire's screams still rang in her ears. Scrubbing crusted blood out of her eyes, every bruise and scrape throbbing in time to her wildly pounding heart, but oh she'd been alive, high on the fact of her own continued survival.

Before finding out the price, that was. The world was full of snares just waiting to grab a woman, freedom only ever a temporary condition.

It irritated her to lose another laptop, a few rolls of emergency cash, and the stake, as well as some clothes. She hated that the stepstool from her old house was going to be sitting abandoned on gravel until it was picked up, driven over, or rotted. But chewing a limb off to get out of metal jaws wasn't just a coyote's trick; all it took to learn was marrying the wrong man.

Or getting snatched by a vampire. Did this count as a second abduction?

All these fucking vamps so interested in me. Is it my cologne? Neither breath nor energy to laugh; she cut across rolling grassland, leapt a gully—nearly invisible to human eyes, but clear as day to her bright bloodsucking senses, her body taking the jump with swift, unconscious authority—and landed soft as a cat.

The plains weren't flat, though they might look that way from a car window. The grass sea had tides all its own, the movement of wind deceptive as the hummocks and groundwaves underneath swelled and dropped. Still, if she aimed for the smear of low orangish glow that was a town lit by clustered human homes and streets, she couldn't go too far wrong.

Because this town had a truck stop—the Big Horn Watering Hole, to be exact, where she'd recently filled up the RV before setting out to take her last bounty. And Simone, thinking furiously, had pointed her poor, now-burning vehicle in that direction.

She wasn't going to bother trying to talk a trucker into giving her a ride, though that would be relatively easy. No, she'd parallel the route to I-25 and hop aboard a semi heading to Cheyenne.

Wedging herself between a cab and trailer wouldn't be the most comfortable thing in the world, but better than the alternative. She didn't particularly *like* her life as an infected vampire hunter… but it was hers.

It was the only goddamn thing she had left.

And with a fresh cargo of old-vampire blood singing in her veins, her limbs moving fluidly and her hair flowing like a pennant, she would keep running until she dropped.

If she had to. If it became necessary.

❦

Three and a half hours later a refrigerated rig screech-braked all the way down an exit ramp, Simone hit the shoulder with a tooth-shattering jolt, and she was back in the Magic City of the Plains with no cash, no phone, no laptop, no RV, and a tiny tickle of returning thirst far back in her throat. Not to mention she was tousled, jolted, head-ringing from the triple drone of wind, tire-hum, and engine-rumble, and a thin scrim of copper adrenaline had replaced the persistent spice-taste in her mouth.

She never used to think herself any good at navigation; maybe going vamp had granted her an edge. On plains and prairie the cities often had room to sprawl, too, so the grid was often fairly easy to figure out. Especially if you'd been through a location once or twice, poking around, looking for signs of the weird.

The *demimonde*, they called it—at least, those in the know, an old piece of slang deployed to prove at least initial bona fides. And it contained multitudes: Vampires, werewolves, sponta-neous combustion, Mothman, ghosts, little green men, and a whole host of other creepy shit.

Some bits were entirely imaginary, sure. But the parts which weren't? Oh, those were mean as hell.

To be fair she was one of the latter now, her conscience only pinching hard instead of stopping her outright from blurring up to a big chain bank's drive-thru ATM, ripping the facing free, grabbing the cassettes which *didn't* reek of dye packs or degrada-tion fluid, and vanishing into the distance almost before an alarm could sound.

It was far better than robbing a credit union at gunpoint—

there was federal insurance, and naturally the bigger banks scammed everyone so relentlessly their profits were astronomical. This was a drop in the bucket. Plus, the security footage would get quietly filed under 'weird shit' and disbelieved like countless other urban legends and myths.

Her own aptitude for superpowered criminal activity was unnerving. She was trying to work an honest job—such as it was —but how long until she started finding reasons to simply do whatever the hell she wanted?

Simone's desires had always been what she thought of as entirely modest. A small house with a garden, or a quiet condo. Just enough money for rent and groceries. Time to knit, to read, to watch period dramas and pet neighborhood cats. Her fantasies had sometimes involved a husband who didn't strew dirty laundry all over the floor, didn't keep the television blaring in every room, and didn't think it was funny to fart on you in the middle of the night, but she'd come to the conclusion that such creatures were even rarer than Sasquatch. Plus, she never wanted to be a mother and thus, apparently could not be a good wife. Her one attempt at raising a manbaby had failed—not even spectacularly, simply fizzling out under its own weight, and when Curt started banging that chippie from his office, well, affairs had taken an utterly predictable path.

She was better at being a vampire than a housewife—or a part-time secretary at a dental office until Curt got mad at her not having dinner on the table every damn night whenever he decided to wander in and turn the TV on.

Nowadays the slightly metallic smell of a city at 3am. reminded her of lazy summer afternoons—familiar and almost comfortable despite the reek of human sweat or acute vampire-sense tingles of paranoia. The streets vibrated under her boots like guitar strings, leading her to pockets of late-night activity: the gas station where a yawning clerk behind thick bulletproof plastic didn't take his eyes off a smartphone's face as he rang up a baseball cap, a pair of cheap shades, and a couple paper maps still lingering despite GPS; the fluorescent-drenched 24-7 box store where fright crew was busy stocking and a sleepy-eyed night manager opened a case for burner phones, incurious as only retail workers who have Seen Some Shit can be; the craps game in a downtown alley while a lookout on the corner eyed her curiously; the transit maps on bus shelters she studied while her nerves popped and pinged, still jangled from escape; a railway yard where she could catch another ride out of town in a pinch; the basement bar where she bellied up to the counter for a precious half-hour nursing—not drinking—a bourbon on the rocks, listening to hushed conversation that confirmed this was, indeed, a place she could negotiate certain quasi-legal services.

By then the night was old, dawn approaching like a freight train. No time to acquire more than the hat, shades, phone, and cheap messenger bag with a tough nylon strap; she didn't want a cheap cash-only motel, since housekeeping or fellow guests might walk in while she was passed out during daylight.

So she strolled back through downtown with the particular loose-hipped *don't fucking bother me* gait that seemed to have arrived with vamp infection and warned off all but the truly dumb or psychotic human predators, and dialed a number she'd taken the trouble to memorize into the burner.

Thank God for entirely small commonplace miracles, because her finder was awake at an odd hour. Again.

"Hi, Barry. It's Jane."

"These your new digits, hot stuff?" At least he sounded pleased. "Bounty's cleared, you should see the transfer tomorrow at the latest."

It's already tomorrow. She couldn't wait to check Jane Smith's bank balance; a thin warm thread of relief crawled into her chest at the prospect. "That's good news. You still got that rich nutjob on tap?"

A sound of shifting, creak of his office chair. "Deal hasn't changed. Hour of your time, he'll pay, anywhere in the Lower 48. Or hell, he'd probably fly out to Anchorage if you wanted."

Too good to be true. But if *that* money landed, she could maybe settle somewhere, or at least get a better RV and spend her time hitting hospitals for spare blood bags instead of running bounties. Happening across one old-as-fuck vampire was enough. Her luck had been incredibly good up until now, but she was ready to leave the gambling table.

Another benefit to age, she thought—learning to quit while ahead.

"Denver," she said. "I choose time, he chooses place. 2am, Friday. Send me the location—I'll be there, but if this is some kind of scam, Barry..." No threat was dire enough, so she simply let the sentence trail away into a warning pause.

"Holy *shit.*" Now her finder was definitely scrambling, paper fluttering and something falling with a clink. "That's... okay, that's two days from now. Right?"

"Yes." She wouldn't have known if she hadn't checked the date as the burner powered up, getting its bearings just like its new owner. "I mean it, this had better be as advertised. I don't have time for bullshit."

"I promise, I *swear.*" He sounded ready to slap his hand on a Bible, if one could be found on the hurricane mess of his desk. "This guy's legit, he's funded at least five other crews, including that mad Irish bastard who worked for the Vatican—"

"I really don't care, Barry." *I heard O'Shaughnassey met a bad end on the East Coast.* Her one interaction with the man and his crew had been unpleasant at best, but then again, word was vampires had killed his entire family.

She didn't quite blame him for being wary.

Simone's goal came into view—a hotel on the edge of downtown, right next to the Union Pacific station. An old building, and no doubt ID was mandatory for all check-ins.

Good thing her plans didn't involve paying for a room. "He gets an hour, I get the moolah," she continued, her legs tingling as she lengthened her stride. "Set it up, leave a message at this number once it's confirmed. And, Barry, ol' buddy ol' pal? Listen to me. *Be smart about this.*"

"Come on, Janie. Have I ever let you down?"

We've only known each other a few years, my man. You've got time. "Get some rest," she said, and hung up, eyeing the hotel's brick facade from the entrance of an old movie theater half a block away, its marquee overhead nearly dripping with nostalgia.

No, she didn't have to pay or show ID. All she had to do was get inside.

CHAPTER 10

EVEN HAD HIS MEMORY BEEN CONSISTENT, THE WANDERER SUSPECTED
he had never before trailed such lovely, nervous, elusive prey.
Ruthlessly burning her own home to cinders, leaping aboard a
giant metal monster and staying crouched in an exceeding small
space for hours, then moving purposefully through a vaguely
familiar city, slipping through its cracks and corners—oh, it was
a joy to watch her, thrilling to wonder what she would do next,
an exercise in control and caution to follow the faint scarf of
glorious scent while granting enough distance to avoid her
exquisite sensitivity.

Each time he drew too close she hunched those slim, beautiful shoulders and hurried along, doubling back, slipping
through the terrain with all the swift decisiveness of a hunted
wolf, doing her best to shake pursuit he could not think her fully
aware of.

For a fledgling, she was truly exceptional. Then again, she
was leman. Not only that, but his blood burned in her veins;
another few feedings to further cement the bond and it would be
as if he had granted the Dark Gift instead of the Maker who had
used her so terribly. The taking of nourishment would become

even more pleasant, especially for her as the narcotic effect arrived and became pronounced.

He was momentarily puzzled when she ducked into a building near the throbbing iron pit of the railroad station and its associated tangle of tracks—he remembered, vaguely, having more than once used the steam-snorting conveyances during his madness, moving to new territory when sanguinant instinct demanded. Clinging to the top of a railway carriage was like and unlike riding the petroleum-burning behemoths of this time— now, of course, there were fewer cinders, louder wind-roar, and the constant smell of exhaust instead of coalsmoke.

The night had become old and weary. She did not exit the place; had he finally run his most important prey to ground? Dawn was very near indeed, awareness of the tide-change singing in his own bones along with the thrall.

And, of course, the Thirst. Which could be laid aside for some few hours yet, but so soon as fledgling sleep took her...

As the eastron horizon turned grey he entered the building as well, drifting in mistform. A hotel, and some furnishings were almost, *almost* familiar. Had he hunted here before?

Irrelevant. Her trail led not to the front desk but aside, through a door marked *Employee Only*—the concentration necessary to decipher written words was no longer a wrenching effort —and into the non-guest portions. Downward, turning through corridors, sometimes doubling back again, he followed her trail. His admiration grew as he searched; this was a novel tactical choice, though the risk of a stray mortal bumbling across her rest was still unacceptable.

As he felt the sun's breaching of horizon-line the wanderer coalesced in an old, lightless boiler room, now clearly used for storage. Moldering boxes, tangles of cable, conduit, and pipe, what had to be a modern furnace where once a perfectly respectable coal-fired boiler had crouched—the marks where the latter had been taken out were clearly visible to sanguinant vision, even in thick darkness—stacks of wooden crates, discarded furniture, other detritus, a labyrinth holding not a monster but a pearl.

And there, curled in a far back corner, the trophy. She had made herself small as possible, sitting against the wall, knees up and forehead resting upon them, arms braced around her legs. Her hair, still full of night-scent and grassland breeze, lay in shining ripples against hunched, protectively rounded shoulders.

So fragile, so indomitable. She did not belong here, cast amid the refuse; he longed to give her better surroundings, more comfort, and certainly more safety. This was insupportable. He listened to the hotel above, employees bustling while guests drowsed, and thought over his next few moves.

Following and observing had taught him much—though giant gaps remained in his knowledge of this era, he could begin to guess at their contours. And now he had *her* measure. Were she not leman, she still would have made a formidable sanguinant, perchance even enduring to daywalker strength.

Leman remained ever fledgling, though, never reaching even an Elder's strength or speed. Perhaps it was the price paid for such wondrous gifts.

To approach a sleeping treasure, to crouch before her and take a much deeper draught of that glorious scent, was more than enough reward for any exertion. "Oh, darlin', what a night y've had," he murmured, and remembered she did not care for that particular accent, though the drawl was much in evidence from surrounding mortals during her nighttime ramble.

Perhaps it was only *his* use of the local dialect she objected to, since her own accent was far crisper. He would learn better, which required time. He also needed to feed, a place to hold her in some comfort for the daylight hours, resources to cushion and pamper his prize, a mortal identity for efficiency… the list was near endless, and he was grateful for every item. No more spinning in useless disorientation; no, now he had a *purpose*.

Fortunately she had brought him to a place well suited to

begin his work, almost as if granting her new protector a boon for loyal service.

The first step was to take her in his arms—gently, carefully, though she would not wake until sunset. The second was to move through this building unseen by mortals, find a suitable room, set the seals, and tuck his sleeping houri into a more comfortable bed.

All things should be so easy. He smiled in the darkness, taking a moment to touch a strand of her lovely dark hair, silk slipping against his fingertips.

Once she was settled, he could begin.

The times had changed; instead of introductory letters or simply wearing the correct plumage, something called *formal identification* was necessary. Still, many mortals were perfunctory at best in glancing over proffered items, especially when a moiety of invisible force was applied to their mental state. Information now swirled even more quickly than with telegraphs—he hazily remembered the ballyhoo about the wires' ability to sing across an entire continent, though could not pinpoint if that near-miraculous advance had occurred before or after the fire.

It did not matter. His priority was soaking in as much of this era as possible, avoiding large or cascading mistakes, and returning to his sleeping paragon. Difficult to tear himself away in the first place, especially after he peeled each piece of clothing free with slow care before drawing the bed's covers over her lithe, faintly glowing form, and all day he was occupied with remembering the curve of her hip, the line of her throat, the softness against his knuckles as he inadvertently brushed the side of one satiny breast. Faint, pale marks upon her flanks and upper arms were left from mortal years, slowly erasing as the Gift burnished every inch; she had once been more pleasingly curved. He tried to imagine her well-fed and happy, perhaps in a gown of absinthe green, her hair piled high and emeralds clasping her beautiful throat.

Even her ankles and bare feet, bearing soft crenellated imprints of stockings and the marks of boot-wear, were softly gorgeous. He could not wait to explore at leisure.

Returning an hour before sunset, he arranged his first offerings with care, filling his lungs in deep even swells. Her scent had dyed the suite, rendering its imperfections charmingly quaint, and he sorely needed the balm. His head had begun to ache the moment he left her vicinity, the distracting fractures of attention and coherence breaking through by midafternoon. Other symptoms mounted as well—limb-tremors, the thrall's sharp silver rowels pricking deep in his marrow, the dull heavy nastiness of sunlight on exposed skin mounting to pain as if her absence would cause a daywalker's immunity to reverse itself.

This era's idea of luxury seemed but tawdry imitation—the 'marble' of the bathroom was thin tile veneer, the paneling flimsy, the linens somewhat coarse though adequately clean. The ceiling was familiar, even if its pressed tin had suffered many layers of paint blurring sharp-stamped designs; the drapes, heavily figured with gold roses against cerulean velvet, could have been antique save for their thinness, and the sheers underneath were made of slippery artificial stuff. The carpet was harsh, an insult to the mellow hardwood it overlaid.

Yet the plumbing was much better than he expected, bearing marks of constant small refinement in that mortal art. Galvanism had turned into *electricity* and become even more plentiful than gaslight; small outlets in the walls fueled untold marvels. The mirrors were large and clear, luxuries apparently now held cheap. Mortal food in the many restaurants smelled far more appetizing than it ever had, and the streets were much more cleanly. Information did not need wires to hum through the air, literacy was expected of every class instead of jealousy restricted to the highborn, and even the hovels of the abject held certain conveniences.

All in all there was plenty to enjoy, and he could not wait to begin.

If only she would wake. He was very nearly *in a lather*—did they say such things, still? Skin sensitized, clothes maddeningly tight and irritating, he considered ridding himself of all encumbrance and greeting her at sunset already engaged in dalliance. A pleasant thought, taunting the thrall, and yet he suspected she would not look kindly upon such worship.

Not yet. Perhaps not ever, though it would neither alter his course nor cool his ardor.

Still… it would not do to waste the cloth he had just acquired by tearing it, even if surrounded by a wealth of available goods, textile and otherwise, such as former ages could only dream of. To unbutton, unfasten, unlace, unzip, took no time at all; to gather her into his arms even less. For the short time before dusk he was able to hold a sleeping leman, his nose buried in her spice-fragrant, gloriously tumbled hair, pretending her stillness was acquiescence.

All too soon the sun sank below the earth's rim. He knew the moment she awakened, though she remained motionless for a few long breaths. He let her bolt from the bed, tearing the sheet in her haste, and caught her next to the door leading to the suite's antechamber, her nakedness pressed hard against flat slick modern wallpaper, her arms spread wide, slim frail wrists trapped in his palms.

Gentle enough, but inescapable. He lost himself in the sliding textures, his readiness against the hollow of her lower back, his chin atop her head, denying any movement of retreat, to the side —or forward, through the wall itself.

His leman froze, trembling hard, her scent deepening. After a moment, he could force his true teeth into their camouflage and drop a quiet murmur in her pretty, rosy ear. "Did you think you could escape me?"

He had practiced her accent all through the day, helped along by the vast stew and babble of dialect within the city's cauldron. Perhaps she would find his speech more acceptable now.

At first he thought she had not heard, but she swallowed hard—pressed so tightly, even that slight movement was discernible. "It was…" Her breath hitched, charmingly, and the trembling intensified. "Worth a try."

"I see." He did not have to try to sound amused, and pressed his cheek against her hair, marveling at the texture. She twitched, and his hands clamped her wrists afresh. "Easy now, darlin'. In a little while we shall enjoy each other again, but first I must warn you of a few things. Are you listening? Nod if you understand."

"Please…" A breathless, forlorn little plea. "Don't."

It is necessary you comprehend, my beauty. He had thought much, during the day, upon how to condense the few requirements. "If you attempt to escape, I *will* catch you, and I will take you until you are fully pleased. Any attempt at self-harm will end in the same manner. I am your sanguinant and your protector, we will go where you wish to and do as you prefer, and you are *mine*. Do you understand?"

"Don't." She gasped, shuddering in great gripping waves. The contrast of warm flesh and chill wall was not so intense, yet she shook as if with mortal ague. "Not this way. Not like this."

"Do you not enjoy this position?" He shifted slightly, knowing he could lift her a small distance, pin her against the wall, and sink into her from behind. He tensed as if to do so, his grasp on her wrists shifting. "Pity, it seems rather—"

Whatever he expected it was not sudden, complete limpness, and a high thin sound from a constricted throat. He had heard its like before, though he could not remember just when, and cold dread sawed across the pleasure of holding her so closely.

For the sound she made was the despairing whimper of a fledgling moments before the break, sustaining irreversible physical and psychological damage. Some who created progeny in the Blood deliberately provoked such distress for their own amusement, one more cruel game to stave off calcification. He did not think the strategy wise or worthwhile, not least because callousness was just as much a trap as apathy.

How much more terrible to break a leman, then? To mar a creature so exquisite, so very finely made, would be a greater sin than any he had ever committed, remembered or forgotten.

She trembled yet more as he drew her from the wall, her muscles quivering at the edge of seizure-lock. His true-teeth sliced at his own wrist as his knees folded, blood welling up to quiver with surface tension, refusing to leave the opened flesh; sanguinant and leman spilled to the floor in a tangle of limbs, and he pressed the cut against her mouth.

A fledgling in such dire anguish required careful care; she *must* feed. More importantly, she must be calmed, soothed so far as possible. Even a leman driven past sanity was priceless, to be protected and assiduously nursed. Severe mental unrest could cause physical degradation, triggering a killing catatonia—a superbly sensitive instrument, treated too harshly, reduced to splinters.

He would die with her, of course, but that was beside the point. To lose such a prize through incompetence, ill treatment, *that* was another unholy thing. Her innocent shameless flanks filled his lap, her satin weight too cold in his arms, her lovely head lolling on its slender stem.

"Feed," he whispered, barely aware he spoke in a language she could not possibly know. How long since the tongue of Elam had been uttered by a living mouth? It did not matter. "O my beloved, the cup is at your lips; merely drink, and all shall be well."

I will make *it well. I am sorry, sorry, sorry.*

Sorrow was useless. He must keep her, and if it took every last drop in his veins, he would give gladly, thankful for the opportunity.

CHAPTER 11

SHE WAS IN THE CHURCH BASEMENT AGAIN, THE MONSTER'S GROWL filling her skull, a man on her back doing what men inevitably did, the rattle of handcuffs as her wrists flared with hot slicing agony, the *teeth* in her flesh, champing and tearing. The smell of rotting cardboard and damp concrete, the strobe-flickers as her eyelids fluttered, the deep sickening knowledge that she was about to die but even worse, what if she didn't? And the things… the other things the monster had done…

Someone was talking, low and gentle. "—*jane delam*, all'us well, nothing will harm you. Nothing will e'er hurt you again, I promise, little leman, *atashe delam, jeegaram*, you must feed. Feed, and all will be well."

Which was strange, because she wasn't hungry, and the monster in the church basement hadn't spoken. Just growled, and bit, and *hurt*—

"Light o' my eyes, little darlin', shh, *feed*. You must feed." More strange rolling words, but there was something in her mouth now.

A trickle of heat against the back of her throat. The taste—flaky golden buttermilk biscuits, fresh and dripping with honey. Then it was hot chocolate, the cheap kind with crunchy marshmallows administered after a skinned knee on the playground, and how long had it been since she'd thought about *that*?

"Very good," he whispered, almost crooning. Fever-hot skin slid against hers, scorching; it was strange to be held on someone's lap like this. Almost enclosed, almost… safe? "Just like that, m'darlin'. I hunted well to feed ye, take what y' need."

Her mouth was full. She swallowed, automatically, and instinct took over. Her body knew what it wanted, fastening upon what was offered. A sweet piercing almost-pain as bones moved, the fangs springing free and sliding into flesh, biting *hard*. Did that make her like the monster?

But there was no screaming, no ragged pleading, none of her own voice echoing against bare walls, cries rising to an uncaring God. No insane, world-shaking growl of a rabid nightmare thing as it gnawed her flesh. Just that voice, and the supernova explosion of warmth in her midriff, a wave of heat pushing outward into cold fingers, numb toes.

He was stroking her hair, too. Slow, comforting touches, fingertips occasionally pausing to smooth the almost-curls she'd despaired of all her life, neither one thing or the other. Just waves, stubbornly resisting any changing fashion. But it was nice to feel someone playing with the strands. An intimate touch, really.

Along with the heat came relief. Her muscles unknotted, hurtful tension loosening. A great dark wash of relaxation slid down her back, her shoulders softening for what felt like the first time in decades. She twitched, dreamily, settling her fangs deeper as he inhaled, a soft hiss through sharp teeth.

The steady whisper didn't alter, though now it was all in English, far more crisply pronounced. "Beautiful girl, little leman… good, keep going. All is well, you are safe. Nothing will hurt you, I swear it on my Blood. Take more."

How often had she longed to be held, told such sweet lies? The world was a hurting machine; no matter how you tried to protect anything, existence itself simply chewed and spat. But it was so *warm*, so soft, and the relaxation was like two Xanax and a glass of wine. A lake to float in, silken buoyancy, and she realized she was not exactly sober the moment her fangs slipped free of hot flesh.

Enough, her body said, *that's all you need, stop now*. The blood bags were never like this, flat and metallic, always leaving a trace of that terrible, mind-consuming thirst. She'd learned early and well not to let the dryness get too bad, which would have been easy if she'd had access to this fountain.

He kept stroking her hair; she was sitting crossways, cradled on the lap of a lean, iron-strong frame. The persistent poking against her hip was interesting, she supposed, but couldn't be meant for her. Not even the new Simone in a body thirty years younger, clear-eyed and vampire-strong. She moved, testing—yeah, that was what she thought it was, and with her eyes firmly shut and the incredible swimming lassitude weighing down every limb, she couldn't help but wonder what the cost for this sudden reprieve might be.

Lips pressed to her temple, soft kisses. The caressing hands stayed gentle, careful but more urgent, skating over her cheek, her shoulder, one curving around her waist, rubbing gently. He didn't grab, thank goodness, but his fingers were certainly roaming, and her legs loosened as well.

Someone was moaning, softly, as gravity changed its hold on her and she spilled sideways, nearly boneless, the hands suddenly strong and sure, easing her down. A rough almost-scrape down her back—carpet, and there was a mouth on hers now, wickedly distracting as her knees spread and a hot, insistent finger probed between them, slipping in honeythick moisture.

No, not a finger, because the hands were in her hair now, a body curved over hers blocking out the pain, the memory, the fear. Sometimes, in a bubble bath with the door securely locked, she'd fantasized about this very thing—her hips beckon-begging as her spine arched, her palms skating iron muscles under warm skin, a mouth leisurely feasting on her own with absolute possession, and the first exquisite thrust.

She broke free, shaking her head, hair tangling in carpet, lips parted on a strengthless gasp. Tiny begging sounds as the dream settled into fucking her, almost lazily, each stroke strong and sure, stopping at the crest to tickle her clit with a skin-warm, insistent probing.

Wait a minute, just hold on, I'm not—

She wasn't sober, not by a long shot. The lassitude made it so hard to think, sensations cascading and rippling everywhere, a faint scratch of stubble as his cheek lay next to hers and the voice continued, raggedly, promising her safety, repeating *darlin'*, telling her she was beautiful, wanted, that she belonged.

Was this what other vampires felt? Maybe being psychotic with bloodlust wasn't so bad after all.

The thought was ice water flung into a hot oven, a burst of fierce cold fighting with the coiled tension low in her belly. Frantic squirming didn't help, only intensifying the flood of sensation, and orgasm hit before she was ready, slamming like a runaway semi into solid cement retaining wall. Thrown out of herself, spun and tossed onto sharp rocks, she screamed over and over, high trailing cries.

A coughing roar answered, lionlike, nearly swallowing her own noise. Another monster was above her, head thrown back, throat bared, and Simone was so far gone she didn't care. All that mattered was the blessed, furious release swirling through her along with that warm forgiving painlessness.

Good God, she thought, pointlessly. *Again on the floor.* Then a brief spangled darkness swallowed her.

For a short while she drifted, deliberately trying not to think or remember; it was easier, she decided, being high on blood.

Except she hadn't had this reaction to the red stuff before, had she? Confusing, how the rules kept changing.

One thing was for sure: the old vampire had found her again, somehow, and had fucked the life out of her on what felt like carpet. She'd barely managed a glimpse of blue-and-yellow drapes, striped wallpaper, and a spindly pseudo-antique table before he'd caught her and… pushed her against the wall? Yes, that was what had happened.

Where on earth *was* she now? Where the holy hell had he come from? She hadn't felt him following at all, except for the faintest sense of an invisible gaze two or three times while going about her business last night—easily attributable to her usual paranoia, which was now bound to escalate.

So how? Where? What the absolute *fuck*?

He exhaled, a long shaky breath, and sagged atop her. Sounded like he'd gotten what he was after, except his cock also seemed strangely swollen, lodged deep and pulsing. Simone tested her fingertips, her toes—her legs aching a bit even through the warm analgesic flood, postcoital haze mixing with whatever in his blood had gotten her so zoned out.

Or maybe she was simply going insane. That was a definite possibility.

He nuzzled at her cheek, more strange almost-intimacy—of course, this was about as intimate as someone could get, no matter that they were complete strangers.

"Why are you doing this?" Dozy alarm spilled through the heavy sedation, because she sounded nearly drunk, the words spaced-out and dreamy. "You just have a thing for floor sex?"

"Hm." He sounded almost human, a low, amused near-grunt. "You are so delicious, I cannot resist."

A nice compliment, maybe, but Simone wasn't sure she liked it. She shifted, attempting to ease the pressure on her hips; he tensed, nipping lightly at her earlobe. At least he wasn't using fangs—those were really sharp. And she should know, having bitten her own lip to flinders once or twice during a bounty fight.

If anyone had offered a price on this vamp, she wouldn't have taken it. No way, no day. "Look, can you just... Can I get up? Please?"

"Not for some short while." His movement was arrested; something was *definitely* stuck. "You see?"

"Oh, God. Is that... is that normal?" *I cannot believe I am having this fucking conversation with a vampire. Literally.*

"Yes." At least he didn't sound irritated by simple questions. "At least, once a sanguinant reaches Elder status, the physical changes—wait. Are you uncomfortable?"

Sanguinant. The term was vaguely familiar, especially the way he used it. "You mean vampire."

"If you like." Indifferent, but still not angry. A faint stilted cadence, the drawl vanished and clipped precision replacing its blurred edges. "How is it possible, that you do not know such things? The one who made you, how did they die?"

Screaming in a patch of sunshine, after I tore a few boards off the windows and dragged him to where I knew the light would hit. The blood-sedation was so intense Simone could think about the whole event almost calmly.

Almost.

A shiver slipped down her back. She'd passed out at sundown, tucked in a safe dark corner, pretty certain she wouldn't be disturbed—how the *fuck* had she ended up here? "Badly," she heard herself say, in that distant, bitchy tone that warned Barry she didn't want to talk about it.

You're due in Denver Friday night. Start working on that.

Great advice. But she couldn't seem to scrape together enough brainpower to begin. She hadn't even been this distracted after the divorce, when the depression made it hard to focus on more than getting through one more lawyer's appointment, one more hearing, one more day, one more endless stupid hour.

"Your Maker had no time to teach you, then?" Soft and persistent, almost cajoling. This vamp certainly didn't *sound* crazy, which was also sort of comforting. Maybe she could get some information?

That sounded dangerous as all hell, but what choice did she have? "He didn't say a single word," Simone kept her eyes firmly shut; the woman using her voice sounded tired, colorless. Distant. "Just growled and b-bit me. It hurt."

"Then I am glad he's dead." Quiet and level, each word weighed carefully. "I will allow nothing to harm you, little leman."

So, he has a thing for floor-fucking and also for... lemons? Leee-mons, is it some kind of foreign word? Or maybe his crazy just doesn't show at first blush. "I don't understand any of this." Simone's voice remained a flat monotone; she was just too high on old-vamp blood to care about much of anything at the moment. Whatever he wanted, he'd lose interest before long. She could wait—or so she hoped.

And, as the final indignity, she felt a hot trickle from the corners of her eyes, and realized vampires could cry after all.

CHAPTER 12

SHE WEPT AS OLD SOLDIERS SOMETIMES DO, AS IF SHE RESENTED THE very existence of tears. He would have enjoyed closeness forced by the barb knotted deep in her core, but the urge was negated by her steadfast refusal to open her eyes, acknowledge her own pleasure or physical relaxation. Even the fact that another deep feeding had clearly provided some pleasant languor did not seem to matter.

A few more such bouts, and it would be as if he had given her the Dark Gift himself. Patience was required, not least until the swelling retreated and he could slip reluctantly free of her hot velvet core.

At least the bathtub was of adequate dimension, and the water warm enough—though he suspected she would have made no demur at a cauldron a-boiling, refusing to show a shred of weakness. As it was, she also endured his ministrations, though flinching frequently.

His own ablutions were quick, nearly perfunctory. The flannels were thin, but she scrupulously divided their number to grant him half and scrubbed herself dry far more roughly than he would have, unbending enough to steal tiny almost-peeks in his direction, though never quite reaching his face.

Only when clothed—she chose her former raiment from the neatly folded pile upon the pristine bed, dismissing new items he had hoped would be acceptably fashionable—did she seem a little less uncomfortable. She pulled her boots on with every evidence of relief, and brightened considerably upon seeing the new computer.

Laptop, the signs had said, and the displayed price—strange, mortals did not seem to haggle much anymore—seemed to indicate an item of some quality. Inside were secrets of this new age; he could not wait to begin their unraveling.

Yet she immediately sobered and looked pointedly away, as if expecting to be scolded. Her halting answers to gentle questioning were not quite grudging. It was true—she knew almost nothing of sanguinant, despite hunting miscreants stupid enough to come to mortal notice.

"Eight?" He tried not to sound shocked, and suspected he had failed in quite signal fashion. "In five mortal years?"

"Yeah." Slim, long-fingered hands knotting together, she perched on the edge of the bedroom's only chair, set at a precise angle from the spindly table only barely large enough for letter-jotting. She kept the *lap-top* in peripheral vision; perhaps she longed for its mysterious comforts. "They each felt pretty young, though. Not like you. And they were all… bad. They did terrible things." Quivering with fresh anxiety now, his lovely new responsibility stared at some point just past him, and the crystalline tears continued to flow slow and inexorable. She made no move to brush them away, even as salt drops dotted her cotton shirt.

"A considerable achievement, darlin'." He took care not to drawl overmuch, fastening his belt-buckle and running fingers through his damp hair, shaking to settle the strands. Now that he was no longer lost to unreason, it was enjoyable to be clean. Freed of such quotidian matters for some while, he approached his shy, delightful prize with slow care. "Even among leman you are exceptional."

"Lee-mun?" A quick darting glance, this time at his face, weighing his expression. Evaluating, testing.

As if she expected sudden violence. He throttled a flare of near-incandescent rage at those who had taught her such caution before folding, degree by easy degree, into a crouch before her. Making himself smaller might ease some small fraction of her nervousness.

"*These are the ages of sanguinant,*" he quoted, softly. Even in this modern tongue the cadence wore through, rhythmic and pleasing. "First are the fledglings, children of glut. A few become Elder, free of day-sleep, though prone to the killing dream. A handful become daywalker, facing the Sun. Age matters a little, but strength matters more." So finished the catechism, almost, but there was something much more important to press upon. "And you are leman."

A flicker of green in large dark eyes as her gaze touched him, skittered away. Her hair ravelled upon her shoulders, silken skeins begging for a comforting caress. "What does a lee-mun do?"

"It means *beloved*. There are other names, but it... you are different." Now he must choose his words carefully indeed, avoiding anything which might frighten or disgust a pale, trembling naïf. "The moment the Dark Gift is received, there is danger. A fledgling may glut into bloodcraze, an Elder enter the killing sleep's false visions and starve to death. Daywalkers face the Sun, yes, but at every stage the years weigh upon a sanguinant. We become rigid, stultified, locked in habit. Numb, with the passage of time. Even an Archon—"

"Archon?" A flicker of interest, those huge eyes still brimming and blinking rapidly, her thick dark lashes matted.

"Little is known of those, and better not to ask." He sensed there was enough to occupy them both at the moment. Eventually she would learn. "An old sanguinant will become brittle, stupid, prone to apathy, feeling nothing. No joy, no pain, no emotion at all. Simply greyness."

"Oh." She visibly considered the notion. "That sounds horrible."

"It is," he agreed, gravely. So far, so good—and she seemed to accept his new accent, or at least did not express displeasure at the cadence. "But a leman suffers none of those things. You will be ever curious, ever flexible; you will never know glut or blood-craze, killing sleep or the calcification. Leman are very, very few; to meet one is a miracle."

"Then why…" A slight shake, damp-darkened tendrils swaying heavily as they dried. Now she freed her hands and brushed at her cheeks almost angrily, dashing the tears away. "Assuming I believe all this, why did the others all act drunk? None of them could even *talk*."

"That is a leman's effect on fledglings. Your scent, it is…" He searched for the proper term, shuffling through mental store-houses, hoping he could pronounce each word properly.

Her lovely eyes widened, almost impossibly. "You mean I stink, and it drove them crazy? Great." More head-shaking; she physically recoiled, leaning back in the chair. "So, what are you? One of those Elders, right? And where did the cowboy accent go?"

Fascinating, to witness her quicksilver moods. "Your sanguinant does not fear the Sun," he said, formally. "I spent much of today learning to enunciate as you do, since my speech did not please my leman. And I would ask you a favor."

"A what now?" Now she lifted her chin, and he was once again the entire focus of her attention. Quite a pleasurable sensa-tion, indeed. "This is the way vampires ask for favors? By… by busting into my RV and…" Perhaps at a loss for words, she did not finish the thought.

"When a leman is found, they are bitten and claimed. Always. You are simply too precious to squander." He watched her lean back still further, withdrawing yet another critical frac-tion. "But there, at your elbow. A com-puter, yes? Lap-top." He sought to pronounce the words correctly, was rewarded when she glanced at the item, then back at him, a faint line appearing between her winged eyebrows.

"Yeah, a laptop. Not as nice as the one I had to melt, but okay." Another hint of challenge, brittle bravery, tossing a gauntlet to gauge the response.

"I will provide better in the future. Tonight, though, we have some time." The thrall was sleepy-sated inside his bones, and he thought it wise to accustom his new prize to his presence in another fashion. "Will you teach me to use it?"

Her mouth opened slightly. His leman frankly stared at him, as if thunderstruck. A short, chuffing chuckle made her sway in the chair, followed by more in a cascade, turning to liquid merriment.

She had such an irresistible laugh.

His leman nearly shook with amusement, possibly at his expense. Yet the taunting edge of fear faded a fraction from her scent—not much, a victory nonetheless. Bathed, purified, still anointed with the feel of her body, he stayed in his crouch, watching a miracle trail into helpless giggles, finally covering her mouth like a child, eyes sparkling.

For a few moments he could pretend he had truly pleased her. And it was so impossibly sweet he could not wait to attempt the feat again.

"Just keep an eye on the battery, and you'll be fine." His leman turned her head slightly, still unwilling to look directly at him. Yet his position—perched upon a settee in the suite's sitting room, watching as she tapped at the 'laptop' on a coffee table set at their knees—seemed to ameliorate some of her fear. "How old are you really, anyway? Can I ask?"

It just does what you tell it, she said, as if such a servant were not a marvel unthinkable for most of mortal history. *Where on earth are we right now?* Casual questions, peppering her lesson.

He let her draw out details, enjoying the game. *How did you follow me? What is that invisible-seal thing?*

"Very old, I think, even before the fire." He examined the text upon the screen; letters had been streamlined and spelling strangely altered, but thankfully his literacy had not been wholly impaired even by the madness. Now he better understood the appeal of the bright flat faces. *Electronic, wireless, streaming, data* —wonderful concepts, words new-coined or repurposed, vast new sweeps of possibility. He had missed a great deal as he wandered, raving, in a backwater. "You may ask what you like, my leman. Always."

"So you just… wandered around hunting people?"

"I avoided notice, fed when necessary, punished trespassers in my territory. The fledgling you dispatched, for example—I was already tracking him." Difficult to keep his tone even, neutral, for a leman was never to suffer combat. It was incredible, unthinkable, a violation of the natural order. She could have been rendered not merely ill-nourished and nervous but outright damaged by a fledgling drunk upon her scent or—more likely— by simple mischance, unwanted mortal attention.

Or, worse, claimed by another as he roamed witless.

"He was a nasty piece of work. Killed whole families, and there was one victim in…" His leman shuddered, and closed the laptop with care. Then she rose, unfolding with sweet grace. "Never mind. Oh, hey, my bag."

She had glanced at the canvas pouch as soon as he shepherded her into the sitting room, of course, but refrained from mentioning it. Now she hurried to the overstuffed blue-and-cream striped chair, scooped the satchel up with sweet grace, and turned to face him with a bright, wary approximation of a smile.

"It's getting kind of late," she continued. "I've got to find a place to sleep. So, you can take that shimmer-stuff off the door and I'll be on my way."

For a moment he thought he had misheard. Then, a sumptuous urge to smile swallowed him; she was entirely captivating. "There is an hour or two yet before dawn." The temptation to carry her into the bedroom, spending that fragment of time in most enjoyable fashion, was pronounced.

"I know, but I'm busy, I've got places to be." She settled the bag against her hip; its strap, diagonal across her chest, pulled the soft cotton shirt taut over her breasts. "I'm not doing any more bounties, you don't have to worry about that. Just let me walk out the door and you'll never see me again."

Did she truly think he would let her go, or was she deliberately misunderstanding? "You are leman. *My* leman. When dawn comes, you will sleep inside these seals." There the matter lay, in all its starkness.

"Look, I'm real glad you're better now, honest, and I'm sorry about trying to blow you up." Quiet earnestness, tearstreaked face luminous, her slim form tense. "But you have to admit it was fair, considering what you… what you did."

Fairness, the argument of prey. "You will sleep *here*." He flickered upright, disliking the flash of fear in her so-expressive eyes, the way her mouth tightened, the nervous sidling step of retreat. "Tomorrow night we will go wherever you choose, and I will provide all you require or wish for."

"You can't just keep me here." Her gaze darted for the door opposite the bedroom, and he could not repress a hard, delighted grin.

"I can, and I will, my darling. Go ahead, attempt escape." He glided toward her, step by soundless step. "See what happens."

"Why are you *doing* this?" A forlorn little cry. His leman retreated, herded toward the bedroom; if she broke and ran, the thrall—sleeping sated, yet ever ready to be roused—might be provoked.

"T' survive. Cain't do otherwise." *And to stay in your company some short while longer.* A ghost of the accent she disliked so much crept in, despite his care; he caught it, could have bitten his own tongue with near-frustration. "I suggest acquiescence, but resist if you like. It all ends in the same place." The thrall roused sleepily inside him, prickling-hot.

In the end she did not run, merely backed slowly into the bedroom… and slammed the door. He halted outside, listening intently. Scraping, a whispered curse as she dragged the one spindly chair, propping it under the knob as if she thought it would keep him at bay. Further stealthy sounds as she roamed the small space, yet she was too wise to approach the seals *or* the heavily curtained window.

A pity, that. But he could wait.

He had nothing but time, now.

CHAPTER 13

Pacing in a hotel bedroom until the usual, hateful lethargy of sunrise hit was awful. Even worse was waking up without a stitch on, tucked into the rumpled bed—how in the hell had *that* happened, she might not want to know—and being stared at by an ancient, wildly oversexed creature wearing only a black waffleweave thermal shirt.

The chair she'd used to brace the door was set at the bedside, and furthermore inhabited by said vampire.

Bright blue eyes, mouth tilted in a half-smile, the powerful old bloodsucker regarded her calmly; Simone swallowed an undignified squeak, jolting half-upright and clutching the covers to her chest.

Elbows braced on his bare knees, sleeves pushed up, his hair a gleaming-dark shock without the imprint of a hat, he looked a lot different than the skinny guy appearing out of thin air in her RV. Healthier, certainly—no longer so gaunt, his shoulders filled out and his cheeks high-planed instead of hollow. More than that, though, he looked *awake*, and terribly intent.

Completely, utterly focused. She'd never been stared at like this. Had he been watching her *sleep*, for God's sake? "What are you doing?"

At least her voice didn't break on the last word. But it was *damn* close.

"Enjoying the view." His gaze dropped, leisurely, appreciative almost to the point of ogling. "You must have been lovely even as a mortal. No doubt many pursued you, men and women both."

Her cheeks scorched as she made sure the blankets were pulled high; now she knew beyond doubt a vampire could blush. "Not so much," she muttered. *Just another middle-aged divorcée, really.*

Sliding into marriage with Curt because it was expected, keeping the house pin-neat on his salary—entry-level insurance adjustor, a good solid career choice, and as he moved up through the ranks the frequent business trips were harder on his delicate digestion than on her loneliness. Laundry, shopping, cooking, putting up preserves, sending Christmas and birthday cards to his extended family and her paternal aunt Kelly's as well. Simone's parents, having done their duty, weren't the type to keep in touch after unloading her into a marriage, and anyway there was the terrible car accident near her sixth wedding anniversary.

Right in the middle of the Aruba trip supposed to be her and Curt's second honeymoon, as a matter of fact. *Christ, they've got awful timing,* he'd grumbled on the way to the airport, and Simone had stared out the cab's condensation-starred window at tropical scenery, muffling a bright sharp heart-stabbing sensation which very well might have been hate.

Taking her birth control pills on the sly because the thought of swelling up and pushing out a squalling copy of Curt was sickening in a way she never quite articulated even to herself, smiling nicely whenever one of Curt's cousins asked whether they weren't thinking about kids yet, wanting to adopt a cat from the shelter but Curt's allergies forbade, the years piling up like dandruff until one day she looked around and realized she was forty-eight, where had the time gone? And the years of weariness afterward, realizing her marriage was a sham and the rest of her life a desert.

Was that the 'numbness' this old vamp talked about? It certainly sounded similar, though maybe not as intense. After she got fangs, all sensations were dialed into the red and her memories of human life oddly dark, muted.

The sheets were cool against her legs and toes; thankfully, she wasn't thirsty. Had he undressed her? She'd certainly freed herself of nightgowns and all other encumbrances while sleeping on hot summer nights before, but never since getting infected.

What if there *was* a cure, like Barry's billionaire thought? Should she mention it to this old, overwhelming, completely unhinged creature?

"Then they were fools," the old vampire said, as if consigning the whole human race to that category. "We should leave here tonight. I do not like how the mortals keep trying the door."

"Probably want to clean the room." She braced the blanket against her chest, rubbed at her forehead. The invisible seals clearly kept people out during the day; what would she have given for that skill when learning how to vamp? "Wait. Did you… how did you pay for this? You have to show ID, so—"

"They will take anything as identification, with proper inducement. And money is easy, my leman."

Maybe for you. Still, having someone show her a few ropes might not be a bad idea. If she could just get him to stop… stop fucking her, for God's sake. Simone's breath caught; she was very aware of her bare shoulders, tousled hair, the vampire's gaze roaming as his hands had a habit of doing.

It was goddamn *distracting*, to be stared at like this.

Her face must have changed, since his smile widened. "Do you doubt my ability to provide? I hunted well today, and will feed you soon."

Oh, God. "When you say *hunted*… do you kill people?"

"Y'all can learn to drink without killing before the first century." A slight, dismissive ripple of those now-disconcertingly broad shoulders, the merest suggestion of a shrug. "Ah, forgive me. I should say, *you* can learn. Fledglings, that is."

Why is he apologizing? "But others can't?"

"I must have, for the habit mostly carried after the fire." A slow blink of those bright eyes, catlike. "Leman do not suffer the urge to glut, so you have never killed, yes?"

Oh, I've killed. Just not people. "Only vampires." Which was probably a bad thing to admit. And how had her life come to this —sitting naked on a hotel bed, calmly discussing murder and bounties with a bloodsucker so old he didn't remember '*the first century*'? And his casual '*mostly carried*' was kind of concerning. "You've done that too. Right?"

"Of course." Like it was no big deal. "And I will again, if necessary."

Oh shit. Was he eventually going to kill *her*? All the talk about being special, about being rare, might just mean *like veal*, or *like foie gras*.

"For example, if another sanguinant seeks to claim my darling. Or if a mortal distresses her—they can be dangerous in swarms, you must realize. Other creatures are not much hazard, since most of the *demimonde* knows better than t'approach a leman." The smile faded, and now his unblinking blue stare was that of a large predator.

Sharp, alert. Dangerous.

"Look." It was super difficult to sound anything other than petrified at the moment. "You want to leave, and I've got some things to do anyway. So how about I get dressed, and—"

"We shall go anywhere you like." Quiet, but with a note of finality. The vampire tensed, leaning slightly forward, and if his gaze had been direct before it was downright scorching now. Not just undressing her with those bright azure eyes but laying her bare, as if the sheet, blanket, comforter didn't matter. "But first, my darling, I must please you."

What the hell does that mean? She had a suspicion. The sinking sensation in her middle met a curious, dark excitement, quickly repressed. "It would be really pleasing to get dressed," she said, hoping it would work.

And staying very, very still.

"Afterward." He began to uncoil, slowly.

Simone's breath caught. She scrambled backward, her shoulders smacking the headboard, and seeing a half-naked man leap onto the bed, crouching to balance easily, should have been ridiculous.

It wasn't, mostly because he was so controlled. Knowing exactly how strong he was, how fast, was both alarming and an odd, mordant relief. There was nothing to be done; he was a hurricane in vampire form, and she a rowboat caught on the waves. "Wait," she pleaded, edging clumsily sideways, the mattress giving an alarming groan. "We can talk about this, we can—"

"You'll fall," he noted, mildly. "If you want to be taken on the floor again, I do not mind."

Simone froze. Miraculously, he did as well, and that smile was back. He certainly seemed to be enjoying himself. Worse, there was a traitorous trickle of heat between her legs. She couldn't get in enough air; her skin seemed at once too tight and absurdly sensitive. Her nipples were hard as ice chips, standing to attention, and a terrible, volcanic thrill shot through her.

"Well?" A bare whisper, his lips caressing the word. "Bed, or floor, darlin'? Choose."

Her nerve broke. Simone pitched the opposite direction, and a heartbeat later he was on her.

A spinning, a disorientation, rumpled cloth and mattress sinking under her and the shadow of him looming above, his mouth finding hers in a delirium of hunger. Her claws sprang free, skidding along hard straps and sheaths of muscle, refusing to catch; she squirmed desperately, knowing it was hopeless, helpless to stop. His cock found what it wanted, burrowing into hot slickness, and his hand was under her right knee, lifting.

Her legs parted almost eagerly, her ankles finding each other and locking at the small of his back. He braced himself, a lion-purr rumble vibrating in his chest, and thrust, *hard*. Her throat filled with a scream, vanishing into his. Greedy kisses, as if he liked it.

As if he couldn't get enough.

Her body knew what it wanted, eager to blot out the uncertainty, the fear, the constant questioning. She writhed in concert with a monster, forgetting everything but the fire spilling between her nerve endings, the need pulsing in her most secret parts, the desire to be filled. He took direction eagerly, every slight shift and begging twitch of her hips answered without hesitation or resistance, and she actually hissed when he freed his mouth from hers because she wanted to be kissed.

She wanted distraction while he fucked her, so she didn't have to breathe or think.

But he made a swift movement, and suddenly the scent exploded in her head—warm, delicious, coppery, coating the back of her throat, the fangs popping free.

Blood. *His* blood.

And oh God but it was good, the warmth sliding down her throat, the tastes overlapping and combining as she swallowed, as she squirmed underneath him.

As she *fed*.

Building and building, taking its time, his rhythm almost leisurely as she gulped at the flood, and finally a burst of lava spread in concentric pulses, every thought and fear blotted from the universe as she came again and again, arched and shameless as a cat in heat, safely trapped underneath a hot, muscular weight.

Simone had never understood how some people could crave sex, do risky, embarrassing things just for the sake of getting laid.

But oh, God, now she did.

CHAPTER 14

HOW MANY NIGHTS HAD HE WANDERED WITH ONLY THE THIRST AS A companion, the dust of ages accreting on his body, his perceptions, his very soul? Now the madness was gone, the fractures no longer thinly scabbed but very nearly healed, stray snippets of memory rising at odd moments as he followed his leman from the hotel, aware she was careful to avoid undue mortal notice.

Hovering at her shoulder, drenched in the heavy sweet perfume laced with a smoky tang of his own blood in her veins, throbbing from crown to soles with the memory of her pleasure as she writhed and cried out underneath him—all of it, *all*, turned the darkness to noon even more surely than sharp sanguinant sight, filled the mortal buildings with secret delight, transformed windows, streetlights, and car-lights into jewels set about the brightest, most beautiful lamp ever made.

Naturally her acceptance was only temporary; he was not fool enough to think her resigned to captivity. Yet at least she had enjoyed his attentions, fed to completion, and settled the new laptop in her bag. The clothes were not inadequate, she declared, but she *traveled light*.

He could not argue. He climbed onto a giant, lumbering metal coach after her—a bus, she said, and he stored the term away, vaguely aware of such conveyances elsewhere, pulled by teams of horses. Or had that been in the more-distant past?

It did not matter. His leman was beside him, dropping into a hard plastic seat and gazing outward through a window which would have been prohibitively expensive some few centuries ago. The cleanness of her profile, the line of her throat, her shoulders loose and relaxed under her dark jacket, all so beautiful he could do nothing but stand, struck motionless next to a metal pole, watching as she swayed with the vehicle's motion.

This was no mere mortal world but a savagely delightful garden, and if every night with a leman were even a fraction so glorious he could spend an untiring eternity thus. Now he remembered other sanguinant proverbs, and the whispers of what it meant to claim a leman.

"God, I miss coffee," she murmured, staring out the dust-glazed glass. Her hands lay decorously in her lap; her hair was alive with golden highlights against the deep, glossy red-brown.

"Coffee?" He carefully wrapped a hand about the pole as a few other standing passengers did—the vehicle was relatively full, and every wan, lackluster mortal face bore the marks of age, hovering disease, shadowy incipient death-rot.

They had such brief lives. She would have shone among them starlike and glorious, ready to be claimed the moment a sanguinant happened across her path—or perhaps, chance and rarity being what they were, she could have gone unnoticed all her brief mortal days?

That prospect chilled him to the marrow.

"Used to be my favorite thing about the day, a cup in the morning with the paper. Or while looking out the dining room door." A sigh caught the last word, perhaps unaware, and she hunched her shoulders, glancing up at him. "Can we even drink coffee? I never got around to testing it."

To be so young, so afraid, struggling with a fledgling's thirst and no doubt terrified by her introduction to the Gift... he knew nothing of her former life, if her Maker had violently broken it, or if she had been alone there as well. "Mortal food is pleasant enough. Not nutritious, though, and does not help the Thirst."

He realized, somewhat belatedly, that she had said *we*. It had a lovely ring, that single inclusive syllable, however reluctant.

"What about garlic?" Her eyebrows lifted slightly, ripe lovely lips parted. Waiting upon his answer, and the sweetness threatened to strike him down as battle, glut, madness, the Sun itself could not.

"Mere seasoning. Crosses are useless, flax seeds easy to count at a glance, and silver only affects very young fledglings." His face felt odd; it was so very strange to smile instead of simply baring fangs in dominance or glut-display. "We do not feel the compulsion to untie nets either. Only *some* folklore is useful, darlin'."

"Guess so." She stirred, patting the aisle seat with delicate fingertips. "You can sit down, you know. It's okay."

Did he dare take such a sweet, hesitant invitation? A moment later the bus lurched and it was too late; she had turned away, her eyebrows drawing together and mouth tightening, all luminous interest withdrawn.

He contented himself with reading the street signs, listening to the thumping pulse of each mortal—unique, the sounds strained through mood, heredity, body shape, density, diet, carrying reams of information concerning prey's fitness or weakening—and absorbing the varied panoply of night. So far he had sensed one or two others of the Blood in this city, but a sanguinant of his strength was well able to deflect interest or awareness. Covering her scent was a matter of reflex; no others would be able to track her as he had.

And he had almost lost the golden thread several times, distracted by the madness. Some kind divinity had impelled him, or perhaps it was a matter of mere chance.

Mortals had ever considered Fortune a goddess. He might well join their number before long.

The bus stopped, started, wallowed, creaked, rumbled,

belched along. Even that cacophony was music, for his leman was nearby and tranquil, watching the night as well.

His lovely prize had a destination in mind, and once they left the loud, lurching omnibus she set off in decided fashion down a wide, deserted sidewalk, barely glancing to mark his position— almost as if she had learned to take his presence for granted, accepted her protector's attentions as natural or at least inevitable.

He knew it was not so, and yet.

"No night bus—Greyhound *or* Trailways—and no direct train connection." She shook her head, her hands thrust deep into her coat pockets, and lengthened her stride.

So, she would teach him how mortals traveled. He could of course bear her a great distance at speed… but clearly she was unaware of the fact, or unready for such an event.

"Are there no hired coaches to be had?" It was enough that he could make a reply, hopefully inducing her to further conversation. "I seem to remember that being common enough."

"Not these days. Taxi and rideshares aren't a good idea." An amused side-glance, dark eyes now flashing with less tint of green or yellow, lacking the kiss of bright electric light. "I did think the airport would be a better bet for what we need, but when I looked it up last night, it's too small."

Airport? Flight was a modern mortal miracle, though far less efficient than mistform or simply skating the terrain. He had hazily understood the purpose of the giant silver beasts coursing the stratosphere even in his madness, seeing them far above; the smaller, lower, buzzing craft sounded venomous but were ultimately harmless. "We will not be… flying, then?"

"Nah." Despite her seeming unconcern, his leman was also sharply mindful of their surroundings. She must have perfected the skill of covert awareness while hunting other fledglings.

"Never liked it even when I was human, and it's never really on time. If I pass out at dawn on a plane, it could end badly."

"Indeed." He considered the problem carefully. "What of a private plane, as a railway car?" The latter was an expensive habit of very wealthy mortals, he seemed to vaguely remember from the time of the fire—a flash of knowledge there and gone in a moment, yet leaving a promise of return.

Healing proceeded apace. Soon he might know more of his own history. Which did not matter, but was still a reasonably pleasant prospect.

"Only if you've got, like, a billion dollars." Rich amusement in her lilting soprano, bubbling with restrained laughter. "No, trains are always better, and buses too. I can hop off anywhere and find a place to rest."

She was teaching him already; the pleasure threatened to undo him. "I see."

"But best of all is a car." She indicated what had to be their destination, a large, ugly concrete cake of a building. A sign on its scabrous hide buzzed desultorily, repeatedly announcing **PARKING - SHORT/LONG TERM** in silent stutters. "You ever stolen wheels before, Mr. Old Vampire?"

"Not that I can recall, darlin'." He could not help the endearment, though it was much easier now to mimic her accent. "I'd love to learn."

She studied the mechanical arm and control box imperfectly blocking a cavernous exit before slipping past a grimy sign proclaiming *No Pedestrians*, turned hard right at the end of the ramp, and set off into the depths. Night wind moaned at the corners of the building; traces of sandy dust lay against faded paint-lines, settling on crouched metal shapes. She selected an inner door and the metal slab swung wide, revealing steps turning back and forth, stretching both up- and downward.

They descended, surrounded by faint echoes. Her small faithful boots sometimes tapped, sometimes remained instinctively silent; he would teach her finer control soon. The stairwell was dirty, ill-lit with buzzing fluorescents, and more than one mortal had apparently urinated in the corners; the smell was atrocious before he filtered it from consciousness.

How much time did she spend in places like this, a solitary doe moving through a jungle of iron, concrete, reeking filth? Her very presence hallowed the environs, yet he did not like them at all.

She deserved so much better.

"What we want is long-term parking." She peered through another heavy, battered swinging door, wrinkled her nose. "Generally on lower floors, since nobody wants the weather getting to their ride. Here we are."

He could sense no danger in the echoing concrete cave, though he *also* did not like how she seemed careless of such elementary precautions as checking before leaving cover. Much to instruct her in, and he anticipated the lessons being enjoyable.

Particularly the rewards for fine performance, should she deign to grant any.

"Want something sturdy enough to go through the boom," she said, softly, slowing to a stroll. "And look there—security camera, but it's more than likely a dummy. Not even plugged in."

"No electricity," he confirmed, barely bothering to glance at the grimy plastic box bearing a clouded glass eye, tucked in a high, prominent corner. "If there were, I would already be blurring us both, my darling."

"You can do that?" Sweet surprise lilting in her tone, only slightly mocking. Another of those darting, apprehensive glances, gauging his reaction.

"They used to call it galvanism." He was almost cheered by her small sarcasm; he could be chaffed so all night, but only by her. "A natural force, like light or air. Easy to affect."

For some reason, that provoked her attention. His leman halted, turned to regard him fully. "Any electronics, or just cameras? What about film? Can you shock people? And light-ning, what about—"

"Lightning is dangerous to fledgling and Elder, film is sensi-tive to light and may be ruined with small effort." Photographic plates had been a different story, he seemed to remember, and could have followed that thread into the labyrinth of splintered memory. Yet her questions took precedence, as did bathing in the honor of her notice. "I do not need to *shock* mortals, and yes, most older sanguinant can affect all manner of phenomena, physical or electrical, according to age and skill. I shall have to teach you most carefully, and from the beginning."

"Huh." Did the prospect entice her? She shifted from one foot to the other, wide-eyed, begrudgingly interested. "Let's see how you are with car alarms, then?" A tinge of uncertainty, as if she expected—or feared—refusal.

What could I ever deny you, beautiful one? "At your service, darlin'."

CHAPTER 15

EERIE AS HELL TO SEE A VAMPIRE LAY ONE HAND AGAINST THE DOOR of a brown Toyota Celica with license tags three months out of date, hear the power locks chuck up and the engine start—choppily, since it had clearly been left down here by someone who didn't care to renew their registration. No need to mess with the steering column's innards, either, since apparently he could unlock the wheel as well.

Even more thought-provoking was him leaning nearly into her lap from the passenger seat, staring fixedly at the payment terminal, and the credit card reader blinking in semaphore. She didn't even need to produce the discarded paper ticket clinging to the dashboard. The machine's LED display scrolled *THANK YOU* as it emitted a soft, happy beep, and the mechanical arm across the exit lifted by stagger-degrees.

That close, the old vampire's body heat brushed against her right arm. He smelled like dusk, fresh grasslands wind, and male, a peculiarly clean musk triggering recent memory. In fact, Simone had to squeeze her knees together, her entire body threatening to turn liquid, and concentrating enough to pull out of the parking garage was momentarily difficult.

Especially with what felt like a toasty, pulsing pool of his blood settled behind her breastbone, sending out waves of relaxation. She hadn't felt this calmly zen about the world in... well, *ever*. Relaxed yet alert, trying not to think that her own perceptions could be hopelessly altered at the moment.

Fortunately, she didn't have to roll more than a city block without finding a sign for I-25; she hoped she wasn't doing the vamp equivalent of DUI. A few more blocks, a left-hand turn—the green arrow popping up almost as soon as they approached the stop line—and traffic at this hour wasn't bad at all, even this close to downtown. Merging was no trouble, and there was even a big friendly green sign announcing the miles to Denver with conspiratorial glee.

He hadn't even asked where they were going. For Chrissake, she was in a dirt-colored, probably abandoned Toyota with an old, freakishly powerful vampire, the engine chopping along but doing its best, and instead of making plans to shake the bloodsucker, she was... what?

What exactly was her goal, here? Sure, she had to make the meet with Barry's billionaire, but what then? The payment was walking-away money, fuck-you money, the best *kind* of money—if it was real.

What about the idea of a cure for the infection? It was a good thing she was driving; she needed time to think, and there was nothing better than freeway piloting for that particular activity. Some of her best ideas had come during long road trips.

Of course, there had been some real howlers as well. Hard to tell the two apart when an idea struck.

"So," she said, settling more comfortably now that cruising speed had been achieved in the far right lane—good practice, especially since even the big rigs would probably want to pass this poor rinkydink car as soon as the city fell away on either side. At least the gas tank was full. "Do I get to know your name, Mr. Vampire?"

He was silent for a few moments, one hand resting on his knee, fingers twitching as if following a private, internal beat.

Maybe he suspected she was going to try to blow him up with this car, too.

If she was thinking rationally, she probably *should*. What had happened to her commitment, the burning focus on bounties, on making the world a marginally safer place? A few rounds of athletic sex, coming almost despite herself each time, and she was suddenly... what? Driven insane by hormones?

"I don't remember," he said, finally. "Call me what you like. I'll answer."

How is that possible? Was it the numbness he talked about, or leftover emotional damage from that fire he kept skipping over, barely giving details? "How can you not remember? It's your name."

"I must have had one as a mortal, yes. No doubt I had several after the Dark Gift, for camouflage or... other reasons. After the... the misfortune, it simply didn't occur to me." He shifted, settled into that eerie motionlessness. "Choose a name you like; I shall wear it."

"What if I pick one *you* don't like?" How on earth was she even having this conversation? The freeway lifted over a slight rise and dropped, still running ruler-straight under the headlights' white cone. No need to touch the brake if she kept her following distance nice and ample, but that was an invitation for assholes to cut into her lane.

As usual.

"I doubt you will." Calmly, as if he'd thought the whole matter over at length. The words were far more fluid now; only a ghost of the drawl remained. "And it does not matter; I will accept any gift from my leman."

This whole lee-mun thing was getting weirder. Still... it was sad to think of someone wandering around without a name, even a vampire. How deep was the trauma if it erased something so basic?

Are you actually feeling sorry for a bloodsucking killing machine? The power of hormones, maybe. But they were stuck in the car for at least another hour and a half, so she might as well play nice.

She had a contender in the name game already, too. "How about John? It's simple, doesn't go out of style. You can be Johnny if you're feeling frisky, and Jonathan if you're formal."

"Jonathan. John." Testing the word. No excitement in his tone, but no disgust, either. Simone couldn't sneak a peek at his expression, needing all her attention for the road. A low-slung red sports car roared past to the left, weaving slightly, no doubt fueled by both cocaine and hi-test unleaded. "Very well."

Lord, give me something to work with here. I'm trying to be nice to a vampire. She freed her right hand from the wheel, extended tentatively across the armrest. "Hi, John. I'm Simone." *Crap.*

She'd meant to use *Jane Smith*, keeping it professional. But her real name slipped out, polite as you please—maybe because she was fairly relaxed from gorging on old-vampire blood, or from lingering post-orgasmic endorphins. She expected confusion on his part, or a businesslike shake, but instead his fingers closed around hers and he bent, leaned slightly forward. A soft pressure against her knuckles, a zinging thrill all the way up her arm.

He literally *kissed her hand.*

"An honor and a pleasure to know your name, my lady Simone." A faint brush of breath branded the words to her skin before he let go; she retreated to her side of the car, suddenly aware of blushing—again—in the darkness.

Given vamp senses, he could probably see. Which was embarrassing as fuck.

Her tough-girl image might never recover. "Wow, you really are old." *Oh, hell. That sounded way better inside my head.* "I mean…"

"I am." Quiet agreement, no hint of anger or wounded ego. "Yet I'm learnin', and I have the most beautiful of teachers."

Maybe he's just practicing his small talk. And he hadn't asked where they were going, either. Which was entirely for the best, sure, but also concerning. Darkness stretched to either side, waves of grassland lit up to vampire eyes, breathing in billows under the night wind.

"Can I ask you something, Jonathan?" She might as well try. "Without all the lee-mun stuff—why do they call it that, anyway? No, never mind. Can I?"

"*Leman* is an old, old word; to the sanguinant, it means *beloved one*. Ask me anything, darlin'."

Nobody had ever called her *darling* before, and certainly not this frequently. Curt's deepest endearment was *babe* and sometimes *honey*—neither were bad, but didn't have quite the same ring. "If you could be cured, would you?"

"Cured?" For once, the old vampire sounded honestly baffled.

"Of the infection. Vampirism. Of being… sanguinant." Where did *that* word come from? It sounded vaguely French, but accented weirdly. Did vampires have a secret language? She had the whole time to Denver for getting information; he couldn't very well attempt any canoodling while she was driving—or so Simone hoped.

She really wouldn't put it past this guy.

"A curious way to put it." His stillness had returned, almost as if he forgot to move while concentrating on her questions. The shoulder rolled by outside his window, reflectors popping up at precisely measured intervals. "There is no return to mortality, ever. It is endurance or true-death. That's all."

"But what if it's possible?" she persisted—carefully, quietly, knowing how much men hated to be challenged or disagreed with. "Would you?"

"Give up the Gift?" Now he sounded faintly shocked, though she couldn't peek over to tell for sure, and a thread of unease invaded the warm haze. "No. Of course not."

Well, that's pretty definitive. If Barry's billionaire had a line on a possible cure, she might have to do some quick thinking, not to mention fancy footwork, and hope she could keep this vampire away from all the humans involved. "I was just asking."

Lights arched over the road, each patch of glow merging companionably with the next. It used to be gaslights, Simone thought, and before that, torches, lamps, and candles. Darkness was ancient, and a few recent, puny bulbs wouldn't drive it back completely, or for good.

It lurked between stars, too. Ever ready, endless bleak black emptiness.

"Would you?" He was watching her; she felt the gaze of the vampire she had just named, a heavy weight against her right side, pressing against her cheek, sinking into her hair. "If it were possible?"

Yes. In a heartbeat. The words got caught up in her throat, dammed behind the grimy, stuck-rock feeling of a possible lie. *Why can't I say so?*

That was far more frightening than a vampire appearing from thin air in her RV, than waking up naked and vulnerable, than being spread out and nailed under a creature who probably had more anniversaries under his belt than quite a few modern nation-states. The vast impersonal glitter of Cheyenne receded into the rearview mirror, even its suburbs becoming an orange smear on the night horizon, and the plains spread to either side of a thin concrete stream.

Were there vampires still alive from before Rome was built? Before Babylon? Before humans crossed the land bridge from Siberia? If they could walk around in sunlight, what else could they do? Simone prided herself on being relatively blasé nowadays when it came to the world's hidden, carnivorous weirdness, but...

So much for conversation. The silence thickened, the car rumbled unhappily, and Simone suspected it would be an uncomfortable ride to Denver.

She was right.

CHAPTER 16

His leman withdrew, sharply and totally, all that glorious interest and animation gone. Still, he could not help but feel some small progress had been made.

Simone. A lilting, lovely sound, all the more charming because it was *hers*, vouchsafed to her protector. And *Jonathan*— the word held no ring of recognition, yet was not wholly unfamiliar. He could even be relieved, for it was an ancient truth that to name something was to claim it. To belong—finally, at last— was a comfort.

On some level, she must realize her own power. Sanguinant would tear each other to pieces merely to approach her, to inhale a single fragment of that dizzying, drunkening scent—and he would do much worse, destroying any who sought to even catch sight of her shadow. He was ill-acquainted with this era, true, but in a short while every luxury it possessed would be laid at her feet.

Did she wish for wealth? Power over mortals? To build an empire, or to destroy one?

He would provide; *Jonathan* would make it so. He stared out a dust-shrouded window at the plains rising and falling like the back of a slumbering creature. Listened to her breathing, the soft thunder of her pulse, the hum of the rattletrap vehicle.

Yet her question troubled him. Give up the Gift? Impossible. The changes, physical and otherwise, were far too deep; the Blood was irrevocable. He plainly saw her shyness at the quite natural act of feeding, perhaps even understood it intellectually, but distaste did not change necessity.

Ever.

Green metal signs counted off town-names and distance, an amazing achievement in both cartography and mathematics; mortals had advanced wonderfully during his almost-absence. After a short while she reached for the middle section of the instrument panel, granted him a nervous glance, and withdrew; five precisely numbered miles later, she did so again.

"Is something not working properly?" A neutral enough enquiry, he hoped.

"It's better to drive with music." Her shoulders were no longer so relaxed; she was not quite wary, but upon the border of that state. Her chin settled in decided fashion, instrument-glow from the brightly decorated panel before her limning each curve lovingly. "But you might think I'm trying to blow you up again."

The notion hadn't occurred to him; she was indeed a canny creature. He studied the knob she had been reaching for, the blank face of an electronic servant waiting to be summoned. Music, yes. Radio, he had discovered the term; so this was how they brought it inside cars. He longed to know more. "We're past that now. Aren't we?"

"What if I'm not?" She stared at the road before them, leaning incrementally closer to her door. A thin, rough thread of dark-red fear wove through her scent, plucking at the thrall dozing in his bones.

The urge to protect was twisted through mating instincts, after all, warp-weft vines of passion and possession. "There are much more pleasant games to play, sweet Simone." He enjoyed the taste of her name, even if a camouflage or grudgingly given.

"Is that what this is to you?" Now a tone of challenge, just as fascinating as every other aspect she displayed. "Some kind of sick game?"

He wanted to observe that in a certain sense existence itself was a game—rules and goals, players, tendencies and escalations, an interlocking pattern of action and reaction vast as night itself. The most chaotic of deadly battles obeyed its own consistent logic; even madness had its own buried, incoherent principles. "Far from, darlin'. You are a very serious fledgling."

It was, of course, the wrong thing to say. Her chin set with stubbornness instead of mere decision. The car's engine was running far more smoothly, though a truly annoying knocking had developed in its thrum.

Ah. Understanding arrived as he studied her profile—a pleasant pastime, indeed. She might weary of his attention, but he was far too fascinated for turning away. "You're uncertain," he continued, "and it annoys you."

A small, dismissive toss of her pretty head. She didn't reach for the knob again, but the orchestral rhythm of her pulse was all he needed. Finally, his dulcet leman spoke again.

"You haven't even asked where I'm going."

"No need." His fingertips ached, longing to brush the shoulder of her jacket, to use gentle strokes as if soothing a frightened feline. Horses required firmness and a certain scent-balance between *master* and *cohort*, but cats were to be coaxed. "Any destination will do."

Denver, the signs said, and he recognized the name. No doubt he had hunted here, before or since the fire. Or both. The sense of familiarity was strong, though not overwhelming, and small flashes of strangeness peered through—scenery which should have been bare now choked with houses, concrete road instead of dirt tracks, a half-familiar storefront nearly unraveled by time, cars instead of carriages, a street precisely where one should be peering back at him like an old friend.

Far more intriguing, however, was his leman's behavior. The night was wearing towards dawn, yet she did not seem inclined to choose a resting place just yet.

Instead, she piloted their iron chariot through a few slices of the city, veering away from and recrossing the high road they had arrived upon. Then, she brought the contraption to a stop in a sliver of quiet residential area found seemingly by instinct, leaving the vehicle motionless though still running, and twisted to reach into the back seat.

The movement brought her close, almost touching his left shoulder, and that was quite pleasant, though short-lived. She was after her bag, which settled between them on an approximation of an arm-rest, and proceeded to dig in its maw, bringing out what he could now recognize as a cheap mobile phone.

No need for letters, for telegraph wires, for dusty riders with brimming mail-pouches. What would mortals invent next? Jonathan watched carefully as she prodded the item into wakefulness, then fiddled with it further, raising it to her ear.

"You have one new message," a pleasant electronic voice chirped. A pause, then a recording began to play, with no need for needle or wax cylinder.

"Hey Jane." Male, tinny through the speaker, with an odd humming in the background. *"Hope you're doing good. Listen, the meet's set up. 2am, Continental Hotel's Gunslinger Ballroom."* A rattling of numbers and a street-name, then a harsh exhale. *"He'll bring personal security, which is fair. If you don't show I'm on the hook for the payment, so don't give me any heartburn, huh? Be cool, girlie. Call me if there's any change, a'ight?"*

Her lips moved slightly as she lowered the phone, tapping at its face with intent once more and studying the result before pressing a side button to render the small appliance inert once more. "All right," she said, quietly. "I'm going to take a look at a place, okay? There's a meeting, and it's always good to check out the ground beforehand."

"Indeed." Now he was possessed of a name *and* afire with curiosity; this was proving an excellent, most interesting evening. "What manner of meeting is this, may your sanguinant ask?"

A troubled, sideways glance as she replaced the phone, then reached to drop the bag into the back seat once more. This time the operation did not require her leaning close, which was a shame.

"Business," she said, finally. "Not a bounty, so don't worry. Right now I just want to see the place, and tomorrow I'll be there early. Never want to be last to a meet."

"You are quite the strategist, sweet Simone." Nevertheless, this was not an optimal development. "The voice, was that a mortal?"

"It's *my* business, which means none of yours." She busied herself prodding the car into fresh motion. "It's just a quick drive-by tonight, since we're almost out of gas and I've got to find a place to sleep. You're more than welcome to get out now, if you've got somewhere else to be."

Was it a jest? More likely, she still did not fully compass her own position—or his. "Perhaps a reasonably clean… hotel?" he suggested, almost saying *inn* before realizing it was not the modern word. "Or if there is a house you like, the inhabitants are easily—"

Immediate negation, shaking her lovely, finely modeled head, cedarbark hair swinging heavily. "No, no, I can find a place, don't worry. Besides, you can't just take someone's *house*. Jeez."

"Very well." This was all very concerning, but at least she wasn't actively attempting escape at the moment. Not that it mattered, in the end. "But, Simone—"

"What?" She did not glare at him, only because the chariot— no, the *car* was already moving, her attention focused through the front glass. "If you're going to complain or threaten me, save it. I'm not in the mood, *John*." Emphasis on the name, as if high-lighting the gift—how could he possibly protest, when she had been so very, signally gracious?

Mortal entanglements are not good, for fledglings or leman. Any leftover relationships were best severed, thoroughly and swiftly, so soon as a leman was claimed—and any fledgling who would not turn away from mortal family or friends inevitably learned a harsh lesson, either through time or the Thirst itself.

"Neither, of course." He turned his attention to their surroundings, absorbing the terrain, eyeing the sky as dawn approached. Let her retain an illusion or two, at least for the moment.

Yet his chest ached, another sweet piercing. She was still so very new to the Blood.

CHAPTER 17

 the Big Ponderosa Inn had a bone-dry abandoned pool behind a wind-rattled, decrepit chainlink fence, hourly to weekly rates clearly posted, and precisely the right proportion of skeevy disrepair versus focus on profit. Every 'guest' had their own problems, locked their door when they weren't sitting on the threshold to have a smoke, and—most importantly—minded their own damn business.

Circling the place once was enough to satisfy her on the suitability and escape route scores; dumping the running-on-fumes car a few blocks away was strictly routine. Apparently her sense of just how far she could push a sputtering stolen sedan was tiptop too, a far cry from her law-abiding human days. The old vampire didn't say a word, simply followed her from the Celica without a backward glance.

The Big Ponderosa's front desk clerk barely glanced at her, taking a few crumpled bills from her ATM hit and thrusting a key with a chunky red plastic tab through the small aperture at the bottom of a sticky, fly-spotted plastic pane supposed to protect him from armed robbery, bad breath, and acts of God. His green-and-brown polyester bowling shirt said *Curt* in fancy embroidery across the breast pocket, which may or may not have been his actual moniker but was incredibly funny in either case. She hadn't checked her ex-husband's social media feeds in a while.

That was a positive development—one of the few in this recent mess, Simone concluded. She wondered if the chippie from her ex's office had finished draining him of cash yet, decided it was none of her business, yet couldn't repress a tiny, grim curiosity.

The room was on the second floor, at the very end of the breezeway, and neither the cleanest nor the filthiest she'd ever had to deal with. From the scratchy plaid counterpane to the dust-stiff taupe curtains, the arthritic air conditioner to the dark, tiny bathroom smelling of mildew and bleach, it was entirely mid.

Which was perfect. John, however, looked entirely nonplussed. He halted at the foot of the twin bed, holding his black hat in both hands and turning a complete circle to absorb the heavily repainted walls, the cheap television bolted to the wall over a dresser made of plywood and probably nailed fast as well, the chain she slipped on the door, the curtains she pulled and made sure there wasn't a single crack for sunlight to slip through.

Maybe she ought to sleep *under* the bed. Dusty, sure, but probably cleaner than the sheets.

"Hey." She ducked out of her bag's strap, and was glad she didn't have to deal with getting some kind of food at this hour *or* using whatever commode lingered in the bathroom. "Can you do that invisible-seal thing? Show me how?"

If she could figure out how he accomplished that particular trick, not only could she be safer during daylight… but also have a chance at undoing his variety. Which would be ever so useful, and a victory to cap the night with.

She could use a win at this point. Any would do; Simone wasn't picky.

"You mean to sleep here?" Dim light from the weak bulb in the bedside lamp gleamed over his dark hair, glowed in those blue eyes, burnished his skin. In twilight, vamps appeared even more perfect and poreless; it was downright creepifying once you noticed.

Though most regular folks honestly didn't seem to. The truly weird stuff in the world could knock a person loopwise if not aggressively ignored. Maybe inattention kept humans sane.

"This is safe," she pointed out. Dawn was barreling toward the city on greased rails, instinctive warning prickling all along her arms, legs, back. Everywhere. "These kinds of places, nobody asks any questions, especially housekeeping. But if you're offended, I'm sure you can find a Four Seasons or something downtown."

"It…" He made a vague motion, one hand freighted with the hat, which was by now well and truly broken in. "You deserve better."

Oh, don't we all. "By this time tomorrow I'll be able to afford something nice, near a hospital where I can get blood by the bag. At least, that's the plan and I'm really tired, it was a stressful drive. Either do the invisible-walls thingie or get out and find yourself another hide."

He went still, an unblinking statue, and Simone realized that treating a vamp this old and powerful like a not-too-bright vampire-hunting trainee was probably a bad move. Her throat threatened to dry out, completely divorced from that terrible thirsty spot—which wasn't active right now, thank goodness— and her back crawled afresh.

The walls shimmered briefly, that funny colorless ripple springing into existence. She stepped away from the door, nervously, and found the air had gone dead.

Just like under a bell jar. Wow. The thought of being trapped under glass, like a spider needing to be taken outside, was both hilarious and horrifying.

And he was *looking* at her, chin slightly dropped, head tilted a fraction. Simone had never, ever been studied so intently. Maybe he wanted another round of volcanic fucking, and the thought managed to be at once appealing and deeply unnerving.

Her own body was a traitor, but that was nothing new when you were born with ovaries. Between the pain and mess once a month—vampirism had put a halt to her erratic perimenopausal cycles, praise God and hallelujah—and an entire world determined to make you nothing more than a fetus-container, there was almost no room for anything approaching satisfaction, or self-determination.

Getting infected had liberated her in numerous ways, a gift with literal teeth. Which was bleakly hilarious, like so much else about this stupid, endlessly eerie situation.

Come on, Simone. Distract the male, before he starts getting ideas. "How do you do that? Will you teach me?"

"The seals?" Slowly, enunciating with care. "Ah. When you are old enough in the Blood, I shall indeed teach you. But are you certain you wish to stay here? This is…"

"It's cheap, it's safe, and it's right in a zone where I can get to the meet easily tomorrow, okay?" She weighed the advisability of telling him anything more, decided she could probably risk a bit of explanation. "I don't want to keep doing bounties, you know. I want to retire, which takes money. This meet is about getting enough."

"I told you, money is easy." It was the first time he sounded thoroughly modern, and wouldn't you know, it was because a lightly poked male ego was the same all throughout history. "Do you doubt that I will provide?"

God, give me patience, and give it to me right-fucking-now. Simone decided getting him to set up the invisible seals was either a blessing to keep neighbors from listening through paper-thin walls or a major miscalculation since she couldn't just slam the door and find somewhere else to bed down.

She had proof positive the latter tactic wouldn't work, anyway. "I just met you, and you didn't even have a name. So back off on the *providing* stuff, mister. And anyway, a woman needs her own money. This is enough to set me up, and I'm taking it."

There were different names for a woman's best defense, but Simone liked the simplest: *walking-away money, fuck-you money.* Even a man who loved you and swore never to leave could get in a car accident, and then where was a girl who had kept house, smiled prettily, gotten old, done what she was told all her life?

Entirely fucked, that was where. And not in any even remotely pleasurable way.

The only real friend a woman had was cash. She'd figure out the problem of investing for a long-ass lifespan later, but she needed the lump sum now—assuming this meet was legit. Barry said he was on the hook for the payment, and sure she could ghost as soon as she had confirmation the moolah had hit her account. But that was a dick move, and she also had to think about the problem of withdrawing a substantial sum and vanishing, since Jane Smith wasn't doing any more bounties.

Which was also a relief, even if she was abandoning any pretense of high-flown principles.

"Grant me a few nights." John's strong, callused fingers had tensed on the hat's brim, though the rest of him was calm as a stone. "I have already begun preparations, and shortly will be able to give you anything you wish. Simply say the word, Simone, and it will be yours."

I cannot believe we are even having *this conversation.* And what kind of 'preparations' could he possibly have made? "What, you fuck me a few times and think it makes you something special? You could vanish tomorrow, *John.*" She drew the name out, sarcasm not just dripping but outright gushing. "You might even decide to leave me stuck in these seal-things when you do it, and I'll starve to death like a rabbit in a hutch. No dice, Mr. Old Vampire."

"You are my leman." The worst thing was his air of bafflement instead of anger; his reactions weren't anything close to predictable. "I will never leave you, nor will I harm you."

I've had it with this leman nonsense. "Clearly we have differing definitions of 'harm'." She sounded nasty even to herself. "You show up out of nowhere, you do… what you did, to me, and to be fair you're the only other vampire I've met who can even *talk* and I'm not thirsty anymore but that doesn't mean I don't know where the blood comes from and I just… I just…"

Her fingers were starting to numb up, announcing sunrise and her own helplessness. So were her toes; she hated the feeling. Simone shut up, set her jaw, and stalked away from the door. Getting past him promised to be tricky, but she stared past his shoulder and extended her very best urban *don't mess with me* body language.

It worked—sort of. He backed away four whole steps, before moving aside between the bed and a nicotine-stained wall.

But he also put his arm out, neatly barring the bathroom door. "Simone. Please. Simply grant me a few more nights. Two, three at most. I swear, on the Blood and on my leman, that—"

"You can show me, *after* I go to this meet." *There. That's as far as I'm going.* The relief was intense—just like telling Curt they were getting a goddamn divorce, for real and no takebacks. There was a kind of relaxation in discovering she couldn't be pushed any further, just like the moment when a bounty sighted her and she was committed to fight-or-die. No compromise, no middle ground, no bending for another person's needs or desires.

It felt wonderful each goddamn time. Which probably meant she wasn't a good person, sure. But that fact, however lately discovered, had helped her survive.

John didn't leap on her, but he also wasn't giving up. "Mortal entanglements are unwise." Whatever *that* meant.

"This is non-negotiable, Jonathan." The name rolled out easily, as if she knew him. Which was weird, but maybe just a function of being around someone who could talk coherently about vampire stuff.

Even bloodsuckers had to get lonely. And what if he was right, what if she'd been the reason the other ones had acted all drunk and psychotic? Though the bounties had done terrible things *before* she appeared, it was still chilling to think she'd mistaken her sole edge in the situation.

What else was she missing? What else did she need to learn, and could she trust this bloodsucker to give her a few lessons?

His arm lowered a few degrees, then a few more. "You forget I am daywalker, sweet Simone. I have not been… idle, while you rest."

Good for you. "I suppose you could just drop me in the sunshine somewhere, if I don't cooperate." Probably best to let him know she'd considered the notion, and was on guard against it. Although what on earth could she actually do? "Is that it?"

"Of course not." Did he actually sound shocked? His baby blues widened, almost comically. "I would never—"

She shoved past him. "Just stop. I'm tired."

The lock-button on the bathroom doorknob didn't work at all. No windows, and the fan was probably too choked with dust to provide any real ventilation. The bleach-and-mildew bouquet could've been worse or, conversely, a whole lot better.

But the plastic bathtub didn't have a ring, at least. She left the lights on—only two out of three bulbs in the strip over the sink worked—and clambered in, boots and all, curling over her bag as the numbness of sunrise mounted in leaden limbs.

All I have to do is get to the meet. She'd hear the billionaire's pitch, then decide. If there was nothing to this 'cure' idea, she'd figure out a way to give John the slip and set herself up in a cottage somewhere. If there was anything real or actionable, though, she'd have to get creative.

Really creative.

She was trying to decide which she hoped for most when dawn seized her.

After recent events, it was almost startling to wake up with her clothes on, let alone in a questionably clean bathtub.

Simone stayed very still, eyes closed, breathing deeply. Folklore said vamp sleep looked like a particularly fresh dead body until you hammered the stake in, but she'd never been able to test the assertion.

Wonder if John would tell me. A silly question, sure. The air was still and dead, two of the bathroom's walls—the outer edges of this home-for-an-hour—bearing that invisible almost-shimmer. Maybe she ought to be grateful he hadn't forced her to settle on the bed, or moved her there like a tired toddler once she was out.

Now she had to get to the meet. After she'd possibly antagonized an old vampire who could probably keep her bottled indefinitely, and was perfectly aware of the fact.

While she'd been snoozing, though, some part of her had apparently been busy coming up with ideas. One sprang, full-blown and awful, to the forefront of her brain.

Oh, God, that's awful. But it could possibly work. She'd done more difficult things, both before and after infection. Of course, a good girl wasn't *supposed* to fight dirty, to kill slavering vampires and demand prompt payment; a lady shouldn't be threatening or rude. A good girl was supposed to be patient, long-suffering, wait to be rescued.

Getting to middle age meant discovering—and internalizing—there was nobody coming to save you, so you'd damn well better do it yourself.

The hardest part was stripping, folding her clothes neatly, and piling them next to the sink, her bag and boots tucked against the facing underneath. Deliberately not looking in the flyspotted mirror, she waited for the shower to gurgle into life.

Great water pressure, even if the spray never got truly hot. She wrung her hair dry and didn't bother with the towels. Not part of her plan, and what she was about to do was nasty enough. No need to add whatever was on anemic, faintly mildewed terrycloth to the mix.

Watch, I'll look out and he'll be gone, that'd be hilarious. It took more courage than she'd guessed to twist the knob, pull the door open slightly, and peer out.

The room was just the same as it had been, except the bed was piled with shopping bags. A large black suitcase lay on the pillows, open and waiting, its lid against the headboard; the TV was on but muted, glowing at the old vampire who stood stock-still, staring at its glass face as if enraptured.

Men and televisions. It's like a bug zapper, they can't look away. Simone hesitated, wondering if the crazy, awful, long-shot plan was worth carrying out.

Black jeans, black shirt, plain silver belt buckle, plain black boots. His hair bore no crimp of the hat's sweatband, turned into a half-tousled mass balancing the harsh planes of his face. Not gaunt anymore, but there was nothing soft about him either. An oblivious human might peg him as thirty, thirty-two tops, a rawboned good ol' boy unremarkable save for those straight eyebrows and piercing blue peepers.

What did it take, to live a long time as a vampire? To get so old you could walk around in sunshine—what would a being like that want with *her*? All that leman stuff had to be horseshit. Some kind of con game.

He turned, a swift, graceful movement. His hat was on the cheap nightstand; at least he hadn't left it on the bed. Did he know about the old superstition? Maybe he was older than a folk belief or two.

The idea that those blue eyes could X-ray right through the flimsy door was immediate, and hideously unwelcome. Simone froze.

"I, ah." He made a short sound, almost like a nervous cough. "I brought you gifts."

Really. Simone tried to process this, her brain briefly sputtering like a flooded engine.

"I don't know what women of your era prefer," he continued, reciting near-breathlessly as if racing through a prepared debate opener. "I will learn. All I ask is a little… a little…"

A little what? Simone realized she'd opened the door slightly further than she'd meant to. He was getting an eyeful of what infection had done to her body—best nip-and-tuck around, except for the faint fading traces of old stretch marks on her thighs and the sides of her breasts; the ones on her arms were almost gone, along with her varicose veins.

Hopefully the remainders wouldn't interfere with her plan.

Simone let the door swing wide, padding into the motel room. The carpet was worn down to the weft in some places, delightfully scratchy save for the hint of grease lingering on nylon strands. She was still damp, but thankfully summer-scorch and winter snow both rolled right off vamp skin to a certain degree.

She pretended to examine the bags on the bed. *Well, can't lay on that, or at least, I don't want to roll around on plastic. So he shops designer, huh. Wonder how he got those past the seals? He doesn't take the shimmer down to pass through, I think.*

So much she had to learn. So she turned, looking up at him, and found out he was closer now, a soft warm breath of moving air brushing her cheek. "You're trying to buy me?" *Should I flutter my eyelashes?*

"To *please* you," he corrected, and she found out it was entirely possible for an ancient being on a liquid-red diet to look hungry. John stared from under lowered lids, his lower lip pulled slightly in, blunt human-seeming teeth touching lightly. All his attention focused, those blue eyes nearly incandescent, and yes, he did appear absolutely… well, famished.

He said bloodsuckers could eat human food. Once she got

through this, she was going to test the assertion with a bacon mushroom cheeseburger, a mountain of waffle fries, and a cookies-n-creme milkshake.

With *loads* of whipped cream. Any digestive trouble afterward would only be what she deserved.

For now, Simone regarded him with what she hoped was cool measurement. He could probably hear her heart hammering, but maybe keeping a straight face was worth a point or two. "Why?"

"You're my leman." As if that was supposed to mean something.

"But why?" she persisted.

His throat moved as he swallowed. Simone began to get the idea she had some kind of weird advantage here—unless he was indeed lying. But then again, maybe a male vamp could be led around by the little head instead of the big one, just like human guys.

"Are you all right?" The urge to laugh bubbled in her throat, was ruthlessly pushed down, and died somewhere behind her breastbone. *If he says yes I'll probably die of embarrassment.*

She was, after all, stark naked.

A deep thrumming slowly intruded on dead-air silence. He was staring at her, and *starving* didn't even begin to cover his expression. A faint crackle accompanied ripples sliding through his cheeks, muscles on his jaw flickering.

She might have been overconfident, Simone thought. Just a little. *Oh, what the hell.*

More courage was necessary to step close to him, to place her palm flat on his shirt. The vibration in his chest slid up her arm —like a massive jungle cat, purring.

Those have fangs too. Oh, Simone, be careful.

"You can have what you want." Hard not to coo, or flutter her damn eyelashes. She felt ridiculous. "But it has to be how *I* say." *Are you really doing this?*

He leaned into her touch, gaze fastened on her lips. A heady feeling—this powerful monster, old enough to walk around in sunshine, right at her fingertips. Waiting to be unleashed.

A slight change in his weight, inclining toward the bed, and she understood as if he'd spoken aloud. "No," she said. "Not on the floor, either. And you'll need to take your clothes off—"

Fabric tore. Her bare, still-damp back hit the wall next to the bathroom door, and the fact that the paint was stained with ancient cigarette smoke didn't matter because his mouth was on hers, a thin thread of copper-taste from his bitten lip stroking the spot in her throat where dormant thirst roused in a sheet of blinding crimson. Lifted and held, the growl rattling into a sonic haze—she wondered for a moment if the neighboring room could hear it through the shimmer—and warm skin sliding against hers, her fingers clutching, full of silken strands as she plunged her hands into his hair. Her legs wrapped around his waist, and her hiss at the sudden heavy, stretching first thrust was lost in the flood of sensation.

Oh hey, this isn't bad—

Then there was no time for thought, just clutching and writhing, her body determined to get what it could. He seemed to know which way she'd move, each convulsive move closer to shattering, her clit ruthlessly massaged by that wicked, knowing extra protuberance and the wave building, lightning slamming up her spine to detonate in her head.

This time he waited until her shudders eased, his breath hot against her ear, whispering something she couldn't hear through the pounding of her heart, her own ragged gasps. And when he tilted his head, guiding her mouth to the pulse beating hard and high in his throat, her fangs sprang free of their own accord, burying in the insistent throbbing.

He held her impaled, pinned to the wall as she fed, shudders passing through them both with each mouthful, each twitch of her sheath clamped tight around him. For a few brief moments Simone didn't have to think about the meeting, a possible cure, how to keep her balance on the edge of an unpredictable hurricane in vampire form.

It was over far too soon.

CHAPTER 18

A WRENCHING CHANGE OF DIRECTION, ANOTHER MIRACLE. THE shock left him dizzy, barely able to concentrate, for she had approached him—not quite fearless, yet bravely, a shepherdess taming a snarling lion. She had been *willing*, and not only that, but afterward, soft and languid with the double opiate of release and his blood filling her veins, she looked over his small offerings and pronounced them *not bad, I guess you know how to shoplift for quality.*

Pointing out that he had paid for each item brought a long, solemn appraisal, her beautiful forest-eyes dancing, the corners of her mouth trembling slightly, suppressing a smile. He watched, uncertain of just what to do with his hands, his voice, his very self as she packed the suitcase with swift dancing movements, and his remark that he had acquired another car gained another lingering look.

She kept glancing at the red numbers of the clock wired to the nightstand, a thread of nervousness appearing in the spicy gorgeousness of her scent. Each time she also looked at the door or the walls, where the seals held firm. A rare, wondrous bird, weighing whether to batter itself against the cage.

Jonathan knew her apparent willingness was likely a bid to

establish some manner of control, perhaps the beginning of a more complex attempt at escaping his presence and protection. Whatever this 'meet' consisted of, its import to his leman was clear—and high indeed.

"There's plenty of time." He was gaining facility with the speech of this era—not least from listening to the telly-vision's endless flow of chatter, information, exhortation, enticement. "I will accompany you to this *meet*, and once you have what you wish, we will—"

"You aren't part of the deal." She fastened the suitcase with swift grace and straightened; the bed now stood drifted with bags and discarded packaging. "It'll only take an hour. We can rendezvous somewhere when it's finished."

He could easily keep her trammeled until well after the proposed time, though this filthy little room was increasingly unappetizing. Moving a somnolent fledgling during daylight was reasonably easy, with a few elementary precautions. By dawn tomorrow they could be in another city; she would wake under seals, and no matter her protests the pattern could continue nearly indefinitely.

She did not belong in this rundown hostel reeking of desperation, smoke, cheap burnt food. A leman was to be kept in comfort; she belonged behind pierce-carved porphyry screens, lounging upon silken pillows, cosseted with gifts and fed to repletion, her every whim indulged and delight procured. To think of her moving in patterned moonlight, her hair swaying, long legs and softly curved belly overlaid with delicate shadows, was at once a pleasure and a torment.

If he spirited her away in that manner, how long would it take before she approached him of her own will again? A few centuries, half a millennia?

Never?

Though she had packed the offerings neatly, she chose to wear her own rumpled clothes. Well-fed, her eyes bright, she was still uncertain, nearly flinching when he made a restless movement. She was so new to the Blood, having little idea of a leman's pricelessness or place, and he wished there were other sanguinant to ask of such things while understanding quite well why there were not. Why there could never be.

Even the whispered proverbs were of limited aid. He was forced into the uncharted territory of *this* leman, the deeply reluctant sum of every dream or desire he would ever have.

"If there are other sanguinant present—" he began, hoping against hope she would be willing to listen.

"There'd better *not* be." Her hands settled on beautifully rounded hips clasped in worn denim; the trousers clung lovingly to long, lithe legs. "It's just humans, okay? And I can handle a few of those for an hour. Once it's done, maybe we can meet back here? I'm gonna need a place to sleep."

He decided in that moment never to allow a return to this sorry, claptrap hole. Still, there were far more important questions to settle. A leman's mortal entanglements were to be cut away, smoothly and swiftly as possible—but it seemed an unachievable ideal in this particular situation. Jonathan fought the urge to clench his fists. "I will not interfere with your *'meet'*, darlin', but I will be nearby—invisible to mortal senses, of course. It is impossible to do otherwise, with a leman." Inspiration struck. "My instincts will not allow it."

"What sort of instincts?" Her chin lifted, vexation sparkling in those striking woodland eyes.

"In mortals, they are connected with mating. In a sanguinant they are much more intense, as so many other—"

"*Mating?*" To see the blood drain from a fledgling's face was an uncomfortable experience, made far worse when it was one's cherished, still-so-frail leman. "What, are you after little vampire babies? I, uh… no, nope, that's not okay."

It was alternately charming to teach one so naïve and maddening to think of how adrift and lonely she must have been since gaining the Gift. Jonathan shook his head, carefully. "Of course not. Fledglings are only of the Blood, not the body. Mortal pregnancy is quite impossible once the Dark Gift has been granted."

"Oh." She studied him closely, perhaps searching for evidence of falsity—but why would she suspect such a thing? "That's good. Do you have, uh, fledglings?"

"Not that I remember." Now was perhaps not the time to explain that any sanguinant approaching her, even one granted the Gift by his own design, was to be destroyed without mercy. "The instincts are protective, and absolute. I will linger nearby, and I will not allow the mortals to see me. Please, be reasonable."

Her mouth worked for a moment, as if she were struck speechless. Which was oddly adorable, and he stared at her lips, tempted to taste her afresh.

Not just that part of her, either. Soon there must be time to worship properly, with every instrument his body or imagination could provide. The surface of desire had barely been scratched, and he enjoyed the idea of exploring even the shallows of that sea.

Let alone the depths.

"Reasonable," she muttered, finally. "Right. You don't even know if you have kids?"

"Fledglings," Jonathan corrected. "The fire took much of my memory. For what it's worth, I suspect I have none." *None which survive, anyway. And none to trouble you.*

"Well. That's a relief." Sharp tinge of sarcasm, but her shoulders softened. She half-turned, reaching for her faithful satchel, and ducked through the strap. Then she shrugged into her dark, rather severe jacket, freeing her hair from the collar with a harsh, casual yank that made him wince inwardly. "Is that what you're wearing?"

"Is it inappropriate?" The clothing was comfortable and functional; he quite liked the hat. "I've seen some rather garish belt-buckles, and several other styles of dress. This seemed rather tame by comparison."

"Tame, he says." His leman addressed the air over his shoulder, and her patent amusement was worth any amount of mockery. "Don't worry, it's fine. Can we go now? I want to get there early."

"Of course." A sharp, precise flower of relief unfolded inside his chest, along with nebulous apprehension.

She had agreed to his terms far, far too easily.

The Continental Hotel was a high-crowned wave of glass and steel struts flanked by a pair of similarly vitreous wings, no doubt full of glittering glare upon sunny afternoons. At night the central bulk was a glowing blue-and-gold jewel, the vast airy foyer gleaming. Boxes with transparent walls rose and fell along several stacked balconies—mechanical lifts, trundling slowly, regularly as deep sleepy breathing. The front desk was split into two portions, blue velvet ropes on brass posts ready to restrain an invisible crowd from assaulting any false-mahogany grandeur. Potted plants stood sentinel near small groups of furniture too uncomfortable for true conversation, and an entrance with strangely antique swinging wooden doors sat under a similarly distressed sign for *The Gunsmoke Lounge*, the space beyond full of murmuring as last call warnings filtered through a haze of alcohol both spilled and metabolized.

Posted signs gave schedules for conventions and conferences, reflected in the polished faux-marble floor; blue carpet lay in strips to indicate pathways and gathering-spots. The meeting rooms were capacious, and the hotel apparently boasted four ballrooms—a truly excessive number, but every era held its plenty as well as poverty.

He could not wait to discover this age's secrets, with her.

His leman had already made a survey of the hallways, moving in patterns he found strange until he realized they were to evade several electronic eyes. He must teach her to blur such things in her vicinity, the instant she reached an appropriate age in the Blood.

As it was, he performed the service while drifting in mist-form, observing a polite distance. A few more feedings and she might well sense him nearby despite any and all precautionary measures; she was so exquisitely sensitive.

For an hour and a half she roamed the hotel, not only familiarizing herself with the place but showing him how to do so, teaching him by example the best escape routes, what to look for, what to avoid. He saw her slip past weary mortals intent upon cleaning duty or other tasks, watched her stand motionless at the end of a hallway as a pair of drunken mortals, involved in a kiss so feverish as to nearly approach sanguinant intensity, fumbled to open a door and all but fell through, their moans suddenly muffled as it swung shut. Witnessed her peer down a stairwell of functional concrete, clearly not meant for guest use, and shake her head slightly, cedarbark hair rippling—what test had it failed, what passing thought had occurred to her?

He burned to know, could not ask.

A lovely game, especially when she glanced suspiciously in his near direction. Perhaps she already sensed him; her scent vine-wound through his, for just before every sunset he had taken a mouthful of sheer glory, erasing the fangmarks with assiduous care.

If she were so shy about her own feeding, he did not care to think upon the likely reaction to *his*, let alone his addiction to her taste. It was a matter for another day.

Sweet Simone dug in her bag, checking the handheld phone —marvelous that it could speak through empty air, a matter of *frequencies*, it was said, and he would discover more as soon as possible—and her movements took on fresh, subtle purpose. Another staircase, a more luxurious specimen though decked with faint traceries of ever-present plains dust, and she exited carefully at the end of a short hall leading to double doors.

"Hell yeah," she whispered. A change, rippling through her

slim frame—shoulders back, chin rising, her beautiful dryad-eyes flashing. Her steps loosened, hips shifting with sinuous authority, and Jonathan nearly lost mistform, nearly forgot to hang back. Now she prowled as a lioness, showing no trace of the uncertain, nervous, trembling leman.

An infinity of surprises lingered within his prize; Jonathan longed to swirl about her, tease at the glossy cascade of her hair, let her know she was within his protection, that she need fear nothing.

But *stay back*, she said; he had promised. He lingered, watching her push the double doors wide with a popping ping, breaking whatever lock held them fast and strolling into a cavernous, glass-roofed space beyond.

The hotel's largest ballroom, the pride of the establishment, and the location of the 'meet'.

Jonathan let his mistform thin, spreading in the dark hallway, and listened.

CHAPTER 19

Ten human pulses, each readily distinguishable, sang in her sharp vamp ears. They were amped, but that was pretty reasonable if you were going to meet a bloodsucker; also, the deal had been six to eight security, and she wondered why they were pushing it until she spotted a familiar mop of ginger hair.

He was taller than she'd thought, only having seen him seated onscreen before. And next to him stood a bandy-legged male shape which had to be the mysterious rich client.

The Gunslinger Ballroom had a very nice wooden parquet dance floor—the pictures on the hotel's website carefully showed it to advantage—currently covered by thick protective matting, dustcloth-shrouded tables and chairs stacked between the doors studding the left wall. A truly magnificent view of Denver spread into the distance past the floor-to-ceiling windows to her right, twinkling ferociously. The roof was glass as well, a marvel of modern architecture. At the far end three steps rose to an empty stage big enough for two warring rock bands and their respective mosh pits, flanked by what had to be two freight elevators for bringing up supplies, false screens pushed aside.

All other decorations were put away; the space could be

turned into anything, the hotel's website gushed, and Simone bet it was true. Renting it even at 2am was bound to be an expensive proposition. But rent this guy clearly had, because several of the recessed lights were on—dialed to low, in order to show the view to best advantage—and the motion detectors weren't sending out that funny high-pitched whine which meant *live*.

So, eight security, plus the client. And an additional surprise.

"Barry." She halted, hands on her hips, and gave her very best *professional, so don't try it* smile. The lingering relaxation of old-vamp blood was deep and soft all through her body; she felt loose, ready for almost anything. "Fancy meeting you here. And wow, you weren't kidding. This is Elton Huske, right?"

Low light conditions might give humans trouble, but were high noon to vamp eyes. Four of the security—big and beefy, just the thing for a nervous billionaire—had night-vision goggles strapped on, their heads insectile shadows. Two more were tucked into what they probably thought were good hiding places among cloth-draped furniture. Another pair flanked the client, and figuring out his name was no big trick.

It was the face on a thousand promo shots, after all—close-set goggle eyes, nose clearly re-sculptured by surgery at some point, jowls treated with expensive skincare to give a greasy glow masquerading as youth, a haircut so bad it had to be expensive as well as aggressively self-chosen. And there was the eternal fleece vest, half-zipped over a T-shirt no doubt chosen for quirkiness by an underpaid assistant, and the slightly bowed legs in expensive stonewash Levi's ironed to provide a crisp crease front and back. Birkenstocks and black socks completed the uniform, and to top it all off, there were four fancy 'smart' X-OL rings on his left hand, not surprising since he owned the company, plus a high-end smartwatch with a nylon strap *and* an earpiece that was probably a X-OL prototype as well.

Car manufacturing, ultralight planes, 'smart' wearables, his very own social media platform only his fans and yes-men were allowed on—yep, it was Elton Huske all right. In retrospect it made a kind of sense, since he certainly had the cash to burn.

Still, several thin, tickling claws of unease walked down her back. The sensation was subtly different than the sense of *being watched* she'd felt at odd moments while she cased the hotel, which might be John keeping an eye on proceedings despite his promise to stay the hell out of her business.

No, this was something else, familiar from her human days. An atavistic reminder—*one of* those *guys, be careful.*

"Wow." The billionaire actually clapped, soft dutiful cupped-palm smacks used at ribbon-cuttings or the end of particularly boring office meetings. And he strode right for her, brand-new sandals squeaking counterpoint. "Jane Smith, a huge pleasure. I'm a big fan of your work, very big."

A trace of accent—the puff pieces made a big deal of his family's roots in foreign mining—lurked behind the almost-nasal California flatness. It was, she discovered, more irritating than John's cowboy drawl, because at least the ancient vampire hadn't sounded… well, *fake.*

Just old, and painfully stilted.

"Really." Simone still gazed at Barry. Her finder had the grace to look uncomfortable, slouched in jeans and a camo fatigue jacket, shifting his weight from one Converse sneaker to the other. "Always good to meet an admirer, I guess."

"Oh yeah. The drone footage is really great, *excellent.*" Huske seemed to get the memo, stopping at a reasonable distance—which was pretty wise of him, all things considered. "Goes real well with popcorn and a good sauvignon blanc."

"Drone footage." Simone had never before been able to raise a single eyebrow, Spock-fashion, but she felt like she was getting close.

Barry's fidgets intensified. Now he was almost swaying like a kid at a rock concert, and his fingers were twitching as well. "Last three bounties," he muttered, and did he look almost *ashamed*? "Tracking the targets, Janie, not you."

Simone had never heard any propellers. Yet she'd often felt *watched*, the sensation also slightly different than that just before John showed up. Now she realized that crawling, unhappy sensation was akin to the feeling of live security cameras, dismissed because she took care to lure her bounties into deserted, pre-scouted locales.

It's not paranoia if they're really spying on you, right? The deep relaxation of powerful old-vamp blood thinned, turned brittle. Behind it rose a rasp of dislike—and outright unease.

"Yeah, the way you vanish after each kill, it's really impressive." The grinning billionaire stuck out a heavily lotioned hand. "Let's make it formal, a'ight? Elton Huske, pleasedtameetcha."

He was either brave, stupid, or both to get so close to a vamp. Plus, the way he said *kill*, almost salivating over the single syllable, was disgusting. Simone smiled, the way men were always telling women to; a slight crackling sound, and her fangs were out as her fingers blurred up, grabbed his, and squeezed.

Very lightly, so she didn't turn the small bones to paste. Still, Huske gulped audibly.

The sharp teeth went back into hiding far more easily than usual, which was great even if she knew why.

She wasn't thirsty. Not in the slightest. "Jane Smith," she said, and watched the sweat spring up all over the rich man's face. The smell of fear excreted as salt moisture was cloying, mixed with expensive aftershave, organic deodorant, a faintly greasy all-natural fabric softener which probably didn't do a damn thing for how new clothes always itched. Along with those entirely civilian aromas was a tang of metal and gun oil. She was betting he had a pistol stuck in the back of his waistband, and that it made him feel like a big man.

His pulse spiked, pupils dilating—a human animal recognizing an infected predator, and was she even more of a monster if she found the instinctive reaction perhaps a little funny?

"I hear you're researching," she said, softly, and let go of the moist little paw. Hopefully John wasn't close enough to listen;

she'd meant for him to wait across the street or at least down in that ridiculous kitschy hotel lounge, but now she was almost certain he'd trailed her through the entire Continental. "For a cure."

"Well." To give Huske credit, he shifted from fear to schmooze in less than a heartbeat, backing up a few creaking sandal-steps. His hand twitched, as if he wanted to wipe it on his expensive navy fleece vest and stopped just in time. "Yeah. So, you… wow. Okay, so you see the biologicals are tricky, but we've got some very promising work. What I had in mind was a partnership."

The kind I thought I had with my finder? Simone listened to their pulses, all galloping along. One guy had a congenital heart murmur, the sound a whooshing rasp; another was clearly on steroids, a metallic edge to the high pops of his cardiac muscle slamming shut. It was amazing what you could tell just from that single sound, a pump working from before birth, day in day out until the ghost gave up through accident, injury, disease.

How long would her own significantly slower pulse last? "I'm not big on team projects." Simone suddenly wanted to be out of this empty, echoing ballroom full of nervous men—especially the ones with rifles. Were they vamp hunters? She was *fairly* sure anything up to the experimental fragmenting ammunition wouldn't be a problem, but if this guy had indeed done his research, he might also have supplied his backup with some fancy bullets.

She could get through the door behind her in a twinkling, or maybe right through the glass wall to her right. It had to be hardened in some way, like skyscraper-sheathing, and the drop afterward might be uncomfortable.

Really uncomfortable.

"It's like this." Huske stuck his thumbs in the vest's side pockets, a habitual pose from his publicity pictures. "The same work you're doing with Barry here, but just *slightly* different. We need research subjects."

Is this dumbass for real? "What, you want me to go in with a clipboard and interview them? It doesn't work that way. Vamps are fast, they're mean, and…" She tried to think of John interacting with this guy, and drew a complete blank along with the urge to laugh.

Nervously. At length, and very close to screaming.

"Well, yeah, and they're cautious. No human team can get near 'em the way you do—believe me, we've tried for a few years now. Anyway, all you'd have to do is bring them to a predetermined point, and then *pow!*" Now Huske's hands jerked up, spreading, another familiar public-relations mannerism. "We've got some techniques for, like, getting them relaxed. We take some samples, administer some tests. It'll move us along like lightning."

He was warming to his presentation, his pulse easing. No change in the security detail, but that was to be expected. The only wrong note was Barry, sweating freely, jittering, eyes popped and gaze roving. He looked like a man undergoing either forced detox or a nightmare; of everyone in the room he knew *exactly* what a vamp could do, and how dangerous it was being so close to one.

Even her.

"You want to use me as bait?" It wasn't that different than her usual operation, sure.

But Simone still didn't like the idea.

"Oh, no, no. Just *encourage* them to cooperate, you see? Look, you know first-hand how stunning the physical effects are, right? Strength, speed, cell regeneration, and that's just for starters. It's the next step in human evolution." Huske was really getting into his rhythm; Simone stared, wondering if her ears had gone haywire. "It's all right there in the folklore. Blood is life, and all that—and imagine the patents. What if it's not an *in*fection, but a *per*fection?"

He's nuts. He was looking to profit off the monsters after all. It was almost depressing to have her suspicions brought to life.

Nobody was ever disappointed by expecting the worst, after all —make that the second and final piece of wisdom she agreed with her ex-husband about.

Simone had to close her mouth with a snap before actual words would form. "You know what vamps can do. You must've seen it—Barry, you've shown him the files, haven't you?"

"Vamps!" Blinking rapidly, Huske beamed at her. "I love it. Man, some of my friends, they refuse to believe in the weird shit. My head PR girl Shelly, she's always telling me not to talk about things going bump in the night. I used to think people had a right to know, right? But they don't want to. Sheep, right? Just sheeple."

I've had about enough of this. It hadn't yet been an hour, but oh well. "Well, this is certainly… an idea." She hated having to use the placating, plastered-on smile; at least the old vampire didn't yammer on like a fucking car salesman. "Thanks, I'll think about it. If I decide to take the job, I'll let Barry know."

She turned, disliking the slight grab of her bootsoles against the floor's protective coating, and headed for the door. Her back itched, her attention settling on the rifles.

"Wait." Clearly, Huske was used to a very different reaction, everyone nodding and telling him how handsome, smart, wonderful he was. "No, just wait a second. Barry, for Chrissake, tell her to wait."

"Janie?" Barry, sounding strangled. "Janie, *please.*"

Oh, hell. She'd thought of her finder as an anomaly—the single, solitary creature who might be called a 'friend' once she walked away from her old life. He'd been the one to pay her first bounty, posted on a dark web forum holding what she thought was a little less bullshit than the rest; developing enough mutual trust for video chat had been a long, careful two-year dance. He'd been her only real, unfeigned human contact since the night she'd been attacked.

Simone wasn't quite proud of the bounties—they were, after all, murder—but to suspect that maybe the real money hadn't been in getting rid of rampaging nighttime monsters but instead tracking *her* was still a punch to the gut.

A whisper of cloth, as if Huske was windmilling his arms. Maybe an obscene gesture at her retreating back, tale as old as time, a man unhappy at rejection. A curious *pop* like a champagne cork bursting free, and the strange thought that the billionaire was about to throw a predawn party just summed up the sheer unreality of the past few days.

Even for her own nighttime existence populated with crazy shit, this was fucking *absurd*.

A spear of ice jabbed deep into her back. It dilated, a burning cramp; Simone sucked in a breath to cuss—how had any of the humans gotten close enough to stab her?—before a giant seizure raced up her spine, turned her arms and legs to noodles, and the room wheeled around her in eerie slow motion.

What. The hell.

A bump, a metallic squawk-jangle. She was lifted, head lolling, and the cramps were *awful*. Worst was the way her throat was a pinhole, only allowing a single straw's worth of passage to air she suddenly, desperately needed. A slow, horrid thumping inside her ribs, watery and ragged, was definitely her own heartbeat.

She was still wondering what the fuck had happened when there was a whoosh, a mechanical chime—*elevator*, she realized dimly—and another rattling. Huske's face, sheened with heavy glimmering moisture, swam into view. The edges of her vision wavered and blurred; the burning was so bad, a raging fever almost like during the initial transition to full vamp, every part of her afire while bones creak-cracked and moved around, nerves screaming relentlessly, and the thirst, the awful throatcut scorching—

Wait. No thirst, something else, what is this?

"See?" Huske's voice, warped and slowed like a glitchy voicemail. "It works. It fucking works!"

"Oh, shit." Barry didn't sound happy. "Shiiiit. She don't look too good. What if you've killed her?"

Yeah, what if you have? Simone tried to blink, to force her brain through the a sudden soupy haze. A fluttering, a buzzing of fluorescents—the freight elevator was rising, but they were already so far up.

Roof. To the roof. Okay, so—

But she couldn't *think.*

"Don't be a pussy," Huske hissed. "See that? Says her vitals are still going. Just watch the line. Great shot, Kovacs. Went right in, right fuckin' in. You get a raise."

A mutter that might have been *yessir.* Crackle of static, someone gabbling, the sound distorted over an electronic whine. Five human pulses were crowded around her, but Simone wasn't standing. She was strapped to what felt like molded plastic, and every time a coherent thought managed to form another wave of volcanic pain swept through her, muscles locked hard, her body no longer a vamp's strong, responsive instrument but a tar-pit trap.

Paralyzed. Tranquilizer, that must've been a dart. Got to be strong if it'll knock out a vamp, but—

Burst of cold air, a glimpse of night stars stacked in dizzying spirals, whorls, and glowing cascades. Her eyes watered, a thick hot trickle she hoped wasn't blood. A buffeting, a deep drilling whine, a rhythmic thopping, the wind intensified to a gale and she was lifted, jolted, spun, each movement a starburst of sheer agony.

CHAPTER 20

THE HUSH WAS FULL OF MURMURS, THE HUM OF A LARGE OCCUPIED building at night, the ticking of its mechanical systems, his leman's pulse in the near distance audible against the more frantic thunder of mortal hearts. Jonathan listened intently from the hallway's end, drifting back and forth in mistform at the margin of sweet Simone's watchful caution, and scanned the rest of the hotel almost idly.

Nothing amiss. Why was he so uneasy?

Perhaps it was her insistence upon meeting with mortals. He could pour through the door and render them corpses in short order, but she… well, even the distraction and near-frustration of his tentative, wary, beautiful treasure entangling herself in this fashion was a pleasure in some aspects.

The lady had merely requested a small indulgence, after all.

Still, he did not like it. Her scent hung in the hallway, powerfully soothing. More noises—freshly awakened machinery, soft clatter, mortal voices in earnest conference. Her silence was now marked, though her pulse remained even, regular.

Was this another escape attempt? His patience snapped, and he streamed through the minute cracks under, around, between the double doors she had so thoughtfully warped with a single blow.

Aren't you enthusiastic, darlin'. A pleasure to name her thus.

A faint whoosh issued from the far end of a half-glass cavern, the song of his leman's heartbeat receding upon its stream. Closer, and far louder, were five mortal males, all in a strange costume he could now identify as *tactical*. They gathered in a tight knot near what seemed a bandstand or dais, and the reek of reined bloodlust was strong.

"—fuckin' amazing, man." A large blond specimen, standing a-spraddle as if possessed of a virulent rash upon his nethers, pumped his fist in the air. "Just *pop*, and down she goes. We gotta get more of that shit."

"Experimental." A dark, ferret-faced fellow cast a nervous glance across the vast shadowed space, as if he sensed Jonathan's presence. "An' I dunno, bitch might wake up in transit. Wouldn't want to be stuck on a whirlybird with *that.*"

"Cut the chatter." The chief of their small group was blond as well, bristles standing up aggressively on his close-cropped head, his scent full of shaky dominance bearing a burnt-metal chemical edge—some manner of medication, Jonathan surmised. "Hooper? We good?"

The lantern-jawed mortal so addressed was staring at a small flat rectangle—*smartphone*, that was the proper word—and nodded, his thumb lovingly stroke-tapping its glowing surface. "Payment's landed and verified."

"A solid night's work. Let's move ou—" The chief blinked, watery blue eyes widening, swelling like poached eggs. Jonathan noticed the gleam at the man's throat—blackened metal rings worked very finely indeed, chainmail snugged against flesh. The collar was ingenious; yet unless constructed of true silver it would not turn aside even a fledgling's fangs, merely causing allergic reaction to one new in the Blood.

Jonathan pulled his hand back, twisting his wrist to loosen muscle suction. It was so simple to stop a mortal's inmost clock;

the ribs were not reinforced as a sanguinant's, the sac enclosing the organ fibrous instead of bone-shielded.

The other blond male's chainmail collar produced a single spark against the drag of Jonathan's claws before parting, only slightly more resistant than water. Next came the ferret-face, who alone of his group had the presence of mind to begin moving, although unfortunately he chose to stagger backward, heavy-soled boots catching upon the lowest dais step.

Ferret-face was dead upon landing, head lopped free, and before the arterial spray reached full gush the heretofore-silent fifth male—owl-eyed, his heartbeat speaking of some small congenital flaw which might or might not cause problems were he to survive past this night—was flung across empty space with precisely enough force to hit the vast windows running all along the northwestern wall, producing a bonesnapping *crack*.

The impact, precisely gauged, was not enough to break or even spiderweb the glass. The mortal's interior architecture was not nearly so lucky.

Which left only the lantern-jaw and his phone. Said jaw was loose as the mortal stared, fishmouthed, attempting to absorb the sudden whirlwind of violence; Jonathan leaned close, gaining a deep whiff of the mortal's very particular scent—weak and harsh at once, so far from the perfume of his leman.

His strike was comparatively gentle, gauged just a hair over necksnapping force. The phone described a high arc, flipping end over end before dropping to land in Jonathan's waiting hand as its former owner spun and crumpled.

Not an escape. He was almost certain; after all, she would either be far more direct or cunning, not this middle-road effort. Blurring mistform again, pouring through doors into the lift shaft, drawn upward upon the golden thread, and when he burst onto the roof a flood of night wind bore only a single trace of her along with a puff of exhaust and a fading thump-shirr noise. A complex wash of other male mortals—prey, and now he could pinpoint an additional detail, alerting him to the true nature of this disaster.

The golden thread held an acrid note, something inimical attempting to metabolize through skin and breath. Poisoning a sanguinant was difficult indeed, most drugs and illnesses simply eaten by the Gift.

And yet mortals were endlessly inventive, and this an age of technological wonder.

The fleeing shadow made a distinct rhythmic noise to the northwest, a deceptively inelegant bee bumbling along. One of the strange aircraft with whirling blades, staying aloft through science indistinguishable from magic, wheeling due west as if chasing a sun long retreated.

Or fleeing swift-approaching dawn.

Even in mistform he might not catch up before the sun rose. Were the mortals intending murder, or something far more daring? He should have listened to their conversation, instead of refraining from politeness to his sweet Simone.

He was still holding the phone, he realized. Plumbing its secrets could wait. He slipped it into a pocket—wonderful, really, the clothing of this age was agreeably convenient in that regard—and took to the sky.

CHAPTER 21

IF SHE FOCUSED WHILE THE CRAMPS WERE ON AN UPWARD SPIKE, Simone could just about taste what they'd dosed her with. Acrid and oddly sweet at once, two overlapping auras and a funny sugary afterburn, it lingered as neither blood nor alcohol-burn, slow and syrupy.

And painful.

Despite that, she could piece together a few things. The popping sound had been a tranquilizer dart, she'd been loaded onto some kind of plastic sled by men who did *not* take the opportunity to feel her up—which said they might possibly have understood just what they were dealing with—and now she was on a swooping, jittering helicopter while Elton Huske yelled over and over about how smart he was.

"—Mojave Green and pufferfish," he crowed, muffled by a helmet which no doubt had a radio mic in it—she could tell from the slight whine of feedback, and the way the pilot kept muttering on a separate channel. "Really cool, huh?"

"Yeah, it's great." Barry, along for the ride in a helmet of his own, didn't sound happy. Of course he wasn't a big fan of heights, and Simone was wearily unsurprised that she knew that about him but hadn't figured out he was tracking her for someone else. "You said you were just gonna make a pitch."

"And if she'd listened, we wouldn't be doing this." Huske let out a short, blurting whoop, like a toddler glimpsing a birthday cake. "Didja see the way she just fell down? It works, it absolutely works. Genius stuff, just *genius*."

The cramp released, a blinding relief. Simone had a moment to goddamn *think*, and her first conclusion was that she had to hope whatever they'd poisoned her with wasn't fatal. The second was that she was tied down pretty tightly. A wide metal band was bolted over her throat, and dozy, prickling heat poked through the general lethargic pain whenever her chin brushed its top edge.

What the hell, man? She couldn't even talk, her jaw was locked, and the faint crackle-shifting as her fangs slid free and retracted in short uncoordinated bursts was lost under the helicopter's irritating buzz.

Huske kept blathering about what a brilliant move this was, how many different versions of the poison—not a sedative, actual *poison*, Simone was too busy focusing through the wracking waves to do more than hope her vamp infection could fight the shit off—his staff had tested, the amount of trouble he'd gone to.

He certainly seemed to be having a wonderful time.

"What about the money?" Barry finally piped up. The helicopter shifted, banking, and the sound of its rotors changed. Gravity pressed against Simone's shaking, twisting body, and a new, wholly terrible thought rose through the chaos inside her head.

Fuck the money, what happens at sunrise?

"Soon as we have some samples, that'll be a drop in the bucket. But don't worry, there's tracers on her payment, right? We'll get that back, and you'll get that percentage because I really value your contributions, my man." There was a faint smacking sound—either Huske was clapping again, or he was pounding Barry's shoulder like an excited sports fan.

Metal rattled—Simone braced herself for another seizure, but a gush of cold sweat flooded her skin and she realized her vamp-infected body had fought off most of the crap she'd been injected with.

Oh, hey, thanks. A delirious thought, addressing the infected, patient meat she hauled around on a daily basis. *We haven't always seen eye to eye, body, but you're doing really well at the moment.*

An experimental twitch, her fingers obeying and every savagely tired muscle in her arms and legs trembling with relief. Yep, she was a *lot* better now. Tied down on some molded plastic sled, sure, and something about the straps was concerning, but she was back in the driver's seat. Her muscles were listening, and that was a blessing.

"And just think of the defense contracts…" Huske's babble trailed off. "Uh-oh."

"Oh, shit," Barry muttered, maybe too low for his mic to pick up. "What's *uh-oh*?"

Just give me a few more seconds. Simone tested her arms, found them comparatively weak but willing. First, she had to get her upper half free, then she could—

Another ice-spear jammed deep into her left thigh, and she screamed. The howl was long and glassy, possibly edging into ultrasonic, and the helicopter jolted as if startled. Someone cursed, another man let out a short horrified cry, and for a moment she wondered dismally if she was going to have to survive an aircraft crash tonight.

Then her limbs seized again. The motherfucker had jabbed her with another dose of poison-whatever.

Oh, goddammit.

Dawn approaching—she was dimly, instinctively aware of the fact through a screen of agony. The cramps were more intense this time, requiring all her energy and attention to keep breathing through the waves, monstrous ripping sawteeth at every peak. Sweat had long since crackle-dried on her clothes, and now she knew why the metal band at her throat burned.

It was silver. Not entirely, of course, but a layer of sterling over something much harder, which apparently, go figure, was one bit of folklore that actually had a claim to truth. Blisters rose wherever the metal touched, bursting and re-forming with agonizing regularity as her wracked body tried to escape both the bonds and the terrible foreign substance busy making her every vein a stream of twisting, convulsive fire.

What had the old vamp said? Something about young fledglings—but that was useless, he was left behind in the Continental Hotel, and Simone couldn't even begin deciding if this was worse than being trapped in an airless space behind 'seals'.

At least he hadn't *hurt* her. Fucked her to hell and gone, sure, but not poisoned or… or betrayed her. Maybe he was actually honest about what he wanted or intended?

The point was, for a bloodsucking hurricane of a monster, ol' blue-eyed John was looking comparatively good right now.

She barely noticed when the helicopter landed, despite the jolt wringing a miserable half-choked cry from her raw throat. The whine of the rotors slowed; a metal shelf shuddered, rattled, and the plastic sled was drawn out into a burst of cold predawn air redolent of pine, freshness, and a peculiar thinness meaning *high altitude, don't go for a jog just yet*. There was a squeak and a groan as the sled was thumped atop a metal cart, its wheels rattling over what felt like frost-heaved pavement, and she tried to blink, to gather impressions.

A mountainside cresting like a dark wave, blotting out the horrible, dangerous grey haze on the horizon. Smaller electric lights blinking, the helicopter's whine cut off clean as a knife-slice, a gush of gasoline smell accompanied by a patter of running feet.

"—make it downhill to Aspen for breakfast," someone called, before the waning stars were blotted out by a roof. Simone was hauled into a giant mouth carved from sheer rock, her entire frame shaking and shivering as the vamp infection fought with poison, hoping he wouldn't jab her again.

The wheels smoothed out, clattering against smoother flooring. More heartbeats and running feet, excited voices. Simone's hands ached, fingers contorted as her claws slid free and retracted in spasms like her fangs, and now a new and more terrible torture was rising.

The thirst-spot at the back of her throat dilated all at once. In a moment between waves of muscle-grip wringing, she tried to turn her hands, to drive her claws into the sled. The urge to rip, tear, strike out wildly even if her limbs wouldn't fully obey because they were locked by toxin-flooded muscles poured through her, the last desperate attempts of a tied-down animal sensing the approach of black nothingness.

"What the fuck?" Barry, nearly hysterical. "It's killing her, you can't… Jesus, man, it's killing her!"

"Get this into the lab!" Elton Huske bellowed, for once without that nasal, wheedling California accent. "I'll fire every fuckin' one of you if we don't get some fuckin' samples, now *move!*"

Dawn grabbed Simone while her body was still convulsing, and the thirst followed her past the threshold for a few moments before dropping away.

Nothing, then. Not even relief.

CHAPTER 22

Tumbling to earth as the sun lifted its massive fiery rim from hoary, mist-drenched horizon, then Jonathan's boots landed heavily next to a small, glass-clear mountain stream, dislodging a spray of pebbles. His eyelids fell closed; he groped internally for that subtle unmistakable whispering of the Blood's connection, strengthened by deep feeding yet lost as a fledgling's daylight sleep took hold.

His leman must be unconscious now, possibly gravely wounded. Had the mortals left her to the sun's not-so-tender unmercy?

If they have, I will find them and make them regret it before they die. Then I will kill every other mortal I can reach. I will wipe this entire world clean before I die of calcification, and those of the Blood will starve or grow stupid upon animal claret. The thought was cold, crystalline, and clove a tide of rising whispers with its sharp razor gleam.

His skull was full. The madness was returning, not in tiny dribs and drabs with the slow passage of mortal years but trickle-to-flood as a melting glacier. Eventually a jagged crack might open in the floor of his consciousness where the animal of survival lived, the creature grown strong and ruthless with aeons of hunting, drinking, hiding.

He opened his eyes. The chase must now continue under different conditions; fortunately, there were other methods.

Which required careful decision.

Aspens shivered in strengthening golden mistglow; the stream chattered happily. Perhaps the landscape was beautiful, but all Jonathan saw was rock, dirt, wood, the entire world a soulless painted panel unblessed by his leman's presence. If she were beside him at this moment…

But no. Addiction tugged at his veins, the thrall running sharp rowels all along his bones. A fading ghost of her scent clung to his clothes, his fingers, his tongue; he strove for a moment of stillness and clarity, in order to use any following effort most efficiently.

Bitch might wake up in transit, the ferret-faced man had said. At the moment Jonathan—he clung to the name, an anchor amid dark, unsteady waves—had been laboring under the assumption of an escape attempt aided by mortals, which he could see now was certainly not the case. This was a *capture*, and *transit* meant they had taken his treasure elsewhere.

Most unwise, to touch a sanguinant's leman. Even more so to *take* one. He had been traveling in a reasonably straight line so far, chasing the whirligig-craft.

Helicopter. Use the proper words; do not forget how she likes you to speak.

A shake of his head, one hand flashing to close around the bole of a slim sapling leaning to look at its own wavering reflection. A slight groan, bark and inner tissues compressing, and its branches' shimmer was reminiscent of his leman's trembling, hopefully with pleasure but more likely with overwhelming fear.

How can you not remember? It's your name.

He had not yet time to teach her even the barest of essentials, and had not learned more than a few tantalizing hints of her past and preferences. If he were ever to discover more, he must be swift and canny now.

No, it was not like his cautious Simone to be thus taken in—or was it? Her method of hunting fledglings had clearly been to wave herself before them, unaware that her very scent made them desire-drunk; perhaps she risked herself as a matter of course?

A habit he must deter; he would never again allow her to wander past arm's length.

Then think clearly before acting wisely. You must reach her, and soon. During the slender remainder of the night, the pull of his almost-fledgling's Blood had not altered, the vehicle carrying her presumably flying in a straight line. Jonathan eased his fingers from the aspen's bark, barely noticing the marks—not splintered but compressed, so the tree might eventually heal from insult.

It had not been mercy or conscious restraint, though some part of him was aware she might care for the trees' beauty. Absent-mindedness alone had kept him from doing greater damage.

Half-familiar mountains crowded his current shelter, stone thrusting itself skyward. Had he ever wandered over these slopes?

It did not matter. He could still move at some speed without mistform, and would have to be careful of deviating from the path. Of course, as the kidnappers neared their goal—whatever *that* was—they might turn one direction or another. He did not know enough of the fuel capacity for the… that what?

The word for the craft now lingered at the tip of his tongue, stubbornly refusing to coalesce. He could not dig it free, and rescuing the phone from his pocket did not help, for its screen remained stubbornly 'locked', asking for a numeric code he had no idea of.

There were limits even unto magic, of course. The item was reduced to splinters quickly, with a convulsive movement of his fist, and he tossed it away with a sudden savage twitch.

Old ways are best. Follow the line to your prey, and if all else fails wait for dusk. Once the sun falls she will wake, and when she does the call will resume.

Yet if it did not…

Jonathan did not care to think upon that prospect. He studied the rising, broken ground before him, hopped over the streamlet, and vanished into the thickening forest.

CHAPTER 23

AT FIRST SHE WAS ONLY AWARE OF FUNNY LITTLE FLICKERS BELOW
her skin, little mice feet pitter-pattering. Her eyes burned, barely
able to blink aside a heavy crust; her teeth throbbed with
horrible sensitivity, sharp edges pressing lightly against chapped
lips and swollen tongue. Every muscle felt savagely over-
stretched. Even her bones ached, a feeling she vaguely remembered from being human.

A child might call it growing pains; a middle-aged woman
would know it was mortality chewing at her bones.

After a few attempts at orientation, Simone discovered
herself attached to a vertical metal surface by tight restraints
made of some kind of flexible woven material which burned
relentlessly wherever it touched bare flesh. Ankles, above and
below the knee, hips, a band over her ribs scarcely allowing
enough room to take a middling breath, shoulders pressed hard
to the wall by a strap passing just under her armpits and
mashing her tits unmercifully as a bonus, a choker snugged to
her throat, another ribbon cutting into her throbbing forehead.

Her arms were spread wide, jacket- and shirtsleeves cut
away, and the burning from the strap passing over her biceps
was awful. Even worse was the wrapping on her wrists and

hands; blisters swelled there, the slightest twitch sending hard zings of pain all the way up to her shoulders as they popped.

The light was a fluorescent glare from white industrial fixtures; the entire giant room reeked of disinfectant, pain, and a zoolike undertone she might be imagining since her nose was so stuffed. Stainless steel tables, likewise surgically gleaming counters and cabinets, strange shapes that had to be machines of some kind, and a virtual jungle of glass beakers, tubes, test tubes in racks, rolling cabinets, wire cages, and other weird shit turned the entire space into a cross between a veterinary clinic and a mad scientist's laboratory.

Fully stocked, too. A collection of smeared shapes hurried back and forth, most in bright white lab coats, some with clipboards and serious expressions, more with tablets they frowned at and thrust before each other with simulated enthusiasm.

People. Human beings. Okay.

It took Simone some while, peering from under heavy, itching eyelids, to realize many occupants of this strange anthill were doing not very much at all despite their frantic imitation of busywork, and every blessed one reeked of fear and tension. A giant windowed observation deck loomed over the room, and the shape pacing back and forth behind the glass, stopping to glare down every once in a while, was a blurred but distinctly recognizable Elton Huske.

Fuckuva fishbowl you've got here, buddy. Her senses were muffled, her vision full of strange amorphous blobs intruding as she struggled to focus, and her ears felt stuffed with cotton. It was probably a blessing; vamp-sharp senses, when they came back, would make the bright light and nasty smells even worse.

Assuming she could heal from this. How far did her infected body's ability to erase damage go?

Looks like we're gonna find out.

A rhythmic but unmusical beeping and booping came from a vertical panel hung to Simone's left, just within her peripheral vision. Marching across its top third were lines that looked a lot like a heartbeat and… was that brainwaves? Along with respiration and maybe blood pressure, yeah. Her own vital signs, somehow communicated through the metal slab or straps?

What the fuck is going on? But she knew—she was a lab rat, and these people were supposed to figure out how to extract whatever Huske wanted to sell. The tiny trickle of scent slipping into her snot-packed nose screamed of barely controlled anxiety; so did the buzz-thump of nervous human heartbeats.

Presumably everyone in here knew what vamps could do, and was justifiably a bit jumpy. Hard not to believe in the demi-monde with a fang-bearing specimen strapped down right in front of you. She was, as the kids used to say, the Real Deal.

Oh, God, I'm already sounding like an old lady. Truth in advertising, she supposed.

What had they done while she was out? She hurt, sure, but she didn't feel… well, there was no evidence of outright assault, to put it one way. And she didn't smell blood—human, *or* vamp.

Yet the thirst was back, scratching at her throat. At least she wasn't poisoned now—had she slept it off, like a college hangover? What would happen if they jabbed her again?

They didn't leave you in the sunshine, at least. Think, Simone. Stop being scared and use that brain that got you out of that goddamn church basement.

But she was *terrified*, and the last few days hadn't helped. Whiplash was cumulative, whether physical or emotional. As soon as she escaped one trap another closed on her, and wasn't that the way it had always been?

Fresh scurrying warned of something new afoot. The big glass observation deck had gone dark, and a knot of lab-coated shapes crowded at a featureless steel door across the vast space, clearly visible from her vantage point. A luminous dial overhead said something was descending, and she had an idea of what.

Great.

✺

The elevator opened and Elton Huske stepped out—bloodshot and blinking, though he'd changed into a fresh set of ironed jeans and T-shirt, his fleece vest now dark green instead of blue. His jowls were tight with anger, his hair aggressively mussed under a payload of what had to be very expensive gel. Instead of Birkenstocks, there were brand new sneakers, probably custom, squeaking in a different register than the sandals had. The billionaire stalked through the flutter of lab coats, his gaze fixed past them.

Nailed, in fact, to her own sorry self strapped in T-pose like the most fucked-up crucifix imaginable.

The only surprise was Barry beside him, rumpled, pale, and bobbing alongside in imitation of an agitated stork, mouth moving at a mile a minute. Simone strained through the murk of overlapping voices; her arms and legs twitched, and the beep-boops changed intensity.

"—look, man, just let me talk to her. You don't have to do all this." Barry Jessup, bless his mercenary little heart, sounded downright upset.

"Shut the fuck up," Huske hissed, his already-thin mouth now nearly lipless with tension. He probably never showed this narrow-eyed glare in board meetings or breathlessly adulatory journalistic interviews; no, Simone thought, this expression was saved for anyone unfortunate enough to be labeled 'the help'.

A rolling rattle alerted her to one of the lab-coated humans— a willowy brunette with a set expression, her gaze refusing to settle on a tied-up vampire—pushing a shining metal contraption, coming to rest just at Simone's right. It looked like a goddamn dessert cart, but its stainless steel top shelf held a tray of polished implements instead of sweet treats.

Nothing nice about the offerings here, no sirree bob. Several large scalpels arranged by size, a rack of big syringes with elephant-sized needles... was that a bone saw? Clamps, a kidney-shaped dish with smaller scalpels, surgical scissors—

Simone didn't want to think about what was in the drawers underneath.

Especially since the top also held a shining metal blowtorch, the type used for creme brûlée, resting on its own pad of bleached, presumably sterile paper.

A gangly blond kid behind the woman was pushing a wheeled pole, a complicated contraption festooned with tubing and hanging blobs Simone recognized.

Blood bags. Needles topped the tubes, oversized as the huge syringes, and there were other bags of yellow plasma. She couldn't smell the red stuff in the closed sacks, but knowing it was there… God, that was almost as bad.

She was even thirstier, now.

"This isn't what I signed up for," Barry persisted, his hands flapping like fish just dragged from a pond. "You said you were just going to make the offer. You could've let her think about it, you could've—"

Simone saw the twitch of Huske's left arm, a motion stopped just in time. Looked like the billionaire had a teensy anger management problem, no doubt kept under careful control when there were reporters or fellow investors around. He reminded her of Curt, in fact—all smiles and schmooze around clients and corporate visitors, passive-aggressive to any underling who didn't seem likely to ever fight back, flat-out aggressive to wait staff or retail workers.

This guy seemed like her ex-husband dialed up to eleven, and the only surprise was that even this variety of cowardly, bullying asshole had the courage to get close to a vamp. Then again, Simone was apparently a failure at being a finely tuned killing machine; all her experimentation and laborious logical testing of boundaries clearly hadn't been the right kind of survival strategy.

Maybe she should have stayed with John, learned a thing or two. He was no doubt chasing some other girl vamp now, calling her *leman* and *darlin'*.

You can't honestly be mad about that, can you?

"If you don't shut up I'll have Security drop you in the middle of the mountains. With no pants." Huske continued striding along, and the dismissiveness in the threat was almost as bad as that little twitch. Something in his tone said he might have done it before, and of course with enough money you could make people disappear, couldn't you? A helicopter ride into the boondocks of Colorado could even be called comparatively cheap.

Her neck ached, her forehead burned. Simone coughed, wishing she could move—if she developed a sudden itch, being strapped down like this would quickly become unbearable.

What do you mean, quickly? It already is.

But they'd noticed the monster was awake. A cringing wash of terror rolled through the scent of massed humans, so intense it filtered through her blocked nose and scratched against the thirst, *hard*. The brunette next to the cart flinched; the blond kid swallowed visibly, his grip on the pole white-knuckle and the entire apparatus swaying, blood and plasma bags swinging grapes on a shaken vine. Several of the lab-coated crowd stopped or backed away, staring wide-eyed at the lab rat who had just made a noise.

"Elton Huske," Simone said, loud and clear, scraping each word from the bottom of her lungs. "Typical. When you can't buy your dates you drug 'em, right?"

It got his attention off Barry, at least. And Simone had no idea why she was distracting Huske from carrying out his threat, when all things considered her treacherous redheaded finder had been the one to talk her into this ambush.

That, and your own greed. Be fair.

She didn't want to be fair. The only thing she wanted to do was tear these restraints off, leap on the nearest throb-thumping human pulse, and sink her aching, overly sensitive fangs deep. The first hot gush would be heavenly, and she might not be able to stop no matter how much John insisted on her being a super-special lemon-scented fledgling.

Bet he says that to all the girls. It was hard to concentrate with the thirst rough-pulsing in her throat, and the machine recording her vital signs was emitting all kinds of interesting noises now.

The billionaire stopped in his tracks, still staring at her. His pupils were dilated, and through the reek of fear as well as the crap in her nose Simone caught a high, sawing metallic edge—some kind of drug, a tranquilizer if her vamp instinct was right.

Dried sweat crackled on her skin. She tried to blink away the crust on her swollen, tender eyes; the machine's noises were getting *fucking irritating.* Just as she thought so it began to whine, static crawling through the displays.

Huske's Adam's-apple leapt up, dropped, and his grin held no amusement whatsoever. "Glad to see you're awake!" he crowed, and a rustle ran through the lab coats. A portly man on the other side of the room backed up, triggering an automatic door into whooshing patiently aside; he vanished through, probably relieved as hell to have got while the getting was good.

Simone could second that emotion. Her gaze roved, taking in the gigantic room's dimensions, and she wished again the goddamn machine would stop its cawing and beeping.

"Elton." Barry was giving it another try, the sheen of nervous sweat on his forehead coalescing into fat drops. "This wasn't in the deal, okay? Let's just all calm down and talk about—"

"Barry, you're fucking fired. Someone get him out of here." Huske approached the hanging slab, his sneakers squeaking more loudly now; the socks under them were still creased from packaging. So goddamn weird, that he didn't wash before wearing—but maybe whatever employee laid out his clothes didn't like him enough to clue the boss in on that little life hack.

John hadn't washed his new clothes either, but that seemed different. She didn't want to pin down just why at the moment; no, Simone had all she could handle.

She studied her new captor, denying the urge to blink. Her

aching, split upper lip twitched, rising, and it was quite possible she was sneering.

Huske, of course, was just the type of asshole to be overly sensitive to even the faintest flicker of disdain on a woman's face. Another bright false smile slid into place, exposing his expensively capped teeth. "Jane Smith. You know you're kind of famous? Nobody can decide on your real name, if you're really a sanguinant—"

He knows that word? She couldn't help but twitch. The machine reading her vital signs whined, burped out another cascade of beeps like the world's crappiest slot machine.

"Will someone turn the sound on that down? Thanks." Huske addressed empty air, shifting to stare vaguely at a point past Simone's right shoulder, and the blond kid fiddling with the pole of blood bags and plasma hurried to obey.

She heard the kid's footsteps, passing *behind* her, and that was valuable information—she wasn't mounted on a wall, the slab was a free-standing structure. Not that it did much good, but any detail could be the critical one allowing escape, a lesson learned in an abandoned church's daylight basement as she worked at handcuffs cinched to bloody wrists, hoping the snoozing monster who kept attacking her in the dark hours wouldn't wake up.

Sure, this situation was bad; it was arguably worse than being held down and athletically fucked on the floor of her RV. But Simone found out, with a weary useless variety of relief, that it wasn't as terrible as the nadir of her entire existence, those endless morning hours as the sun rose and she tore at her own flesh, discovering her willingness, her own determination to survive.

No matter what.

Two more lab coats—a man and a woman, both with glasses and matching harried, hunted expressions though the woman was a bottle-blonde and her compatriot shiny-bald—hurried up to take Barry's arms, muttering at him. Barry cast a single agonized look in Simone's direction… and let himself be hustled away, probably grateful to get the hell out of this madness.

Which was about all you could expect from anyone, so it was silly to feel a thin, cold spike go through her chest. There were more immediate problems, like the burning in her arms, across her forehead. Her wrists, elbows, biceps were slippery, blisters swelling and bursting, swelling again.

There was no give in the restraints. What the hell were they made of, under the silver?

A strangled squawk, a muffled curse in a young, near-breaking male voice, and the machine stopped its warbling. In fact, its glowing screen died completely, becoming a blank dark glass pane; Simone suspected he'd just unplugged the damn thing, and mentally applauded the kid for solving the problem in the most direct way.

Huske, still blinking rapidly, didn't notice—and appeared to have immediately forgotten all about Barry as well. "I've done my research, you know." Despite his great show of unconcern, he edged sideways instead of approaching her more closely, and finally stopped staring at her long enough to check out the surgical cart. "It's taken a decade and a half, plus a *lot* of resources; even the young ones are so fucking hard to catch. To be honest I thought ol' Jessup there was running some kind of scam. They're all over, especially on the dark web. But he wasn't, was he. You're the real deal."

If I wasn't, would you have shot me with that tranquilizer? But Simone knew the answer. "Can the goddamn monologue," she said, wearily. "You're not a supervillain; you're just a kid who lucked into Daddy's money."

The hush became profound. Every lab coat in the room had frozen in place, and it was depressing that she could guess with near-perfect accuracy what button to push on a middle-aged man.

She had, after all, been married to one.

"Maybe." Huske extended a hand, his well-buffed fingers

wiggling to brush the blowtorch's canister, almost lovingly. "But I'm also the guy who finally caught himself a real live vampire. I'm going to live forever."

Bullshit you are. Simone couldn't help it. She began to laugh, harsh chuckle-caws shaking her against the unforgiving restraints.

Huske's face congested. Another pair of lab-coated workers saw their chance and made it through the automatic door at the far end, its whoosh covered by her hoarse, scraping chuckles.

"Shut up. Shut *up!*" His scent changed, a harsh purple-red tint invading the drug's caustic screen; he snatched the blowtorch and heaved it at her. The willowy brunette let out a short, squeaking cry, the cart rattling as her hip bumped the pushbar.

Pow. A good throw, all things considered, the canister's bottom bouncing off the strap over her eyebrows. It didn't hurt; Simone had taken worse during any number of bounties. Face-hitting a vamp was a good way to break whatever you were swinging at them, or your own damn hand.

So he'd been trying to catch vampires for years, huh? It just went to show how irredeemably stupid the man was. Whether the money atrophied his brain or it had been useless to begin with was an open question, really. Which made her laugh even harder, and God but she suspected her own sanity was about to snap.

She might become just as foaming-psycho as the eight young bloodsuckers she'd killed.

Huske stood stock-still, ribs heaving as she continued to laugh. Finally the fit passed, and she found she could breathe a little more easily. She couldn't shake her head, but Simone hoped the impression was there.

"Dumbass," she croaked, in what she hoped was a pleasantly dismissive tone. "You absolute chuck-fuckling dickbag dipshit. You won't ever be a vamp; you wouldn't survive a half-hour."

Huske's nostrils flared, color draining from his face until the skin turned chalky-yellowish all the way down his neck, every pore and hair visible even with her eyes so badly crusted, along with the flutter of his raging carotid pulse. There was no swelling point of wet crimson light in his pupils or spreading to engulf his eyeballs, no sense of cold, prickling, absolute focus. No superhuman speed, no superstrength, not even the advantage of enough fierce, uncompromising human willpower to rip his own flesh to ribbons, yanking hands through too-small metal cuffs.

He was just another small-dick midlife crisis, albeit a variety with enough money to make everyone around him miserable. Of course he wanted to get infected, of *course* he thought it was like the movies, living forever and getting everything he wanted. Just like a toddler might want an entire birthday cake, throwing a tantrum when other children got reasonable pieces.

Maybe he'd manage it, with some kind of transfusion—that looked to be his plan, what with all the blood bags, tubing, and plasma. Maybe he *had* figured the details out, or someone working for him had, but Simone didn't think so.

This didn't seem like a fully functioning evil scientist's lair, after all. It was just a stage set to massage a single manbaby's ego.

"Get set up," Huske said, in a strangled, unnatural rasp. "We're going to tap this thing like a keg ,and drain it dry."

So that's his plan. Simone let her eyelids droop, sagging against the restraints.

Except for her left hand, which twitched inside its wrapping. The bands over her forearm, elbow, biceps, and chest were fractionally looser on that side.

CHAPTER 24

Sharp stone masses reaching skyward, their feet emitting low groans of tectonic activity, these mountains cared little for any small drama played upon their flanks. Shadows accumulated in every hollow, painted the eastron face of every tree, rock, and rise. Dusk was an indigo-strengthening hour away, collecting ever more quickly at lower elevations. Masses of aspens drew away in shaded spots; spruce, pine, and fir were more than happy to spread in their stead.

And a wanderer had found a road. More precisely, he had stumbled across a pair of small shacks at the bottom of a steep incline. Between them, two armatures barred entry to a rising stripe of pavement. Inside the shacks a quartet of mortal males sat and yawned, desultorily glancing out the windows at odd intervals. Dressed in matching uniforms, a strange badge upon their breasts—an X in a jagged circle, no symbol Jonathan knew or cared about—they also bore ungainly modern rifles, slightly different than the variations carried by mortal deer-hunters during his madness.

Guards. Which seemed an encouraging sign, though it took him a short while to decide against draining them dry. He must be subtle in his stalking; he settled for passing unseen and following the road.

The treeline was some distance above, and this passageway obviously laid at great expense. It was well-kept, prior frost-heaves and cracks assiduously patched; mounting in switch-backs, it seemed to be traveling in the correct direction. Instinct tugged at him, seeking to draw him in a straight line across its zigzags, but he hesitated as twilight thickened.

Two shining, oversized black vehicles had already passed, skittering downhill like frightened insects. His finely tuned senses discerned fear upon the occupants, an emotion quite divorced from reasonable appreciation of any wilderness dangers. He could have halted both automobiles and fed upon their contents, but again, instinct halted him.

It was necessary to catch his greater prize unaware.

Jonathan. Simone. One name guttered like a candle, drawn away down a long dark hall as the fractures threatened. It took a great deal of concentration to remember larger considerations; however, the other name beat under his strong, ageless pulse, a blade driven deep enough to reach the animal crouching at the very bottom of his soul's well. The madness whispered, taunted, stole what it could while his attention turned outward as a wary predator's must, but it could not touch the bond—even so new and fresh, the tie was indissoluble.

Simone. Simone. Simone.

So he loped easily through the forest a stone's throw from the road, at a pace even a mortal would find reasonably comfortable. Wildlife clearly disliked this area, since all trails were old or overlaid with the heavy reek of caution; wolf or bear, deer or coyote kept their distance. So did any smaller beast, even the most foolhardy or flighty.

Interesting. His own scent held close as a wrapped mantle, he passed like a burning shadow through tangled undergrowth, between pillared trees, across bare rock or thin soil.

The sun touched horizon as the road crested a rise; the paved ribbon hesitated, then dove straight into the mountainside. A cunningly concealed entrance, though a thick reek of petroleum exhaust hung in a simmering haze, fooling no creature with a halfway sensitive nose. It *had* to be what he sought—or did it?

Mortals did strange things as a matter of course, and the hills could be honeycombed with their secrets—not to mention older, fouler things. There was no hint of a familiar shining scent-thread drawing him to his leman. Where was she? Alone, vulnerable in a fledgling's daylight torpor, lost in a hive of mortals...

A thrill dark and fragrant as unwatered wine shot through his limbs. While he lingered, studying the opening, the great eye of day had finished its downward passage. The call of a fledgling he had fed deep—and willingly—tugged at his veins, an exquisite glassy thrill, and the pull was no longer attenuated by great distance.

The golden rope was before him, and it led into the mountain.

He did not hesitate. The wanderer burst into mistform and raced for the carefully screened aperture.

A vast cave housed a different forest, this time of concrete pillars. A fleet of heavy black metal chariots stood among the stone trunks; for a moment time folded upon itself and he was with his beautiful leman as she searched for a vehicle to her liking. But there was no wind moaning through the upper reaches of an open structure, no reek of mortal urine, and most importantly, no hint of her gorgeous, mouthwatering fragrance.

Each car was alike, parked in serried rows; half reeked of petrol, the others held a drowsing electrical readiness. Tucked along one side of the cavern was a fluorescent lit gallery with a sign overhead shouting *FUEL - CHARGING STATION*; he gave a single glance at the letters, noting irregularities of spacing, and moved on. At the rear, a bank of steel doors led to six mechanical lifts, half of which breathed softly with activity above, lurking in the bulk of the mountain.

To the right, a set of different metal doors loomed, both bearing round glass portholes. A powerful animal stink lingered in that direction.

Hermetically sealed, the doors trembled as mistform pressed against them. A metallic click as he found a hidden switch with the same invisible pressure used for laying seals or denying electronic eyes, and steel slid aside. Passageways divided and reformed around him, and he could *feel* the blood-pull from above.

She was alive, and somewhere overhead.

The walls drew away as he poured through another slowly opening door, mistform turning heavy and visible as a greenish fog. The stink was massive, titanic, and a chorus of babble engulfed him.

Cages. Rank upon rank of containers to every side, aisles and stacks stretching toward distant walls. The stink of terror and captivity vied with the effluvia of imperfect cleansing, a bright hot hungry panting of starvation and mute terror. They had not been fed in some while—perhaps their captors had other concerns—and the beasts were growing desperate.

Now he knew why wildlife avoided these environs. Not only did the soft pink bipeds with their cruel machines and incomprehensible weapons linger here, but also the horror of durance, the invisible fume of baffled, uncomprehending fear. The wanderer hesitated.

Things had been *done* to these creatures. This was an abattoir, but worse, it was also a torture hall.

Some animals, small or large, huddled trembling in the back corners of their cages. Others showed their teeth or howled. A few watched unblinking, hopeless yet waiting for any chance, no matter how small, to strike back at their tormentors. All, *all* longed for escape, though most did not believe it possible.

And they reminded him, in some foggy way, of a pair of

lovely wide forest-eyes, a fall of cedarbark hair. *Not this way*, she had choked, pleading without hope of mercy. *Not like this.*

A momentary flexing of his will, a signal sent along branching galvano-electric paths. Heavy thunks and buzzes sounded, wire-woven doors swinging open, glass hatches raising, soft puffs as pneumatics engaged. Not only that, but the doors he had passed along the way opened as well, their controls overridden.

The wanderer's scent belled forth, spreading from the greenish fog in a haze of chemical communication. *Go*, it said. *Leave. Now.*

A scurrying, a scrabbling, a fresh clamor. Even those who had been maimed or mutilated, even those upon the verge of expiring from fatal despair gained a sudden burst of energy, knowing something far older and more terrifying than the mortals had passed by, was issuing a command.

The wanderer floated. Shapes slithered, jogged, dragged, fluttered, hopped along the aisles, a river of fur and teeth, feathers and scales, all seeking egress. There were even four mangled simian forms, screeching and showing their fangs as they moved in a tight pack; a single rail-thin wolf, its fur matted and singed with caustic burns, stopped near the entrance to this *chambre des horreurs* and looked back over its scorched shoulder, showing its own canines. In the flat goldgreen glare of its gaze was no gratitude, nor any ruth.

It merely wished to make certain of unpursuit, or perhaps it was swearing vengeance.

Do not worry, the wanderer thought, a moment of sudden clarity amid the hail of fractures spreading through the rest of his consciousness. *What they have done shall be avenged.*

The wolf lifted its tail and rejoined the flow of cringing, creeping creatures given a new lease upon life. The wanderer sent out one last pulse, making certain every cage was empty and every door upon this level open, the way to the outside clearly marked, then returned to his own hunt.

His prize remained, waiting in this warren. All else he found would be crushed.

Somewhere above, an irritating noise began to blare. An alarm of some kind, triggered by his actions or another event.

Simone. Mistform thinned, and the wanderer had indeed forgotten his own newly acquired name.

No matter. He did not need it.

<h1 style="text-align:center">CHAPTER 25</h1>

FOR ALL THE MONEY CLEARLY SPENT ON THIS PLACE, THERE WERE some piss-poor design choices. Like the fact that the slab Simone was strapped to was fixed in place, so the blond kid who had turned the screaming vital-signs machine off had to teeter on a hastily fetched metal stepstool while attempting to shove a needle into the hollow of her right elbow.

The young man didn't seem phlebotomy-trained despite his nicely pressed lab coat. Several more of his brethren had slipped out through that automatic door, but the escapes had halted when Elton Huske turned around to glare at his underlings. Half froze in place, rabbits under a hawk's drifting shadow, and the others redoubled their frantic though not very productive activity.

It was bleakly funny—the moment their boss swung back to bark at the kid on the stepstool, at least two more employees scurried for the door. The crowd was noticeably thinner now.

"Should've done it while I was sleeping," Simone said, and watched Huske's fury rise again. "That's what rich boys like, right? Date rape drugs."

A vein in the billionaire's forehead was throbbing; if he hadn't had a blood pressure problem before tonight, he certainly did now. It was depressingly easy to enrage this kind of a noxious asshole, and while he was boiling he didn't notice the slow, subtle twisting of her left arm.

Which hurt like hell, bright scarves of agony twisting up from her palm, her raw-hamburger wrist now weeping pink-tinged trickles as the blisters popped, re-formed, and were torn again. Her arm on that side was similarly slick, rubbing against the metallic weave.

Silver. Gotta be. What Simone was about to do would hurt even more than the blisters, than ripping herself free of handcuffs.

She didn't care.

The blond youth dug at her inner elbow again, the needle prodding but unable to pierce. Vamp skin was tougher than its poreless perfection seemed and this wasn't a tranq dart going at speed; plus the kid looked definitely greenish and the thin trickle of scent from him, working its way into Simone's clogged but sensitive nose, reeked of juicy, copper-colored fear.

There really was no point in being conciliatory. Especially once it occurred to her that Huske might not be able to load her up with that awful poison again, since tainting the blood he was planning on shooting into his own veins was a bad idea.

Of course, he could get angry enough to try it, which was a risk she was ready to run. Especially since the fluid wrung out of the popped blisters was so very slick, and the strap material that *wasn't* silver was saturated. Felt like nylon, not a lot of stretch… but maybe, just maybe enough.

"Sir?" The brunette near the cart had a lovely, clear fluting alto. "There are protocols. Maybe we should—"

"You're *fired*!" Huske barely turned his head to yell. Spittle flew in a fine spray, and that regularly twitching vein had turned nearly purple. He lunged for the cart, scooping up the largest scalpel, and Simone had to shove down a thick, braying laugh.

It was goddamn liberating to have absolutely nothing left. Her mortal life, her RV, her finder, her career as a vampire hunter, pretty much all of her dignity—all gone, lost in a rising tide of dry scratching thirst. The only wonder was that she'd played by the rules so long, doing everything expected of a reasonably good girl, up to and including simply accepting a pittance for alimony because digging in and fighting your ex-husband made you a bitchy old dried-up harridan.

Oh, she'd tried, even when middle age had arrived with perspective and very few fucks left to give. But now she was faced with the knowledge that it had always been a lost battle.

A good girl didn't drag the vamp who had spent several nights biting and assaulting her into a weak bar of sunlight coming through a filthy daylight basement window, or feel a savage sense of *serves you right* when the thing began to writhe and bubble-burn, streaks of dust racing through its tissues. A good girl didn't at heart *like* ripping rabid young vamps into ribbons with her bare hands; a good girl wouldn't deep-down *enjoy* getting fucked by a cowboy-drawling, nameless tramp of a vampire.

Or maybe the very concept of *good girl* was complete fuckery in and of itself. At the moment Simone didn't care, because Huske jabbed at her with the scalpel, roaring inarticulately, and she suspected the blade was silvered by the way it caught in the strap over her left thigh with a sweet starburst of further pain. The blond kid on the stepstool let out a blurt ending in "—ly *fuck!*" as he toppled, and everything slowed down.

One hard straining push, all her remaining, waning strength concentrated in a single burst. Her shoulder popped hard, dislocating with a red flare lost in the general misery, and she barely felt her own skin peeling free as she forced joints in ways they were not intended for, degloving almost her entire arm.

A coyote would gnaw its own paw off to escape a trap; snakes burst and slid out of their hides all the time. The animals were onto something, and what was a divorce really but a painful shedding of the scales over a woman's eyes?

One thing wasn't left behind in the tight, unforgiving straps, though.

Her claws. She swiped first at the band over her throat, nylon and thin strands of metal parting like water, and if the triangular razor edges at her fingertips also slashed her own flesh Simone didn't particularly care. Freeing her right arm was a flicker. She dragged the finger-knives down her ribs, blood bursting free; the sweet candysick scent shouting of pain and illness stroked the thirst's dry-dollar spot at the back of her throat, reaching down and yanking at something old, something very nasty living in any woman who had made up her mind to fucking well survive.

It seemed almost leisurely to her, but vamp speed and human reflexes were two very different things. The straps over her torso parted, and the thick band over her hips was sawed through in less than a heartbeat.

Sure, the restraints all *looked* good, very aesthetic. But none of this guy's shit *actually worked*, except for maybe the tranquilizer and that was questionable at best. Still, Simone was pretty sure that cocktail of bullshit had nearly killed her, and maybe if she hadn't been sucking at old-vamp blood for a couple days the helicopter ride might have gone a lot worse.

Her temples throbbed, the band over her forehead slipping, and she managed to cut her legs free on the way down, a swift stripe of bright spangled sensation up her ribcage as the scalpel was torn from Huske's trembling, sweating paw. Simone hit the ground, arms and legs not responding as they should for a long, taffy-stretching moment; the thought that maybe she'd expended her final burst of energy on simply thrashing like a landed fish was bleakly funny as well.

All of this was so fucking *dismal*. Even the floor, which was indifferently mopped for a place with so many pretensions to scientific or medical cleanliness. Simone realized she could see as much because her only slightly injured right hand was rubbing the crust from her eyes, and she blinked furiously as the first cries rose.

Human screams, accompanied by a general rush for that automatic door. And somewhere nearby a red light began flashing, an electronic warble pouring from porthole-shaped speakers.

A shattering metallic crash was the blond kid, knocked from his perch to land on the stainless-steel not-dessert cart. The brunette froze—at least, for a very brief span of time before the wheeled contraption, obeying the dictates of physics, hit her amidships and sent her ass-over-teakettle. The stepstool skidded sideways, its indifferently padded feet losing their grip on featureless metal, and headed for a slice of blank, smooth concrete wall.

Simone's left leg pistoned out, a completely instinctive movement. Once more, her body knew what to do and she was just along for the ride; her boot kissed Elton Huske just between floating ribs and hip, sending him careening across the floor in loose tumbledoll fashion before he tangled with the still-moving cart. The maneuver produced a terrible cascade of bonesnapping sounds, audible over the hideous, continuous blatting.

Someone pulled the fire alarm, she realized. Which made some kind of strange sideways sense, even if she wasn't sure this place would have adequate, OSHA-approved exit routes. *Motherfucker didn't even take my boots off.*

Then again, Huske had to be really excited. A real live vampire after years of effort, strolling right into his rented ballroom; he probably had never, ever considered that she might be able to wriggle free of the trap. It really was a curse to get everything you wanted, Simone thought. Made you sloppy, slipshod.

All the money in the world couldn't buy class *or* experience.

Her wet, bleeding left palm smacked the floor. Simone found herself flickered up into a crouch, fangs out, a deep rumbling hiss rattling from her ribcage. Growling like any of the vamps she'd put down—had they felt like this, a wildfire inside their skull, nothing but red glow and smoke?

No wonder they'd chased her.

Another instinct lifted her head, peering through strings of brown hair writhing like snake-coils. A quick hard *huff* cleared her nose, then the smells poured in, wonderfully vivid. Even the foul odors were a blessing, because she was no longer tied down. Her eyes, tender and throbbing, blinked rapidly as she shifted, knees wide, crouching with turnout a ballerina might sell a soul for, a faint ripping lost in the hubbub as her jeans tore along the inseam.

The crowd at the automatic door, milling desperately, had hit a snag. It wasn't just that both glass halves had frozen instead of whooshing neatly along their tracks; the bigger problem was a half-dozen men in tactical gear, rifles pointed up as they hammered through the press, trying to get *in*.

The elevator to the observation gallery dinged, its steel doors reluctantly spreading, and there was another clutch of big black-clad male figures. One wore sunglasses despite the hour, and every throat gleamed dully—blackened chainmail gorgets, all the fashion among vamp hunters lately. She'd seen instructional videos on a few forums, a real do-it-yourself project if a hunter had the time, available for a fee if not, and even thought of maybe getting one herself.

But in the end there was no point. She didn't need body armor, fancy toys, crucifixes, rifles; she was what they fought.

Did they have a tranq gun laden with that poison shit?

Be careful, Simone.

Which was a laugh and a half; did she really want to live after all? Why else had she ripped her arm out of the restraints? It stung, rags of flesh left on saturated straps shredding into gleaming grit, the tiny particles falling with crystalline tinkles buried in the racket though clearly discernible to vamp hearing.

But the pain was retreating, akin to the remembered sensation of a deep sunburn as tissues plumped in fast-forward, rebuilding. She stretched the limb, shrugging the dislocated shoulder *hard*, a quick flick of bones pop-crackling back into place.

The hunters burst out of the elevator, clumsy-clunky humans shouting at each other over the din, and her fangs were so far extended she couldn't speak if she wanted to. Because along with the scent of her own spilled-free blood, delicious and wicked, was a thinner though far more enticing note. Salt-hot, deadly sweet crimson, not the cold ersatz from the bags but pumped from living veins—not the taste-shifting gorge-delight from an old vamp either, but good and necessary. Her body knew what it needed, what it craved, and the screaming crowd packed against the far wall was no longer a collection of unique individuals.

Now the crush was simply a mass of bleating, milling, juicy prey.

Simone uncoiled, blurring through air gone tight, hard, and straining against her skin.

CHAPTER 26

THE PLACE WAS A POKED ANTHILL, SEETHING. MULTICOLORED LIGHTS flashed at intervals along the passageways, and the constant klaxon was a mild aural irritant as he followed a soft, almost elusive pull against every nerve and artery. Each time his heart squeezed the call intensified, leading him through the maze of concrete tunnels. Blundering along with a little less than the whispering speed, stopping and doubling back, he barely noted the changes when he burst into what were clearly the habitable places of this heap—a bedroom with black walls and a mirrored ceiling, a long low room with a strange tank full of iron-smelling water, its egg-shaped lid open and a rubber suit like a discarded skin hung upon a nearby, curlicued metal pole, two large functional kitchens with attached plastic-booth dining areas and a smaller, much more expensive dining room with a very large tinted window staring out onto the night, more bedrooms, one reeking of recent fumbling mortal lust with an acrid tinge of some chemical aphrodisiac under a flood of hastily applied cleaning agents. Other rooms held long tables and electrical equipment, screens crawling with static as the various inter-locking fields of visible and not-so-visible flexed and fluxed in response to an Archon's will. And yet more rooms dedicated to purposes he did not care to guess at or even consider, since none held what he wanted.

The most concerning spaces were those full of metal tables and vaguely insectile equipment, reeking of pain and death. More torture chambers with lifts connecting to the animal prison below, simmering with a reek of stinging disinfectant applied slapdash-fashion, unable to wash away the filth.

She does not belong here either. The rage was building, almost colorless in its intensity.

He did not quite realize he was growling until he turned a corner and came nearly face-to-face with a trio of mortals—two males, plus a female with strawlike pale hair. The central figure, ruddy-headed and jittering with nervousness, took one look at him and backpedaled, nearly pratfalling to bony posterior, and the inelegant squeak he let out might have been amusing in another time or place.

The other two, both wearing strange bleached cotton coats, froze in the eternal manner of prey. Their bodies knew before their minds, a sudden drift of glandular terror spreading in a haze—the faint tingling sensation in the wanderer's eyes meant the killglow was upon his gaze, liquid crimson spreading and behaving as no light should, droplets rising upon invisible updrafts at the corners.

"Ohshit," the man on the floor piped, in a choked whisper almost lost in the continued alarums. "It's one of them, it's a vamp, it's a fucking sucker!"

The wanderer recognized that voice—he had heard it through a phone's tinny earpiece, speaking ever so casually to sweet Simone; its timbre was also familiar from the hotel, wafting down the hall just before a leman was stolen.

Ah. The fractures of looming insanity twitched, and his fangs slid free. The two white-coated mortals screamed in odd harmony, one voiding its bladder in a hot gush, and then he was upon them.

Blood hit the back of his throat, jaw distended and teeth

driven in. The claret was nearly tasteless, though it laved the thirst; oddly, the lack of flavor helped the wanderer focus, as it could never approach the nectar he longed for. He drank merely to replenish a day's energy spent searching, dropping the male mortal the moment the body was drained, catching the female as she scrabble-clawed along the hard smooth wall in search of escape. A useless attempt, just like the red-haired one crab-scuttling on palms and heels, blindly retreating.

And upon all three was the very faintest ghost of fragrance. They had been in contact with his treasure, within the past hour.

"Oh please," the copper-furred male squealed. "Ohplease ohplease Janie, *I didn't mean it—*"

Too late. The wanderer was upon him then, draining the mortal in a few casual gulps. The cargo of nourishment made the pull of his fledgling strengthen, tugging relentlessly. Now he was replete, though he should take more to feed his prize when he found her. What state would she be in, brought to this place and enduring an entire day of torment? While he had languished and lingered, betraying his only purpose—to guard what he had taken.

A chatter of gunfire erupted in the near distance, echoing through overlapping tunnel-throats. A faint note underneath the pulse and the annoying screech was something else, and the wanderer's nerves caught fire afresh with recognition.

Now he heard other things as he dropped the skinny male, licking the last traces absently; his skin would absorb splashed nutriment as well. No urge to glut, merely the imperative to find her, to aid his leman—for the song of her killgrowl was as music to him.

Between himself and that melody was the pattering of mortal feet, the soft confusion of mortal pulses, and a high, dizzying aroma of exquisite fear.

Good. One clear, cold thought, flotsam upon the whirling maelstrom. *You should scream, and run, for you tried to hide her from me.*

He streaked into motion, and two junctions later he found the source of the footsteps, a tide of animals far less wholesome than those he had freed.

Claws out, eyes shining with a red haze, he plunged through them as a flame through paper cutouts, tracing the flow to its source.

CHAPTER 27

TERRIBLE TO HURT OTHER VAMPIRE HUNTERS, REALLY, BUT HER BODY didn't care. If they just wouldn't shoot at her, she'd leave them alone—

That's a lie, Simone. Because even if bullets hadn't spattered against the floor, whining crazily and striking sparks, ricochets plowing into the crush near the door where other hunters—or maybe security, since now there was an additional group, men in regular ol' tactical without the chain neck-wraps and wearing silver *X-OL* badges instead—were still trying to get through, the smell was there.

Blood. Fresh, sweet human blood.

Its fragrance cut through everything else, even the remaining zoolike stink, and hit the back of her throat like a runaway semi, lighting a fuse all the way down her spine, yanking her arms and legs with terrible easy fluidity. As if she hadn't been shot full of poison, as if she hadn't been hung up like a bargain-basement imitation crucifix, as if she was no longer tired, or afraid, or uncertain.

She landed in the knot of men near the elevator, her nose twitching as it filled with *male, sweat, gun oil, live fire,* her left-hand claws sending a burst of pain up to jolt in her savagely stretched shoulder as they skittered across the body armor's ceramic plates. Down into a crouch, then, before she erupted as one tried to swing his rifle-butt at her. Throwing both arms and her right leg out, each limb hitting with a solid *crack*. Three bodies went flying, more bullets spewing crazily for the ceiling, and a chip flicked against her cheek. Concrete, metal, ricochet fragment, she didn't know or care; Simone was already on the hunter who seemed to have the most presence of mind, since he'd tried to hit her and now was struggling in a slow blundering human way to level the rifle.

Fury filled her. The fact that he was just a guy doing a job, a fellow bounty-collector, didn't matter. It was always the same, fucking *men*, even if you were on their side they'd lash out. All they saw was a pair of tits, an innie instead of an outie, and that made it all right to do whatever they wanted.

Pow. He crumpled, thrown back against the slowly closing elevator doors, and a warped jangling echoed from inside the luxuriously carpeted box. Sparks flew, different than those wrung free by humming bullets. Simone turned neatly on forefoot, her hair lifting as she spun; her childhood longing for ballet lessons was a sweet strong nostalgic pain.

Funny, the things you think of. Her hands flashed out again, tearing the chainmail from a stocky blond man's throat; he had three bluish teardrops tattooed on his left cheek. Vamp kills, maybe, and as her claws slid through human flesh it wasn't the same as killing a bloodsucker, no indeed. No wet rot turning into gleaming dust but a hot spray of deliciousness she tore herself away from almost as soon as the first droplets sprang free, since the men at the door had suddenly begun firing through the crowd.

The cacophony took on yet another dimension, screams turning hellish instead of merely terrified. Along with the sweet, sweet burst of shining blood came a darker, fouler tinge—bowel-cut effluvia, urine-stink, the brassy stench of death.

This is my life now. Well, she'd made a complete fucking hash of the human one, maybe she should try really being a vamp. What had being restrained, being polite, being *good* ever gotten her?

Tables shattered, glass disintegrating, a thin blue jet of flame spurting from a nozzle—maybe the blowtorch deciding to work on its own, maybe something else? The bullets were bees, humming to shred anything softer than concrete, various substances spilling and mixing, caustic clouds rising, fluorescing to vamp sight as bits of lead and glowing metal plunged through their hearts.

She could have slowed down, watched every chemical interaction and reaction with interest, but the streams of fire were converging and she knew they were using the real ammo, the stuff supposed to bleed a vamp dry in seconds flat, and the moment Simone stepped into one of those chattering metal rivers she would lose more than just a bit of skin.

Then the world shifted, turned over, paused in its steady path through space.

A low foxfire smear bloomed amid the crowd, viridescent smoke pouring, coalescing. A wall of force expanded, dilating from a bar of crimson light with two swelling points.

Eyes. They were eyes. Their gaze raked past her, taking in the chaos with one swift sweep, and all the trouble, the noise, the glaring, the restless motion stilled.

She skidded to a stop, bootsoles smoking, her right hand tented lightly against the floor, fingertips just slightly touching a tangle of shattered glass and clinging nasty wetness as substances which shouldn't mix were smeared together.

I thought I *was fast.* Simone stared, her fangs fully out and sensitive, pulsing in time to her banging, battering heart.

A single streak of motion tore through the shooters, spreading in a streak-cloud, flickering through black smoke to greenish mist, solidifying only to rip open a hard shell of body armor and the flesh beneath or to wrench a struggling lab-coated form asunder. Blood gushed, sprayed, turned to a fine mist, a storm of iron-smelling droplets underlit with acidic lightning.

None of the vamps she'd killed with such wringing, tearing effort could have possibly fought this... this utter catastrophe. It scythed through the crowd, leaving only twisted, dripping fleshrags and sheared bone in its wake, guns clattering to the ground with their smoking barrels split or torqued into sharp curves.

A bullet insect-whined past her ear. Simone flinched, but the streak of killing intent was already blinking across the room with a soft warm whisper of moving air, resolving into a lean shape dressed in black, one iron fist buried in the gut of a vamp hunter who had survived and managed to squeeze off a single shot in her direction.

The old vampire lifted the hapless bounty-chaser, and Simone realized he had punched through armor and belly to grab the lumbar spine. A single irresistible movement, like a terrier shaking a toy, ended with a deep *thunk* of snapping bone.

John dropped the limp form atop a broken pile of other, feebly twitching lumps which had once been vamp hunters.

Ringing, blaring fire-alarm screams coruscated through empty space. Thin, acrid smoke rose in curls. A few struggling heartbeats, weak cries, and a terrible copper stench of blood— the sudden cessation of gunfire and other noise was almost stunning.

Simone's legs quivered. She wanted to stand, stayed nailed in place as John turned, slowly, the crimson glow in his eyes fading until they became shadowed blue-tinted holes, staring at her through fluttering, failing fluorescent light. Half the overhead fixtures were cracked and emergency lighting, vomitously orange, flared and faded in irregular pulses just at the seam between ceiling and walls. The thin crackle of flame merrily snacking on a pool of chemicals was concerning, but she couldn't move.

A puff of breeze stirring her sweat-stiffened hair, a brush

against her cheek, and John again resolved out of thin air, crouched easily before her. He tilted his head, dark hair standing up in wild spikes. His hat was gone, his eyes bright blue, and she was surprised to feel a deep flare of horrible, unforgivable relief.

Even more strange was him leaning forward and inhaling sharply. Something about his stare—wild, vacant, distant and terribly present at once—taunted her.

It was the glare of a wild animal interested in something. Uncertain, warily compelled.

"Simone." Her name rode a soft, wondering exhale. "Sweet Simone."

Oh, hell.

CHAPTER 28

Bedraggled and beautiful, she stared at him as if terrified past comprehension. Of course, his entrance left nothing to be desired in the way of violence; he idly catalogued and monitored the various states of those clinging to tenuous mortal life amid the mess, pleased that none were in a position to harm her.

The scent of his leman bore a warped note, a smoky searing of starvation, battle, and the metabolizing of some acrid mortal potion. Her bare arms were striped with blood, both mortal and her own; his fingers flicked out, drawing lightly down the left limb, and he almost winced at the damage to her luscious skin. A good feeding, rest, and the cessation of all this nonsense was in order.

He pressed his fingertips to lips, savoring the spicy, addictive tang of his treasure along with the strange, sharply venomous substance she had been dosed with. She flinched, lovely eyes gone dark and round with pain, and as the flame of her burned away encroaching madness and calcification he remembered the name again—her gift, all the more valuable after being temporarily mislaid.

Jonathan. That is who I am, to her.

"I..." Her cracked, chapped lips shaped the words so

elegantly, and her voice was a nightingale's warble amid all the furious metallic bleating. "They… I didn't try to—"

"I know," he soothed. He could not wait to feel her mouth drawing against his veins once more, but open flame now crept upon a lake of spilled substances, belching nasty discolored smoke. The killing roar was gone, though the thrall prickled deep in his marrow with sharp silver rowels. There was a swollen, blistered band across her forehead, another at her throat —had they sought to strangle her?

She tensed. Fearing she lacked the strength to stand, he grasped her arms and drew them both upward. His leman flinched again, though his grasp was as gentle as possible, and the rage threatened to return despite the anodyne of her presence, the soothing cloak of her scent.

"There." He steadied her, then let go, slowly, ready to provide more support at any sign of crumpling. "Time to leave, darlin'."

"Yeah." A small shake of her tousled, beautiful hair. "Yeah, I —"

"Bitch," a mortal voice wheezed, from a shadowed ruin of tubes and glass behind her. "Fucking… mess."

Now Jonathan noted the slab with its straps—silver somehow woven into cloth, no wonder she was raw and suppurating. The daring of mortals to do this…

Well, they were dangerous in swarms. Every sanguinant knew as much.

His leman turned, regarding the smaller mess. She took one uncertain step, then another, and Jonathan suppressed a sudden urge to simply grasp her, take flight, and bear them both through the twisting passageways to the clean, forgiving night outside.

The flames were spreading; he did not like their closeness to what he cherished. But sweet Simone's shoulders drew back, her chin lifting proudly, so he trailed in his leman's wake, keeping a wary eye upon the spreading fire. Tiny snippets of memory gnawed at him, were ruthlessly shelved. This was no time to brood upon the past.

Fire could not harm him, but a tender fledgling? She had suffered enough.

When she dropped, he twitched as if to catch her again. But it was a controlled movement, exquisitely graceful even as the betraying hitch near the end spoke of pain. Every instinct but one shouted to simply drag her away, no matter any struggle; the single still, small voice which had led him through the madness, the fractures, through centuries of insanity to finally find the greatest gift of all existence made a different demand.

That voice was hers alone. It spoke again, this time outside his head. "You could have just let me walk away," she said, softly.

The wreckage here was comparatively small, though no less deadly to a fragile mortal frame. A broken form lay speared and crumpled, wheezing as it stared at her. Two additional corpses twisted among sprays of shattered glass and polished steel, smooth surfaces reflecting flickering flameglow and weak fluorescents.

Jonathan peered closer, to discern what held his leman's interest so. Steel bars and crumpled metal had gouged unmercifully at a mortal male with goggle-eyes and a thin, cruel mouth. He had been flung, with some force, into a collection of thin spears and strange sharp instruments. The scent of cold mortal blood from storage was very strong as well, painted in great splashes near a twisted, fallen pole.

Had they thought to feed her? Jonathan's lip lifted at the thought. That was *his* duty, as well as his pleasure and prerogative.

"You bitch," the male mortal wheezed. The voice was familiar from the hotel ballroom as well, though this broken whisper bore little relation to the arrogant, glad-handing tone of before. "You weren't… weren't supposed to…"

"What are you going to do?" A note of genuine interest to her hoarse, supremely soft purr. A thrill slipped through Jonathan, crown to soles; he could, he discovered, listen to her speak so for hours, months, mortal years. "Fire me?"

"Please." The mortal's lungs were either punctured or filling with fluid; he gave another gurgling wheeze. "You… don't understand… I'm supposed to live… forever."

"You really do remind me of him," she murmured, almost too quietly to be heard even with sanguinant acuity. Yet the tension in her was not soft at all. Her strained, strenuous control finally cracked with a thin sound, as a crystal wineglass trod under a careless heel, and she struck.

Like an uncoiling viper, like a stooping hawk. The movement was breathtaking, and she buried her fangs in the mortal's throat so deep it would have been an incapacitating blow even without his various other injuries. Swift and sure she drank, her slim back rippling with each pull, and though Jonathan was glad to finally see her feeding naturally, he disliked the thought of her mouth upon another's skin.

Yes, he disliked it *intensely*. The roar of possessive rage rose within his ribs, was denied for the moment.

Even this, he would gift unto her.

The mortal's heart stuttered, laboring under a triple burden of shock, pressure loss, and a soup of chemical substances wholly unlike that sweet Simone had been subjected to. Perhaps this fellow was some manner of drug addict? Jonathan was about to utter a warning when his leman retreated, springing up and away from her prey almost as if startled, scrubbing at her mouth with the back of her hand, blundering into him and freezing.

Not nearly enough feeding to repair the damage. Still, the air had warmed alarmingly inside this confined space. "Shh," he soothed. "All's well, darlin'. Done?"

She shook her head, a nervous toss, as a thoroughbred scenting fire. The rawness down her left arm was far less glistening now. He longed to know what had happened—if she would speak of it, if she needed or wanted to—but there was one small matter remaining.

"Are y' done?" he persisted. "Tell me, an'..." *Speak as she likes, fool.* He sought the proper cadence, the accent she found pleasing. "Then we shall leave."

A tiny nod, her hair brushing the front of his torn, spattered shirt. "I... didn't kill him." As if expecting her sanguinant to argue.

"No," Jonathan agreed. *But your fangs were in another, and that I will not abide.* "You did not. Stay still. Understand? Stand, right here."

Another small dip of her chin. "Everything's burning." Had she just noticed?

"One moment." His claws were already out. Crack of bone, tearing of gristle, no spray of blood—for she had, after all, drunk deep—he reduced the prey she had touched to anonymous pieces.

As any sanguinant lucky enough to have a leman would.

Through the twisting passageways and strange, stutter-lit rooms he shepherded his reeling, exhausted fledgling, pausing only to gather her into his arms when she stumbled for the second time. The madness retreated swiftly, fractures healing with every deep spice-laden breath, though her glorious scent was now also freighted with smoke. His senses sharpened afresh with each moment, her sweet lithe softness held close as he chose the swiftest path to the parking level.

No few of the vehicles were missing, gaps in their serried ranks. She stirred as he slowed to contemplate the remainder, and shook her head.

"They'll have trackers," she whispered. Pale save for two hectic spots high on her cheeks, heavy-lidded, she trembled now with fatigue and quite possibly shock. Careful care, a place of rest, feeding to repletion—those were her requirements now. "Transponders, probably. Not a good idea."

"Ah, you are a wonderful teacher," he murmured in reply, and arrowed for the hidden entrance.

A cold, clear burst of freshness swallowed them both. He plunged down the slope he had traced her upward so laboriously, and found the guardhouses at the bottom empty, their windows shining with golden electric light.

No doubt they, like other animals, had sensed a paroxysm of vengeance. He followed the road for some short while before veering away, soundlessly leaping the yawning slash of a ravine, landing feather-soft and halting, turning to regard the mountain.

Halfway up its frowning bulk a sullen red glare was visible, peering through heavy summer foliage. A faraway detonation rippled the fabric of darkness; disinterested stars gleamed through a pall of smoke before a fresh gout of black vapor rose. He did not like thinking of his Simone trapped in such a place.

Let it burn.

"Gas." She had turned her head, craning to witness what could be seen of the destruction. "And whatever else he had for running the labs. But cameras in there too. Evidence."

He was cheered at the caution, for it showed she was not entirely lost to shocked numbness. "We shall evade all notice for some short while. Mortals forget things."

"There's forums. Online. They'll hunt us." Barely audible, each word muffled, forlorn. She shuddered, finally turning away from the view, and pressed her face into his shoulder despite the blood, the filth, the evidence of pursuit and battle daubed upon his clothes.

Was it wrong to find the single movement so sweet as to stagger even an Archon? In the distance a howl arose, high and savage—a wolf singing to the absent moon, perhaps drunk with sudden freedom. "Then they will die."

It was quite simple, after all. He bore her into the darkness, already occupied with the task of finding shelter.

CHAPTER 29

BEING CARRIED ALONG BY A MONSTROUS WHIRLWIND WAS STRANGELY soothing. Just holding on was enough, taking deep lungfuls of night air and listening to the wind rush past. Not a leaf touched them, not a twig snapped underfoot, and every so often the old vampire pressed his lips to her temple, a warm forgiving touch.

Yet a hatefully familiar sensation rose in her arms and legs. Dawn approaching, and with it utter vulnerability.

Simone didn't ask about the house—built onto another mountainside, one side propped on triangular trusses, and during daylight probably granted a fantastic view of a valley meandering with the nearby river. The garage was empty save for two snowmobiles under faded, fraying blue tarps, and the decor was a clunky mix of the seventies and several decades leaving their detritus since. It smelled disused but not abandoned—a vacation home, one her ex-husband would never have been able to afford even in good years at the agency.

The power was on, the pipes rattled but eased their protests once enough water gushed free. Even the fridge in the kitchen hummed, though she would have bet hard cash it was empty and dry as a bone.

If even a dollar bill remained in her torn pockets, that was.

Her bag was gone, *again*, along with her coat. She was back to having absolutely nothing, at least until she could get her hands on a laptop or smartphone. Maybe the payment from Huske was still sitting in Jane Smith's laboriously acquired work account, maybe it wasn't. She'd been a fool to agree to the meeting, but then again, what else *could* she have done?

The world gave a woman no real options, ever.

For all the insanity, John looked pretty much the same. Hatless, sure, with tiny spatterspots of blood on his jacket and jeans, a tinge of caustic smoke lingering in the cloth, but still moving with uncanny vamp grace, still full of that terrifying, precisely calibrated and leashed strength. At least he didn't seem *angry*, though how anyone could tell—he'd cut through everyone in the lab without breaking a sweat, and what he'd done to Huske…

Simone shuddered. Once started, the waves of trembling didn't want to stop. Shivers poured through her as she huddled on a lumpy L-shaped couch in what would have been a comfortable den, complete with sunken central fireplace and a prissily closed wet bar on the northern wall.

Would a nip of whiskey help? She was contemplating the notion, hugging herself, occasionally glancing at the crocheted and beaded afghan neatly folded on the short end of the couch when a warm breeze ruffled her hair and he was suddenly *there*, kneeling before her knees and peering at her face with what could almost be construed as an anxious expression.

Eyebrows drawn together, mouth a straight line, that wariness hiding in his blue gaze diminished but not gone. He studied her closely; Simone braced herself for punishment or worse.

She had, after all, technically and temporarily escaped him. Even if it was only by default.

"This is safe enough," he said finally, as if conferring a medium-sized favor. "No fresh clothing, for which I apologize. Tomorrow night the closest city will have everything we need. Will you…"

What was he going to ask? "Will I what?" The thirst, scratched but not slaked, burned in her throat. Her left arm throbbed, the rest of her full of vicious little nipping, clawing pains.

All in all she'd gotten off super lightly. She probably could have fought her way out of Huske's imitation supervillain lair alone, but Simone was forced to admit she was glad it hadn't been necessary.

"Had I been swifter, you needn't have suffered so." Deliberate, pronouncing each word carefully. The stilted cowboy drawl was almost preferable to the hint of laborious care, she discovered. "I promise you it shall not happen again. Will you forgive me, sweet Simone?"

Will I what? Christ Jesus, what a question. How was it possible for an old, old bloodsucker to be *less* of a monster than Elton Huske? Or maybe she was the biggest monster around, and just hadn't known it all this time. "Don't worry about it," she managed, numbly. "I… I just…"

The lab, the fight, the fire, all blurred together inside her head. She swayed, the couch creaking as her weight shifted, and suddenly she outright craved sleep, even if it was like a light switch flicking and the thirst would be even worse when she popped back into resentful, exhausted existence.

"Come." He rose, with slow, infinitely controlled grace, and when he touched her left arm the contact didn't hurt nearly so bad as her heart. He was gentle, steering her up three steps at the den's entrance, down a shag-carpeted hall, and into the main bedroom. Even the mirrored tiles on the ceiling and wall near the bed provoked nothing but weary amusement; so long as he let her lie down, the vampire could do whatever he wanted to her stupid, aching, trembling body.

He paused just inside the door, and Simone had never thought she'd be glad of the sudden shimmer over the walls, the still, dead air now meaning *trapped* but also *safe*. He hadn't shot her with poison and strapped her to a slab; the thought that

Huske might have been afraid he'd killed his golden goose during her daylight sleep was thinly amusing.

She was glad she couldn't remember anything they'd done to her during that stupor. What kind of 'scientists' put up with his bullshit?

At least Barry got out. Though if she ever saw him online again, she might be tempted to do something childish.

"You need to feed," John said, almost kindly. He nudged her toward the bed—king-sized, rustic frame of knotted pine, a red plaid comforter, and at least it wasn't too dusty. She obeyed the pressure, though another wave of shivers hit when she was stretched out on her side, his iron-hard arm snaking under her head, the warmth of him against her back. There was a slight sharp sound, fangs breaking a hard crust, and when his other arm slipped over her shoulder and the cut on his wrist pressed against her mouth Simone didn't hesitate.

She took what was offered, and the taste veered between tangy lemonade to a dripping chocolate cone on a hot summer's day, then shaded into something far more complex as the heat of his blood settled behind her breastbone and began to spread. Not food, not drink, but something soft and frightening.

A relaxation, a release.

It tasted of *safety*, and that was the final straw. She shuddered as she drank, her scraped, reddened left hand clamped against his, holding the flow to her lips. Drank until she could take no more, her fangs retreating reluctantly and a thick hazy relaxation enfolding her, unable to quell the shaking but letting her not care, and she waited for whatever he would do next.

Please. She pressed her lips together hard, unable to speak. Faint rainbow traceries played over each edge glimpsed through her slowly closing, still-dry eyes; maybe it was a residue of whatever drugs had been running around Huske's system. *Please just don't leave. Don't leave me here.*

He held her until dawn, stroking her hair, and it was far more comforting than it should have been.

Near-instantaneous, leaping into consciousness and throwing herself across the room, knowing nothing but sheer animal terror and the need to run, escape, get *away*. By the time Simone realized she was awake, she was trapped sideways against hard cold mirror-tiles, an invisible shimmer turned hard and glassy against her shoulder. Somehow John was there, naked skin sliding against hers, a hot, hard, familiar jab against her hip as he leaned in, effectively trapping her.

At least he wasn't on her back. Simone swallowed a yelp and forced herself to freeze. *Shit. Oh shit.*

Still, she felt a lot better. Her arm didn't hurt, and though her eyes were a bit grainy the immense, sharp vitality of vamp biology had returned.

It was a goddamn relief. She should've known she'd wake up without her clothes, though.

"*Arambash.*" His breath teased at her ear. "Peace, sweet Simone. No need for fear, I have you."

She sagged, full of that deep, unforgivable relief. It had to be some kind of crime, being so comforted at the presence of a vampire. "God." Her voice cracked; the thirst was gone, her throat only near-humanly dry, as if on the downhill slope of recovering from the flu. "Why... where the hell are my clothes?"

"There are machines for washing. And drying. Quite the innovation." He sounded very pleased with himself, leaning in a little harder. "And I must admit I like you better thus. Bed, or floor? Or wall? There is also a bathtub, which I find appealing, though I do not know your thoughts upon the matter yet."

Her knees were *so* not up to this. "Is that all you can think about?" Going from dead sleep to terror was disorienting, and now she had to deal with a nymphomaniac vamp who didn't even know his original name *or* how old he was.

Still, he'd shown up when she... well, needed him? Was that the right way to view the situation? Thinking about the sounds as he tore through flesh, bone, and everything else wasn't helpful at all, especially as his hands began to roam while the rest of him pinned her to the wall. One palm weighed her left breast, the other stroked down her back, fingertips caressing her ribs.

"I have been so very restrained, after all." He nearly crooned the words, sending a cascade of different shivers down her spine. The thought of what else he could do, the strength held so carefully in check, filled her belly with traitorous heat.

Fuck even trying *to be a good girl. Never got me anywhere, really.* "What, you want some kind of reward? I was doing just fine before you showed up."

"I don't think so, darlin'." A rough purr, edged with that rumbling growl. "Choose. Then I will feed you."

Oh, what the hell. "Bed," she whispered, both horrified and excited at her own daring. "But this time, *I'm* on top." Not that she had a chance at enforcing the decision, she thought, but it was still nice to pretend.

Surprisingly, he obeyed. Which meant Simone found herself rocking atop a vampire on a knotted-pine bedstead, his grip on her hips shifting as she moved, and for a short while she was blessedly unaware of anything other than her own pleasure, the vibration of his growl against her feverish skin, her back arching as release climbed from the center of her body to fill her skull.

For a few moments she was in control of the world, and it felt so good she almost didn't mind the echo of smoke clinging to both of them. After a shipwreck, a tornado, a disastrous collapse, any animal wanted to prove itself still alive.

So she did.

CHAPTER 30

ASPEN, THEY CALLED THE TOWN, AND IT APPEARED PLEASANT enough during the short hour or so spent acquiring transport in the dead of night. His leman consented to select a small blue sedan for their most immediate travel needs, and her apprehension at the thought of his steering the vehicle meant he acceded to her driving once more.

Much more responsive than a lumbering stagecoach, swifter than a steam train, Jonathan found he quite liked this new invention. They were also much easier to take than even a single horse from a locked livery, and he was more than ready to continue his education in this fascinating modern era.

She was still nervous, holding the steering wheel very tightly. Well-fed though ragged, she also watched him carefully, mostly sidelong as she steered their conveyance, her attention especially marked when she could reasonably guess him distracted.

The road rose, fell, swooped upon curves like a hawk enjoying summer updrafts. *I always wanted to go west*, she said, and he agreed. Perhaps he might even find something of his own memories there, as small bits of his wanderings before the fire had begun to return with each deep breath of her fragrance.

Soon the closed interior was dyed with her presence, and he relaxed gratefully into that wonderful flood.

"John?" A small, tentative word.

"Hm?" He turned his attention from the cone of white headlight before them. *Woody Creek*, the signs announced at intervals, *Snowmass, Basalt*, with mile-numbers attached. The most immediate problem was selecting another mortal town before dawn, and securing a safe resting place for her therein. Then a busy span of sunlight hours, acquiring various items and solidifying his grasp upon the principles of modernity while she slumbered.

For now, though, he could luxuriate in the closeness of his leman. She seemed almost resigned to his presence once more, and he intended upon using the gift to the hilt.

"You didn't have to, you know." This was a new Simone, biting her lower lip as she coaxed the vehicle into a tight curve. Acceleration pushed and pulled, an invisible dance; he liked the sense of being drawn along with her. "The... Huske, the guy who caught me? He thought he was going to get a transfusion and live forever."

"Was that his plan?" The immensity of the idiocy was almost amusing. "It would not work. The change agents in the saliva are necessary as well; you would have had to bite him with intention."

"With intention," she muttered, darkly. "I guess I did, in a way. But really, you didn't have to... to try and rescue me. Thank you."

Did you think I would not? She did not understand or credit the simplest things, but there was time. Jonathan weighed his next words carefully indeed. "I did have to, and I would again. Though it will not be necessary; I will not allow you beyond arm's reach for a very long while, sweet Simone. Perhaps ever."

"Allow me, huh?" Another sly sideways glance, this time with a faint gleam of mischief. "We're going to have some discussions if you want to stick around, old man."

Old man. Was it mere accuracy, or an endearment? "Whatever you like."

"I don't know how to be a vamp." A catch to her breath, soft and charming, before she corrected herself. "A sanguinant. So, uh, I have some questions. Is that... will you..."

"Ask." He settled more firmly in the seat, scanning their surroundings. So, that was what the mortals had designed upon her. A troubling development, and deserving of caution—there had been others seeking to steal the Dark Gift before, never with much success. Still, now that a single mortal had attempted it in this particular fashion, others would follow. It was inevitable.

He would have to work swiftly, wrap her in safety, accumulate wealth, familiarize himself with the current levers of mortal power.

But first, there was his sweet, priceless leman. She was uneasy; she knew so little of her own strength, let alone his. And she held to silence for a few miles, the vehicle humming happily under her hands.

What creature would not?

"Okay." Enchanting, her glance at the instrument panel, her deep breath to brace herself. Her grasp upon the wheel eased a fraction. "First things first, I guess. Can I have coffee?"

CHAPTER 31

Several months later

A DOWNRIGHT LUXURY, TO WAKE UP ON CLEAN WHITE COTTON percale. No need to leap instantly out of bed, though as soon as Simone rolled over she heard the click and faint whine as the television was turned off, relative silence filling the penthouse. No seals either, since they weren't traveling; John took the invisible shimmers off just before dusk, so long as there was 'no danger'.

He had a *way* different idea of risk than she did, that was for sure.

The first ritual was opening the drapes; it only took a button, but she liked doing it by hand. San Francisco sparkled and twinkled below, spreading down to the bay. The Golden Gate was a strand of yellow stars, and even on this floor she could hear the faint breathing of the city, the hum of traffic, the ever-present surf-murmur of human crowding.

Most nights, the whisper was comforting.

A vintage silk bathrobe, the kind she'd always secretly coveted, was ready on a row of wooden pegs; she yawned, padding down the hall, scraping her soles happily on thick blue carpet. According to the resident expert, the yawn reflex was a holdover from pre-infection.

Mortal time, John would say. *Before the Dark Gift.*

He wasn't kidding about money being easy for older vamps, or maybe he had investments socked away from 'before the fire'. Somehow he'd accumulated enough for this apartment, the furnishings, a new surprise almost every night. Even the cleaning and other chores were handled; no city ever really slept, and with enough money you could get maid service at any hour, day or night.

For the first time in her life, she didn't have to lift a finger. A giant change of affairs, one she tentatively almost liked.

Simone's own nest egg sat tidily in a fresh account under a different name, insulated from 'Jane Smith' by a series of transfers and redirects. Sometimes she called up the statements just to look at them, and each time the sharp swell of relief was the same. All safe, all hers, untouched by daily expenses.

John simply shrugged. *It is my honor to see to your comfort,* he'd say. *And your feeding.*

Which of course generally touched off one of his nymphomaniac episodes.

The penthouse was an open plan, all glass and chrome. He had a fascination with both; Simone was just glad he didn't want to live underground like some folklore vamps. Still, his cautions about completely drawing the heavy blackout drapes in the bedroom before dawn were nearly endless.

The kitchen shone, clean as a whistle. A bubbling, a burbling, the heavenly smell of coffee—it was one of the new pod machines in slick indigo enamel, its lines consciously Art Deco. It worked just fine and the cleanup was easy, one of the very few chores she didn't let anyone else near.

The brewing had just about stopped when warm air brushed her hair; his arms slid around her waist. "I have missed you," he murmured, and nipped lightly at her earlobe.

Her knees went faintly weak, as usual. "Restrain yourself, old man. I need caffeine."

"It has no effect, save psychological." He nipped again, one hand describing her hip under thin silk. Nowadays it wasn't black jeans and button-ups but a thoroughly modern haircut, T-shirts, and butter-soft stonewash, though he kept the cowboy boots. "And you are too delicious. I can't help it."

"Hm." Hard not to feel pleased, not to feel a little flutter deep down in her stomach. The whole leman thing was unbelievable, but she had to admit his story was consistent.

The reaction when she suggested maybe meeting other sanguinant so she could compare notes was thought-provoking as well.

"Be good," she continued. "I decide where and when, that's the deal."

"That is our agreement, yes." Another nuzzle, a very light scrape of his blunt human teeth on the side of her neck, and he laughed softly when she shivered.

The living room couch was vast, dusty blue, and comfortable, her one insistence for the furnishings. It didn't match the sleek coffee tables, Eames chairs, and whole minimalist vibe he had going on, but he never complained about the incongruity.

Miles away from Curt, indeed. She pulled her legs up and settled, tailor-fashion, in her usual spot. And as usual John stretched out, his head in her lap, seemingly supremely comfortable and handing her the remote without being asked.

"What were you watching?" Simone couldn't get over how much an old vampire liked *cable*, for God's sake. Not to mention streaming.

"Nature show." His bright eyes hooded, he went motionless as a cat, nearly boneless as well. If he started to purr she wouldn't be surprised. "One may roam the world without leaving the room."

"Yeah, but you only see what the producers want." The screen lit up, a giraffe working on a high branch with a long dark-grey tongue—when she thought about it, Simone could believe vampires were just one of Ma Nature's little experiments, set loose in the petri dish of a rocky, watery planet.

"True." He studied her instead of the screen, gazing up from her lap as she sipped. "Would you like to travel?"

"Not just yet." Sometimes it was exhausting, all the decisions each night. Did she like this, did she want that, did she prefer, what did she want?

Simone inhaled the steam rising from her cup gratefully, pressed the button.

Channels popped by, the volume at the lowest possible setting. Most nights she didn't want the noise or the bright moving pictures first thing; sometimes streaming old movies with a bowl of uneaten popcorn was tolerable.

She couldn't settle enough to knit just yet.

As usual, John didn't look like he minded her restless surfing. He seemed to enjoy whatever happened; there was, however, always the inevitability of his hands on her, his mouth, her own gasps and pleading, sometimes outright screams of release.

And the feeding. Can't forget that. Finding out that he took a little from her during the day had provoked what would have been a knockdown drag-out fight with anyone else, but he simply listened to her furious spluttering and inquired whether she would like to be bitten while awake, as if it made no difference.

One way, he said quietly, *or another. Choose, sweet Simone.*

She wasn't sure what to think about that yet, either.

Simone skipped past the news, stopped, flicked back. A shiny-haired man with a soothing mellow tenor looked into the camera with what he had to be sure was reassuring gravitas, and in a box to the upper right another man's face floated, promo stock footage from a company event, flashbulbs popping as Elton Huske posed, thumbs in black fleece-vest pockets.

"*—fire in his Aspen vacation home,*" the announcer intoned. "*His company was found to be nearly bankrupt, despite the high stock* *valuations of X-OL and several subsidiaries; investigations are still ongoing. To date, Huske's body has never been found."*

Coffee slopped in the mug as Simone shuddered. John moved swiftly, whisking the remote away, and the TV screen died once more, its electric glow shrinking to nothingness, becoming a blank dark mirror.

He set the remote carefully aside and was suddenly in a different position, his hands on hers around hot ceramic, steadying and safe. An inquiring look, his lips parted slightly as if to speak, and with that expression he was actually, well, handsome.

Or maybe she only thought that because she was sleeping with him. An open question.

"I'm fine," Simone said, forestalling the question. "Really. I promise. Did you…"

Did you take his money? She didn't want to think it was possible for a vamp to learn so quickly, though now he knew his way around a computer and she'd even caught him playing games on his sleek black smartphone, studying the screen with an abstracted air as his fingers blurred.

He'd be hell at a casino. Good Lord.

Huske had more likely blown his fortune on that mountain hideout—which couldn't have been cheap—plus chasing immortality in vampire form. It was also possible X-OL had been a sham, a prettily wrapped present with rotting innards dribbling out the bottom.

She couldn't tell which prospect was most terrifying. Or revolting.

"Did I what?" Funny how anxious John looked. How *human*, blue eyes shaded with worry, straight eyebrows drawn together, a tendril of dark hair falling over his slightly wrinkled forehead, his palms so warm and sure against her skin. "Simone?"

"I wanted to ask." There was no shortage of questions; she was a damn near inexhaustible well, and always faintly amazed that he never seemed to tire of considering each one carefully before answering. "Have you remembered anything else? About the fire?" So far, the best guess was that the event had occurred in Frisco itself, a quake and a conflagration long enough ago to be considered *history*. Which was part of the reason they'd settled here, to hopefully jog his memory.

Though to be honest he didn't seem very interested in the exercise. It could have been Timbuktu for all he cared, though he dutifully went on trips to the older parts of the city with her, looking around with studious attention, far more interested in her own observations.

"Nothing necessary," he answered, as always.

Oh well. She'd try again, soon. Simone nodded, freed her hands, and leaned far forward, searching for a coaster. Once more he anticipated, sliding a square pad of black leather across the glass coffee table, positioning it precisely so she could settle the mug.

With that done, she could draw her knees up and curl into his side. As usual, he accepted with alacrity, his arm over her shoulder like a solicitous boyfriend, resting his cheek against her hair as she waited for the shudders to die down.

Trauma stuck around in vamp nervous systems, just like mortal ones. The apartment building hummed to itself—basement to crown, elevators whooshing up and down, mortal lives lived in a layer-cake of concrete, steel, and glass. If Simone focused, she could hear the heartbeats of the occupants just below.

Unless the seals were active. How long before she asked him to put up invisible force-fields so she could hear herself think without the noise of human beings all around? Did he ever feel that way?

That was a conversation for another night. The shakes drained away; she didn't have to think about the lab, the burning blistering straps, the caustic smoke, the sounds of tearing meat and snapped bone.

Or the terrible, brassy smell of death.

The urge to flat-out burrow into the warmth beside her was overwhelming. She rubbed her cheek on his shoulder, and his stillness was absolute attention, complete focus.

"You know," Simone said, softly, "I don't think we've christened the couch." *It's the only time I don't brood about horrible things. That, and when we're out looking for history.*

"Christened?" John sounded very interested in the concept.

Simone uncurled, tipped her face up, and did not have to wait for a kiss. She never did; and eventually she had to gasp *don't tear this, it's my favorite.*

His reply was silent, but intense. And outside the penthouse windows, the night pursued its own eternal business.

EXCERPT FROM SELENE

Life isn't easy for a sexwitch. Even your own body betrays you. It's bad enough that Selene is partly beholden to Nikolai, the Prime Power of Saint City, but she's got her brother Danny and she's got her job at the college. In the postwar wreckage of an uncertain world, it's pretty much all she's ever allowed herself to want.

Then Danny ends up murdered, and Selene finds herself a pawn in a dangerous game. Indentured to a bloodsucking Nichtvren and helpless, told to stop trying to uncover the identity of her brother's killer, Selene has nowhere to turn. If she's a good girl, Nikolai will leave her a little bit of freedom. He'll take care of her, and she'll be safe—if she obeys.

But Selene hasn't survived this long by being obedient to her cursed powers, or to the clients who buy her body. Her brother was all she had, and now she's ready to borrow, beg, lie, steal or kill—whatever it takes to avenge him.
And if Nikolai gets in the way, Selene will use every tool in her arsenal to make him regret it…

Chapter 1

A SHRILL SCREAM JERKED HER OUT OF THE DEEP WELL OF SLEEP.

Selene fumbled for the phone, pushed her hair back, pressed the talk button. "Mrph." She managed the trick of rolling over and blinking at the alarm clock. *Oh, God, what now?* "This had better be good."

"Lena?" A familiar voice wheezed into the other end of the phone. He gasped again. "Lena, it's me."

Ohno. Not another panic attack. "Danny?" Selene sat straight up, her heart pounding. "Danny, what's wrong? Are you okay?" Sweat began to prickle under her arms, the covers turned to strangling fingers before she realized she was awake.

"Cold," he whispered, breath coming in staccato gasps. "Selene. Help. *Help* you—"

Selene swung her feet to the cold floor, switching the phone to her right ear, trapping it on her shoulder. "Where are you? Danny? Talk to me." She grabbed her canvas bag the moment her feet hit the floor, craning her neck to read the Ident display. *Daniel Thompson*, his familiar number. He was at home.

Where else would he be? Danny hadn't left his apartment for nearly five years. "Keep breathing. Deep breaths, down into your tummy. I'll be right there."

"No," Danny pleaded. His asthmatic wheeze was getting worse. "Cold...*Lena*. Don't. Danger—" The line went dead.

Selene slammed the phone back into the cradle, her breath hissing in. Her fingers tingled—a sure sign of something awful. *What was I dreaming? Something about the sea, again.* She raced for the bathroom, grabbing a handful of clothes from the dirty-laundry hamper by the door. *Just keep breathing, Danny. Don't let the panic get too big for you. I'm on my way.* She tripped, nearly fell face-first, banging her forehead on the door. "Shit!"

She yanked her jeans up with one hand and turned on the faucet with the other, splashed her face with cold water. Tossed her thick blonde mane into a sloppy ponytail and raced for the door, ripping her sweater at the neck as she forced it over her head. She had to hop on one foot to yank her socks on, she jammed her feet into her boots and flung her bag over her head, catching the strap in her hair. *Just keep him calm enough to remember not to hurt himself, God. Please.*

She slowed down at the end of her block, searching for a cab. *One down, nine to go.* Rain kissed her cheeks and made the sidewalk slick and slightly gritty under the orange wash of city light as she sprinted across the street. Deep heaving gasps of chill air made her lungs burn.

Selene crossed Cliff Street, slowing down, pacing herself. *Can't run myself out on the first blocks or I'll be useless before I get halfway there. If this is another one of his practical jokes I am just going to* kill *him.*

It wouldn't be, though. It was far more likely he'd been injured while out of his body—or he was having trouble staying *in* his body even inside the wards she'd built for him.

Three down, seven to go. Selene's boots pounded the sidewalk. Rain whispered on the deserted streets and along the length of her messy ponytail, dripped down her neck as she reached Martin Street and cut across the intersection. There were more streetlamps here, she checked her watch as she ran.

Two-thirty. Santiago City held its breath under the mantle of chill night.

The back of Selene's neck prickled, uneasiness rippling just under her skin.

Why can't these things happen in the daylight? Or when I don't have lecture in the morning? This had better be something good, Danny, I swear to God if you're just throwing another snit-fit I will never *forgive you. Never, ever, ever.*

Something chill and panicked began to revolve under her breastbone. *Getting a premonition.* Her breath came in miserable harsh sobs of effort. *Either that or I'm just spooked. Who wouldn't be at two AM in this busted-down part of town?* She set her teeth, grimly ignoring the stitch in her side. *Danny. Just breathe, please*

God, let him remember to breathe. Don't let him be in the kitchen, there's knives in there. This sounds like a doozy, he hasn't had a bad panic attack in at least six months, Christ don't let him hurt himself. Sometimes pain was all he could use to nail himself into his flesh, and—

"Hey, Selene."

Selene whirled. "Bruce!" she choked, her hand leaping instinctively to her throat. The silver medallion was still under her sweater, warm against her skin. She hadn't taken it off. "Good God, don't *do* that!" She clenched her hands at her side. *If only he was human, I could punch him.*

Bruce grinned down at her, canines glittering in the pallid orange light, his eyes glowing just like a small nocturnal animal's. Beneath his loud polyester sport jacket and eye-searing yellow tie, his narrow spotted chest was pale and hairless. "Don't worry so much, Lena. I wouldn't *dream* of taking a taste. His Highness wouldn't like that one little bit." His lips curled back even more, exposing more gleaming teeth.

Selene's heart slammed once against her ribs. Taking a long deep breath, she willed her pulse to slow. *Focus, goddammit! Danny needs you, you can't fight if you're busy screaming.*

"I don't have time for your bullshit, Bruce. Danny's in trouble."

"I'll go with you." Bruce shrugged and peeled his lanky frame away from the streetlamp. He'd just been Turned, and still looked almost human.

Almost. The feral glow in his eyes and the quick jerking of his movements screamed "not-quite-normal."

Still, for a Nichtvren, Bruce was as close to human as possible. He didn't have the scary immobility of older suckheads. Small blessing, but she'd take it. "That's not necessary—" she began.

Bruce folded his arms, the smile gone. "Danny's under Nikolai's protection too, Selene. And if I let you go over there and get hurt, His Highness will peel off my skin in strips and salt me down." Bruce shivered, his long pink tongue wetting his lips. "Trust me. I'll go with you."

"Oh, for Christ's sweet sake." Selene wasn't about to argue with an undead sucklizard. He fell into step beside her, long legs easily keeping pace as she trotted up the sidewalk. She glanced down. Black loafers and no socks. *All you're missing is a clutch of gold chains and chest hair.* "I don't know what Nikolai's thinking." She sped up. "I'm perfectly safe."

Bruce managed a high thin giggle. "Oh, no you're not, chickadee. You should be glad His Highness took an interest in you." He didn't even sound winded.

I don't need Nikolai's protection. I did just fine on my own.

Okay, so she didn't *want* Nikolai's protection. She'd rather tap dance naked through a minefield singing *Petticoat Junction.* Just because Nikolai was the prime paranormal Power in the city, responsible for keeping the peace among all the other factions of paranormal citizenry, didn't mean anything, right? His Highness Nikolai indeed. Just another suckhead come out from the shadows under the protection of the Paranormal Species Act.

Only this one had an interest in her. A deep, abiding, and *personal* interest. A not-entirely-unpleasant shiver traced down Selene's back.

Danny, please be okay. Don't bite your tongue or cut yourself.

Her bag shifted, clinking when it banged against her shoulder. Steel and salt, the tools she needed to banish anything evil or unwanted; it didn't pay as well as teaching but God knew there was a need for her Talents. She'd been so tired when she got home she hadn't unpacked, poltergeist infestations were like that. Not very difficult, but messy and draining. She pushed the strap higher. "I don't need his...protection or...yours, suckhead."

"That's what *you* think." Bruce grinned down at her, his words soft and even. "Want me to carry your bag?"

"Of...course...not." Selene broke into a jog again. *To hell with pacing myself. Danny needs me.*

The medallion warmed against her skin, reacting to Bruce's presence—at least, she *hoped* that was what it was reacting to. By the time they reached Danny's building, the metal thrummed with Power. Gooseflesh raced down her body; she choked back a final gasp as she rounded the final corner and saw the slim, tall black shape in front of the doors.

Bruce smirked, letting out a soft little snort of laughter. Selene curled her hands into fists, resisting the urge to claw the smile from his face. *Jumping the Nichtvren won't get you anywhere, Selene. Just ignore him, and concentrate on what matters. Danny, my God, please be okay. Remember the visualizations I taught you.*

The tall black-clad shape half-turned, halfway up the concrete steps. *Oh, no. Could this possibly get any worse?*

Of course not. Of course Nikolai would show up now. He always seemed to know when there was trouble.

Bruce dropped back. *At least I won't have to see that fucking smirk on his face. Danny, please be okay, don't be banging your head on the wall again. I'm on my way, I'm almost there.*

Her heart slammed once against the cage of her ribs and her fingers curled into fists. Heat flamed in her cheeks, spread down her neck, and merged with the growing heat of the medallion between her breasts. She fought for control, ribs flaring as she struggled against hyperventilation.

Hands in his coat pockets, chin tilted toward her, Nikolai's dark eyes catalogued her tangled blonde hair, camel coat, scuffed boots. Her fingers itched to straighten her clothes, brush back her hair, check for loose threads. As usual, he was so contained she longed to see him roughed up a little.

I suppose you learn a little self-control when you're a Master powerful enough to rule Saint City. He's the Prime, after all. We all live our little lives in his long dark shadow.

A few strands of crow-black hair fell over his eyes as Selene, impelled by the medallion's growing heat and the pull of Nikolai's eyes, skidded to a stop inches from him. Her ponytail swung heavily, but he didn't reach out to grab her arm and "protect" her from falling headlong on the steps. Her heart actually *leapt*, to see him again.

He's not human, you know that, stop STARING at him!

Nikolai said nothing, the light stroking his high cheekbones. His mouth, usually curled into a half-smile, was compressed into a thin line. His dark, electric eyes flicked over Bruce, who cringed another three steps back.

Selene suppressed a burst of nasty satisfaction. *Serves you right.* She started up the stairs, pressing her left hand against the sudden stitch gripping her side. Her toe caught on the second step.

She fetched up short when Nikolai closed his hand around her left arm, steadied her before she could fall over, and let her go, all in the space of a moment. "Selene." The chill rain-soaked air shivered under the word, his voice soft and irresistible. At least he didn't have the scary gold-green sheen on his eyes tonight, Selene hated that. "Stirling."

"I was on watch." Bruce didn't sound half so smug now. Of course, he was an accident, Turned as a joke or mistake; Nichtvren didn't Turn ugly humans. It was an unwritten rule: only the pretty or the ruthless were given the gift of immortality, and Bruce was neither. Why Nikolai kept him around was anyone's guess, and Selene didn't want to ask. Bruce's doglike attachment and gratefulness for any crumb Nikolai threw his way was telling enough.

Besides, if she asked she had a sneaking suspicion Bruce might answer, and she wouldn't like the answer at all. Not to mention what she might have to pay for it.

Story of my life. Always calculating what it'll cost me to know something. Danny, please be okay.

Selene brushed past Nikolai. Her boots smacked against cold, wet concrete. She reached the glassed-in front door and stopped short, digging in her coat pocket for her keys. *So Nikolai's having me watched. Good to know.*

Her fingers rooted fruitlessly around in her pocket and found nothing but an empty gum wrapper. "Oh, no." Her keys were on the table by the door at her apartment, she had *not* scooped them up on her way out. Just run right past them in her frantic dash. "Bloody *fucking* hell on a cheese-coated *stick*."

"You need to go in?" Nikolai's breath brushed her cheek, the faint smell of aftershave and male closing around her. He was *right* behind her, so far into her personal space it wasn't even funny.

Her violent start nearly toppled her into the firmly shut door. She hadn't heard or *sensed* him, he'd just appeared out of thin air. *Dammit, does he have to do that all the time?* The only place she could escape was through the glass itself. Selene stared at the door, taking in deep harsh breaths and willing it to open. There was a quick, light patter of footsteps—Bruce, making off into the night. "I left my keys at home. Danny called. I think it's a panic attack, and when he gets them he sometimes hurts himself. There's an intercom—"

Nikolai reached around her, his body molded to hers, and touched the lock. The gold and carnelian signet ring gleamed wetly in the uncertain light as his pale fingers brushed the metal. He went absolutely still. The medallion's metal cooled abruptly between Selene's breasts, responding to the controlled flare of energy. She could almost See what he was doing, despite the stealthy camouflage of a Master Nichtvren's aura. The only thing scarier than their power was their creepy invisibility.

I really wish he'd quit crowding me. Her worry returned, sharp and acrid. Her lungs burned, the stitch knotting her left side again. *Please, Danny. Please be okay. I don't even care anymore if it's one of your midnight games, I hope you're all right.*

The lock clicked open with a muffled *thunk* and Selene grabbed the handle before it could close again. Nikolai's hand brushed hers, slid over the handle, and he stepped aside and pulled the door open. She yanked her hand away, her skin burning from the brief touch. *He did that on purpose.*

"Thanks," she managed around the dry lump in her throat.

Stop it, she thought desperately, biting the inside of her cheek. The pain helped her focus. *It's only Nikolai. You know what he is, and why he's doing this. You're here for Danny, remember?*

"My pleasure." His eyes dropped to the medallion safely hidden under her sweater. The metal flushed with icy heat now.

He's looking at my chest like he sees dinner there. Heat sizzled along Selene's nerves. "Oh, stop that." She stepped through the door, sliding past him, suddenly grateful for someone else's presence. Her heart hammered thinly, the taste of burning in her mouth. *Danny. Just remember to breathe, kiddo. Little sister's almost there to take care of you.* "I suppose Bruce called you. And that you want to come up."

"Of course." His voice stroked her cheek, slid down her neck. He leaned back against the open door, his dark eyes now fixed on her face. Selene gulped down another breath, her heartbeat evening out. The familiar bank of mailbox doors was on her right, and the peeling linoleum floor glared back at the dirty ceiling. "It is pleasant to see you, Selene."

Nikolai cat-stepped into the foyer, gracefully avoiding the closing door. Little droplets of rain glittered in his hair, sparked by the fluorescent lights. Under his coat, he wore a dark-blue silk T-shirt and a pair of designer jeans. The shirt moved slightly as muscle tensed underneath.

Selene dropped her eyes, turned away from him. Oddly enough, he wore a high-end pair of black Nikos trainers. *Vampire fashion just ain't what it used to be. Where's the fangs and the black cape, not to mention the evening wear?* Her heart sped up, thundered in her ears. *God love me, I'm going to have a fucking cardiac arrest right here in the foyer.*

"Well, come on, then." She started up the orange-carpeted stairs, sidling away from him. Nikolai followed closely behind, but not too close, letting Selene take the lead. For once.

Given how he's always going on about how I need "protecting," it's a wonder he's letting me in the building at all. But dammit, if he showed up at the door he'd just scare Danny more. He's being tactful for once. Lucky me.

Her legs trembled and she rubbed at her eyes as she trooped up the stairs. Nikolai made no sound. "Would you make a little noise?" She immediately regretted asking. The silence behind her intensified. "God. I just hope he's okay." *He will be, it's probably nothing. He just stayed out of his body for too long and had trouble when he came back, another panic attack and the numbness. He's okay. Be okay, Danny, please?*

Nikolai's footsteps echoed as he climbed behind her. That was a relief, but Selene still felt the weight of his black eyes as they reached the fourth floor. Her thighs and ass burned. Climbing stairs after almost-running ten blocks without rest was a workout she could do without.

Nikolai's arm came over her shoulder again and held the heavy fire door open. The hall was dingy, most of the light fixtures missing bulbs, and a drift of fast food wrappers curled up at the far end. Selene's nose dripped from the chill. She rubbed at it with the back of her hand, tried not to sniff too loudly. Threadbare orange carpet whispered under her boots. The entire hall was so familiar she barely paid any attention. Down the hall a wedge of light speared through the gloom.

Danny's door was open.

❦

Order from your preferred retailer today!

ABOUT THE AUTHOR

Lili Saintcrow currently resides in the rainy Pacific Northwest with her children, dog, cat, a half-feral library, and assorted other strays.

https://www.lilithsaintcrow.com

ALSO BY LILITH SAINTCROW

PARANORMAL ROMANCE

The Watchers

Dark Watcher

Storm Watcher

Fire Watcher

Cloud Watcher

Mindhealer

Finder

The Society

The Society

Hunter, Healer

Sons of Ymre

Erik

Jake

Nigel

Tales of the Sanguinant

Daywalker's Leman

Elder's Prize

Fledgling & Archon

SINGLE TITLE PARANORMAL ROMANCE

The Demon's Librarian

Desires, Known

Taken

Incorruptible

Rose & Thunder

SCIENCE FICTION & FANTASY

Roadtrip Z

Cotton Crossing

In the Ruins

Pocalypse Road

Atlanta Bound

Gallow & Ragged

Trailer Park Fae

Roadside Magic

The Wasteland King

HOOD

Season One

Season Two

Season Three

The Dante Valentine Series

Working For the Devil

Dead Man Rising

The Devil's Right Hand

Saint City Sinners

To Hell & Back

Selene

The Jill Kismet Series

Night Shift

Hunter's Prayer

Redemption Alley

Heaven's Spite

Angel Town

The Dead God's Heart

Spring's Arcana

The Salt-Black Tree

The Black Land's Bane

A Flame in the North

The Fall of Waterstone

Steelflower

Steelflower

Steelflower at Sea

Steelflower in Snow

Romances of Arquitaine

The Hedgewitch Queen

The Bandit King

Single Title Sci-Fi & Fantasy

Moon's Knight

Chained Knight

Rattlesnake Wind

She Wolf & Cub

Coyote Run

Harmony

Blood Call

The Marked

Afterwar

ROMANTIC SUSPENSE

Viral Agents

Agent Zero

Agent Gemini

Ghost Squad

Damage

Duty

Gamble

ALT-HISTORICAL FANTASY

Hell's Acre

Hell's Acre

Rook's Rose

The Bannon and Clare Affairs

The Iron Wyrm Affair

The Red Plague Affair

The Ripper Affair

The Damnation Affair

COLLECTED STORIES

Human Tales

More Human Tales

NONFICTION

The Quill & The Crow Vol. 1

HUMOR

SquirrelTerror

Jozzie & Sugar Belle

WRITING AS S.C. EMMETT

Hostage to Empire

Throne of the Five Winds

The Poison Prince

The Bloody Throne

WRITING AS LILI ST. CROW (young adult)

The Strange Angels Series

Strange Angels

Betrayals

Jealousy

Defiance

Reckoning

Tales of Beauty and Madness

Nameless

Wayfarer

Kin